# ENCOUNTERS OF TRUE LOVE ANTHOLOGY

IF IT WASN'T FOR TONY
MR. WRONG
I JUST WANNA BE LOVED

# Anna Black

Love Changes: Encounters of True Love Anthology

Black House Publishing Editions, October 2013
Copyright © 2013 by Anna Black

Published in the United States by Black House Publishing, Texas.

ISBN-10: 0991152867
ISBN-13: 978-0-9911528-6-5

www.bhousepublishing.com
www.annablack.net

Printed in the United States of America

10 9 8 7 6 5 4 3 2 1

# BOOKS BY *Anna Black*

## *Cole Hart Presents*

Sometimes I'm In My Feelings
Sometimes I'm In My Feelings 2
Fallin For A Dallas Boss

## *Black House Publishing*

Now You Wanna Come Back
My Best Friend & My Man
Hooks In Me

## *Urban Renaissance!*

I'm Doin' Me
Full Figured 10
The Side Effects of You
I'm Doin' Me 2
Foolish
The Perfect Love Storm

# Acknowledgements

TO YOU READER … thank you for your support and I truly hope you enjoy this short story about love and disaster. There will be some head shaking moments and some mouth dropping actions in this story so prepare yourself and keep in mind, its fiction for some, but could be a reality for others. Thank you again for being an Anna Black fan and know that I not only do this for me, I do this to entertain you.

Enjoy!

*Anna Black*

# If It Wasn't For Tony

# Jocelyn

I THINK the saying is "If you love someone, set them free, and if they come back to you, it was meant to be." In my opinion, that is a bunch of BS. How easy is it to let the love of your life just up and leave? Someone please tell me how to do that. Because, for the life of me, I can't let him go. Some days I think I can, but the reality is I can't and I'm not sure if I ever will be able to. Yes, he's gone; he moved on two weeks ago to be exact. It was so hard for me just to stand there in the doorway and watch him load his bags into the back of his Range Rover. The expression on his face before he opened the door to leave is a look I'll never forget, and I still don't know what to think of it.

"Why did he leave?" is your question, I know. But I don't have the answer to that question either. I thought things were fine. When he had kissed me goodbye that morning before we both headed out to work, I had no idea I'd come home to find him packing his bags.

"Tony, what's going on? What are you doing?" I asked when I walked into our bedroom. He looked up, shocked to see me. I had left the office that afternoon a couple hours early because I wanted to surprise him with a romantic dinner for two, but I was the one who got the surprise.

"Joss, I didn't expect you home this early," he said. I could tell by the bulging in his eyes he was shocked to see me. He stopped in his tracks with his toiletry bag, looking at me like a kid caught stealing candy. I was sure he didn't expect me to catch him packing his things to leave me.

"Well, I am, and I see you're going somewhere," I said, folding my arms across my chest, with my brows vaulted.

"Jocelyn, baby, I ... I don't know what to say," he stammered.

"Let me suggest you start with the truth," I said, moving closer to him. I wanted to hear this one.

"Joss really ... I ... I can't explain right now. This will be easier if you don't ask a lot of questions," he said. He continued to pack.

"Easier for who Tony—you!" I yelled getting in his face.

"Yes, easier for me. Now, don't make this into something immense," he said and moved around me.

"Just tell me why." I softened my tone. I figured yelling wasn't going to get me anywhere, so I brought my voice down a few octaves. "I just can't do this anymore. All of this, us, just happened too fast, and I need to fall back. I need some space to figure out if this is what I truly want."

"What ...? Tony, this makes no sense. I didn't force your hand in anything. We both agreed on you moving in," I protested.

"Yes," he yelled, "after you kept pressuring me, Jocelyn, I care about you. You are, like, the sexiest and the most brilliant woman on the planet, but I'm not here, where you need me to be," he said holding his hand to a level even with my heart. "We went out, and not even two months after that, you were naming our kids. And, yes, I know after three months I moved in and that was my mistake, but I can't do this. I want to go back to being single and having my own space. All this couple stuff and living together and not being able to have my freedom is not working."

"So that's how you feel Tony? You don't love me?" I asked, my eyes now welling.

"I do, Joss, but we jumped into this serious relationship too fast. I'm going to move in with Sean until I can find me another spot," he said and went back to gathering his things.

"Hey, Tony, listen," I cried with desperation. "Don't leave, okay? I know you feel smothered, and that's my bad. I just love you, boo. Yes, I rushed things, and maybe I put pressure on you. But from the first night I hung out with you, I knew it was you, so forgive me for pushing you into a commitment so quickly, but I can give you space, Tony, just don't leave."

"I'm sorry, Joss, but I have to," he said.

I could see that his mind was made up, so I stepped back and let him finish packing. I sat on the ottoman and removed my shoes and tried to be a big girl about it, but I couldn't hold my tears back. I wondered if it meant were done, but I was too afraid to ask him. I sat there and sniffled, hoping he'd have a change of heart, but when he exited the room with his two packed bags, I knew he was dead set on leaving.

"I'll be back for the larger stuff this weekend. I can give you back your key now if you'd like," he offered.

I wondered how he could not see that he was ripping my heart out of my chest. "No, keep it. This doesn't mean that we're done, right?" I asked, hoping he'd say we were still an item.

"Listen, Jocelyn, I didn't want it to end like this, but I think we need a serious break. I gotta figure some things out," he said.

Looking into his eyes, I knew he was serious. Tony was always easy to persuade, and a year ago when I asked him to move in with me, all it took was a couple sad faces and sexy girl pouts to make him say yes. Those days were gone, and, sadly, our whirl-wind romance was gone.

"So this is the end," my voice quivered with fat teardrops in my eyes, anxiously waiting to fall.

"Yeah, and I'm sorry," was all he said before he walked out the front door. He threw his bags into the back of his SUV and got in. I stood there frozen, watching him leave, asking myself what in the hell just happened. Why didn't you beg him to stay Jocelyn? Why didn't you pour out your heart to him? I asked myself before I finally shut the door. I went into the kitchen and cracked open the bottle that was meant for our romantic dinner that night. After two or three swallows, I put the glass down and broke down. Yes, it was the ugly girl cry with running mascara, snot, and all. The sounds of a wounded dog or heart, hell, they both sounded similar to me.

I grabbed the glass and the bottle and slid down to the floor, and that's where I stayed until the bottle was empty and my ass was numb. When I found the strength to get up, I made my way to my room and peeled off my clothes. My eyes landed on the picture of us on my nightstand and I picked it up. I ran my fin-gers across his face and let the tears fall, knowing that this was only the beginning of my pain. I hated heartbreak, it was the worst, and there I was again, feeling that same pain I felt when I broke up with Marquez and the guy before him. I remember vowing never to fall for another man again, and then I met Tony.

I was standing in line at Starbucks, waiting to get my fix, and, out of the corner of my eye, I noticed someone tall walk in, but I was too busy wishing the line would move faster to look in his direction. I got what I came for and when I turned to leave, I didn't realize he was so close behind me and I bumped into him.

"I'm so sorry," I said, looking up into the sexiest set of hazel eyes I'd ever seen. He was medium brown, not light at all, so I was surprised to see a set of eyes that sexy on him.

"You're fine, no worries," he said in a voice even sexier than his eyes.

"Thank you," I said. I smiled and couldn't help but compliment him. "Your eyes, they are beautiful."

"So are your dimples," he replied, making me smile even brighter.

"Thank you," I said and walked away. I needed to get to my office, but I stalled by going over to the condiment counter to add cream to my already perfect cup of caffeine. After a couple fake stirs, he was standing right next to me.

"I'm Tony," he said.

I looked up at him. "I'm Joss ... I mean, Jocelyn."

He smiled at me. He not only had beautiful eyes, but he had a sexy smile. "Nice to meet you, Jocelyn," he said, grabbing a couple napkins.

We both headed for the door. I walked towards my Lexus and he went to a Range Rover that was parked two cars over.

"Listen, I'd be foolish if I didn't ask for your number," he said before I got in my car.

"Yes, you would be," I said.

He came over to my car and we pulled out our phones, exchanged numbers, and wished each other a lovely day before leaving. As soon as I got to the office, I filled my girl, Bailey, in on what transpired that morning.

"So, when are you going to call him?" she asked.

"After he calls me." I hoped I could wait that long.

"Joss, please. I know you, and if brother man is fine as you say, you are going to stalk that man."

"No, I'm not, Bailey. This time, things are going to be different.

I'm going to take this one nice and slow; I'm not going to get all crazy over him first," I said, not believing my own lying words. This was the man I wanted to father my children.

"Okay, we shall see. I'll check back with you later and see if you caved." She knew me like the back of her hand.

Bailey and I had been friends since middle school. We both went off to college, graduated and came back home. A couple years after I took my mother up on her offer to work at her cosmetics company. Bailey came aboard after getting laid off from the company she'd been working for. Now, she was the head of marketing.

My job was easy since I was the boss's daughter. I did exactly what my mother would have been doing if she was not retired, and that was approving or disapproving. I simply got a salary for being the last one to sign off on a product. My life at work was like a walk in the park, but my love life … not so much. I hoped I'd hear from Tony by lunch so I wouldn't be the first to call.

By four, I had heard nothing and was about to call it a day, but Bailey stuck her nose into my office. "Soooooo," she said, coming in and taking a seat.

"What?"

"Joss, please. I know you called him."

"No, I did not, for your information."

"What? You didn't call him? That means he called you?"

"Bailey, he didn't call and I didn't call him, so back up off me," I stood up and picked up my purse and briefcase, signaling that I was ready to go.

Apparently getting the hint, she stood up too. "Well, I am sure he will. But, in the meantime, you need to run home and come up out of that suit and meet me for a drink. Today has been one of those days and Momma needs a couple glasses of white."

"That's cool, I can meet you. Let's say … six thirty?"

"Sounds good," she said and we headed out.

I got into my car, tempted to call him, but I tossed my phone onto the seat and drove home.

# Tony

"OKAY THAT won't be a problem, sir," I said and hung up the phone.

I'd had a super busy day and had paperwork up to my ears, but I was ready to call it quits. I wasn't sure if I could keep going at the rate I was going. I knew what I signed up for when I went into psychology, but sometimes this job and this facility made me want to throw in the towel.

After writing a recommendation to increase the dosage of a patient's medication, I hit send and powered off my computer. I had to get out of there. I hadn't had time for lunch or a break and I needed a shower and a glass of Hennessey.

When I got to my Range Rover, I remembered meeting Jocelyn and decided to wait until I got home to call her. At home, I checked my mail and went inside, pulled off my jacket, and hung it up. I turned on some music, went into the kitchen and poured myself a drink, then hit the shower.

After my shower, I threw on some shorts and a tank and gave Jocelyn a call.

"Hello," she answered.

"Hey, how are you?" I asked.

"Great, how are you?"

"I'm cool, glad to be off work."

"One of those days, huh?"

"I have 'one of those days' just about every day."

"Wow that sucks. What do you do?" she asked.

"I am a psychologist; I work with teens at a group home."

"Seriously?"

I laughed, "Yes, is that surprising?"

"Yes. I never would have guessed."

"Well, that's not the first time I've heard that, so it's cool. What about you? I mean, you were dressed to kill and you have to have a prestigious office job to be rocking those sexy-ass heels you had on this morning."

"Well, I work at a cosmetics company, and I don't do a lot of standing."

"At a cosmetics company or cosmetics counter?" I joked.

She laughed. "Oh, you got jokes, huh?" she said. "I work at my mother's company. I'm the CEO now because she retired six months ago. And it is far from being at a cosmetics counter, although I have worked one of those too back in the day, selling my mom's products. And would proudly do it again if I had to."

"That's what's up," I said.

We talked for a few more moments, getting to know each other, until she finally said, "Listen, I promised my best friend I'd meet her for drinks. Would you like to join us?"

"I wish I could, but my boy has a band and we're hooking up where we normally do, at this spot called Genesis."

"Oh, that's cool, no biggie," she said.

"If you and your girl would like to come out to Country Club Hills, I wouldn't mind," I offered. I mean, I did want to see her again, so it was only right to invite her.

"Yeah, I'll hit you back. I'll check with Bailey, and even if she isn't up to it, I'm sure I'll probably come through."

A couple hours later, I headed out. I hadn't heard back from Jocelyn, but then she texted and asked was it still cool for them to come. I replied 'yeah.'

When she got there with another woman in tow—her girl, I presumed—I thought, Damn, that is not the same woman I saw this morning in business attire. She had on a pair of jeans that looked painted on her round hips and thighs. She said something to her friend and they went to the bar. When she turned around, all I could see was ass. She had on a sleeveless, low-cut knit sweater, and I had to make my way over to her before another brother thought it was okay to approach her.

"Joss," I said as if I'd been calling her that forever.

She turned around. "Tony," she said, a beautiful smile appearing. Her dimples looked even deeper.

"You made it," I said and gave her a quick hug.

"Yes, it was a drive, but hey."

"I know, but my girl, Nina, is a barmaid here, and she convinced me to get my guy to bring his band out here on Thursdays."

"It's cool. This is my girl, Bailey," she said, introducing me to her friend.

"Nice to meet you," I said and quickly turned my attention back to Jocelyn. "I have a couple tables over here and Nina got y'all drinks," I said. She followed me to our section and sat down.

Nina was over in a flash. "Tee, what can I get for your guests?" she asked.

They both ordered and I ordered another drink for myself. I couldn't help but stare at Jocelyn for a moment. She was radiant, and I thought she was attractive that morning, but now she was in sexy girl mode and I liked it.

She enjoyed the music and my boy Sean did the same embarrassing shit he normally did when he knew I had a female to come out to see his band. I used to be a part of the band, but I got a real job after college, while they stuck with their music dreams.

"Y'all know we gotta bring my boy and former band member, Tony, to the stage," he said. I turned, and I gave him a look. "Come on, man, you know the crowd loves you," he said. Most of the ladies in the audience applauded. I looked at Jocelyn to see her reaction, and she smiled.

"You sing?" she asked.

"A little," I said, holding up two fingers making a small symbol.

"Gon' … show me what you got," she encouraged.

"Come on Tony P … come on up and let's do this," Sean pressed.

I got up, and I went over to the free mic. I already knew he was going to play the song that normally had women following me out to the parking lot after the show was over. I wanted to laugh, but I held it in and prepared to do my thang. Not that I had to impress Jocelyn, but I was damn sho' nuff gon' give Silk's "Lose Control" the Tony Pierce flava.

The music began and Sean took the first verse as usual. Then I hit the chorus like I wrote the lyrics myself.

"Let me look inside your soul, oh my baby," I sang. The look on Jocelyn's face was one I was used to getting from women, but the difference was I wanted it from her. "I wanna make you, lose control."

The other women were hollering and screaming, but Jocelyn just sat there, never taking her eyes off me. We finished that song and the crowd went crazy. Jocelyn just smiled at me, and I decided to sit in on a couple more songs. When it was time for the band to break before their last set, I made my way back to our table and swallowed the last of my drink and signaled for Nina.

"Tony, you are phenomenal. How in the hell are you not doing this for a living?" Joss asked.

"Because this is not a steady paycheck," I said.

She laughed. "That's a good point, but you sound better than that other guy."

"Well, that other guy happens to be my best friend, and I used to be the lead until I decided to leave the band. It was great when I was in college and five of us shared this enormous loft, working part-time with a gig here and there. After I got my degree, I went into the master's program and after that, bye-bye band," I explained. She nodded.

"So, Tony, is that short for Anthony, Antonio, or what?" Bailey asked.

"It's just Tony, not short for anything. My mom named me Tony," I said and left it at that. So many assume Tony is short for something, but it isn't.

"Okay then, Tony. How many kids do you have?" Bailey asked. I wondered why she was in my business.

"You don't have to answer that," Jocelyn said.

I appreciated her for stepping in, but I could speak for myself. "It's cool Jocelyn," I said and then turned back to Bailey. "I have a son who is now four and lives in Atlanta with his mother. She and I were together for a while, and she decided she wanted to relocate. She chose ATL, I chose Chicago, and my son is with her. Yes, I pay child support. Yes, I see him on vacations and holidays. And, if you must know, his mother and I are very good friends. You want her number?" I asked. I hated when a friend with no business was all up in her girl's business.

"Look, Tony, she didn't mean anything," Jocelyn said.

"I'm sure," I responded.

Nina finally made her way over. "Yes, Mr. Pierce?" she sang sweetly.

"You know what I need, and whatever the ladies want," I said, standing up. "Jocelyn, I'm going to run to the men's room, I'll be right back."

She gave me a warm smile. I didn't have to be a psychic to know that she was feeling me the way I was feeling her. I wanted to see her again. After my bathroom break, the band coming back on, and Bailey making her exit, I knew it was time for me to call it a night. I leaned in and asked Jocelyn was she ready to go and she nodded yes. When we got up, Sean could see we were leaving, so after he finished the chorus to the song they were singing, he sent me a shout, and we left.

I walked Jocelyn to her car. "Did you enjoy the show?"

"Did I? Good looks, sexy eyes, and you can sing? I'm like, how do I make this man mine," she joked. We both laughed.

"So, you're single, as in not seeing anyone?" I figured a woman as beautiful as her had to have a man.

"That's correct. Had a guy, but we broke up about four months ago. I've been out on a few dates, but nothing serious. And you? Are you seeing anyone?"

"I'm not seeing anyone special. Have a couple friends, but nothing serious," I said, being honest.

"So, in other words, you have fuck buddies?" she asked bluntly.

I didn't lie. "You can say that. A man has needs, and until I find the right one, I do what I do. I don't lie to them, they know what it is."

"I see," she said.

I tried to see if that bothered her, but I actually couldn't tell. She hit the automatic start and I took that as a goodnight. "So, can I see you again, or did what I say turn you off?"

"No, it didn't. You're a man, and I appreciate your honesty," she said. I let out a sigh of relief. "And if you'd like to see me again, that's cool. I'd like that." She hit me with that smile again.

"How about Saturday night? We can grab some dinner and maybe have a drink afterwards. Nina also tends bar at this lil' spot in the city, and me and my guys normally roll through there."

"Sure, that's sounds good. But can I ask you something?"

"Shoot," I said.

"Is Nina one of your friends?" She did air quotes when she said the word 'friends.'

I shook my head. "Naw, nothing like that. She's my homegirl from way back. We've just been cool for years," I explained. That was truth.

"So have you ever…?" she asked, an eyebrow raised. I knew she meant slept with—fucked or been with.

"Jocelyn, if I had, I'd never bring you around her. I'm not that dude. I wouldn't have a person that I'm interested in all up in an ex or a jump off's face," I explained.

"I see. And it's nice to know you're interested."

"Well, I did just ask you out," I joked.

She laughed a little. "Yeah, you did."

"Well, Saturday, right?"

"Yes, Saturday," she said.

I opened her door and she got in. I stood there until she pulled out of her stall, then got into my truck, hating myself for staying out so late. One a.m. was my cut off during the week, but it was close to three and I had to drive back to North Kenwood. I knew I'd feel it the next day, but, oh well, I had a good time. And I was looking forward to seeing Jocelyn again.

# Jocelyn

"I THINK I'm in love," I slipped and said to Bailey.

Tony and I had only been out on eight dates, but I already couldn't get him off my mind. He was just so sweet and mellow and I just loved being with him. We talked about everything. I was hooked.

"In love? Joss, see, I told you. You fall too fast. You haven't even known him that long. What has it been, about a month?"

"Yes, a month and four days, but we've been out several times. Plus, we talk on the phone constantly, so why can't I be in love?"

"Because you've only known this guy a few minutes."

"Get outta my office, you hater," I teased.

"I'm not a hater, I just know you, Joss, and you fall in love with every man you date."

"I don't, Bailey, that's just not true," I protested.

"It is, and if I was a hater, I'd sit here and name them all," she said. I was glad she didn't.

"Listen, I know what you're saying, and that may be true about me, but Tony is different."

"What makes him different, Jocelyn?" She leaned in like she couldn't wait to hear my answer.

"Well, for starters, I'm not sprung on the dick and my judgment isn't clouded because of the dick because I haven't seen his dick," I said. Dick somehow hypnotized me, but that wasn't the case with Tony. Not yet anyway.

"You know what, Joss, I will give you credit this time because you are right. You normally utter the word love after a brother has put it on you, but with Tony, y'all have had great dates, so I'll cut you some slack."

"Thank you," I said, throwing up my hands.

She laughed. "Okay, okay, you win. Just don't put the clamp on him and smother him. Tony does seem nice and a lil' different from the rest of them, so can you try to keep crazy Jocelyn in the box for a little while?"

"I can't make any promises, but I'll try," I joked. My phone rang. "What do you know, it's Tony," I said with a smile. Bailey got up to make her exit as I answered. "Good morning," I sang into my Bluetooth.

"Hey, good morning. How are you?"

"I'm good. How are you?" I beamed, knowing I was on his mind at ten a.m.

"Great, I wanted to give you a call early to ask if you'd like to come to a basketball game tonight. I wanted to invite you before, and now that I know you do like sports, I was wondering if you wanted to come see me play."

"You play ball?" He'd told me he was a quack doctor for nutty teens. "Get out. On what team?"

"Not professionally, Joss," he said. We laughed. "A few of my guys and I play at the gym. It's just a team we created a few years back, and other teams formed. Let's just say it's something we do," he said. "Anyway, would you like to come? The first game is at six and then it's like two more after. Depends on whether my team wins."

Feeing special, I said, "I'd love to." When a guy wants you to come around his friends, it's because he likes you or wants to show you off. Either way, I was game.

"Cool, and you are welcome to bring your girl. And you don't have to show up looking like the glamour girl you are. Jeans and tennis shoes are appropriate for the occasion. Afterwards, we go out for a beer if you're cool with that?" he asked.

"Yeah, that's fine. And I know not to wear heels to a basketball game, Tony. I am a season ticket holder," I bragged. I've been to plenty of games and owned a few Bull jerseys thanks to my sports-loving daddy who only had two girls—me and my older sister, Joanna. She was the one who was supposed to take over mother's company, but she decided to move to D.C. and work in politics.

"Awww, my bad. I wasn't aware of that," he replied.

"Well, now you know," I said and giggled a bit. "Text me the place and I'm there. I'll ask Bailey, but she's not a sports girl."

"Well, if she doesn't want to come, I'll introduce you to a couple wives that will be there. You won't be in the stands alone," he said.

"Sounds good, but I'm sure she'll tag along," I said. My other line was ringing. "Listen, baby, it's my mom. I gotta go." Did I just say 'baby' out loud? I thought. I wanted to pop myself in the mouth.

"Aight, I'll talk to you later," he said.

We hung up and I talked to my mom, half-listening to her because I was thinking baby was a bit much. Bailey was right. I had to ease up and take things a little more slowly if I wanted it to work. I did have the fall-in-love-too-quick disease, and I wanted to be cured of it.

"Okay, Mother, I have to go. I will come by this weekend, okay?" I said, hurrying off the phone. My mom was the love of my life, and she and I were close, but since she retired, she has nothing but time on her hands. If she gets you on the phone, it's hell getting off.

The rest of my day went by fairly quick, and I headed home to change. Bailey decided to go to the game with me after I twisted her damn arm. She didn't know a thing about sports and didn't understand what I loved about it.

When we got to the gym, I texted Tony, and he met us at the door. "Hey," he said and gave me a quick kiss. I smiled. Yes, we had kissed before, but it was normally a good night kiss and in private.

"Hey, I see you're suited up," I said, admiring his arms. They looked delicious.

"Yeah, we're about to start in a couple minutes. Follow me," he said, leading me and Bailey inside. I didn't expect to see so many people there, but I guessed it was a popular event that I hadn't heard of. "Y'all can sit here," he said, gesturing toward a couple seats. "This is Dominique, Tracy, and Rhonda." Bailey and I spoke to the three women he pointed out. "This is my girl, Jocelyn, so be nice," he told them and left. Bailey and I sat with them, and I wondered how Tony knew this gorgeous trio. By half time, I knew because they all pointed out their husbands during the game.

Tony played well and I was in the bleachers cheering like he was Kobe. Bailey kept nudging me to chill. "Stop that, Bailey," I finally yelled. She was on my nerves at that point.

"Calm down, Joss. My God."

"Bailey, this is a game. A game is a place where people cheer," I pointed out.

"I know, but you're so damn loud."

"And so is everyone else. What should I say?" I asked. I leaned forward in my seat and whispered. "Go, Tony."

She laughed. "Okay, dang," she said. I wondered if maybe she was jealous.

"So, how long have you and Tony been dating?" Dominique asked.

"Not long." I wanted to ask her why she wanted to know.

"Well, you must be special," Rhonda leaned in and said.

"Why's that?" I asked.

"Because you're the first to get an invite to a game. We've heard of women that Tony has dated, but we've never met one," Dominique said.

"Well, I don't know." I told myself not to jump to any conclusions.

"Well, enjoy, because rumor has it that women find it hard to get over him," Tracy said, getting in on the conversation.

Somebody called a timeout and I looked at Tony. He caught my eye and gave me a little smile. Oh, my Lord, I am in love, I said to myself. He looked so damn good with sweat pouring down his face. I did a body check and even though he had on long basketball shorts, his calves led me to believe his thighs were just as sexy as his arms. Six-one and sexy as hell, I thought. I didn't realize I was staring until Bailey bumped my arm.

"Huh, what?" I said.

"Do you want some popcorn?" she said, standing up.

"Naw, I'm good," I said. The game had resumed and the guys were back on the court. I couldn't wait until the game was over. I wanted to skip the beers and just do Tony. We came close once, but we both agreed it was too soon. Now, I was ready for him to slam dunk in my hoop.

They won the first game and progressed to the second one. I didn't want my man's team to lose, but I was ready to go. When they lost by one, I almost jumped up and cheered, but I kept my composure. Tony came out dressed in a pair of jeans and a button down, and I could tell that he had showered.

"Y'all ready to head out?" he asked me and Bailey when he approached.

"Yeah, if you are," I replied. He grabbed my hand and helped me down to the bottom bleacher.

"Bailey you gon' hang with us?" he asked as we walked out of the gymnasium. "My boy, Dez, asked about you."

"Who is Dez?" she asked with a frown.

"He was number six," Tony said.

Bailey's frown turned upside down. Probably because Dez wasn't a bad looking brother. "Oh really?" she said.

"Yeah, he saw y'all come in and as soon as the first game was over, he asked about you."

"Well, I guess I can hang for a beer or two," she said. We all had driven ourselves, but Tony insisted we ride with him and he'd bring us back to our cars. We headed over to the bar and I could not stop looking at him.

"What's wrong," he asked when he caught me staring.

"Nothing, you were good. I see you are multi-talented."

"I do a lil' sumthin sumthin," he smiled.

"Do you have any other talents I should know about?" I asked with a sexy smile.

"Maybe," he said. My clit clenched.

"Helloooooo, I am in this backseat," Bailey said.

Tony and I just smiled at each other. Our hands were close on the armrest, and I put my hand into his. He held my hand for the rest of the ride. When we got to the bar, all of his buddies and their girls were there. We had a good time. Bailey and Dez had a little connection and I was glad because that got her out of my face. I stood in front of Tony's stool, between his legs. We mingled with his friends, but we also did a lot of whispering into each other's ears and a sharing a few soft kisses.

"Spend the night with me tonight," I said.

He looked at me for a moment "Are you sure that's what you want?"

"Yeah, I'm pretty sure."

"Okay," he said.

"Is that what you want?"

"Yes," he said.

I wrapped my arms around his neck and he kissed me. That time it was tongue. We hung around a little longer and when we were ready to go, Bailey said that Dez would get her back to her car. We left, got my car and went back to my place.

# Pure Pleasure

I STOOD in the mirror and closed my eyes. He was on my sofa. I knew why I invited him and what was about to go down. I hadn't had any in about three months because I hooked up with a loser after my last relationship, thinking I could have sex and be done. But I started to call a brother more than he wanted to be called and he told me to lose his number. That day, I said no more dates, no more sex, no more chasing, and that is what I did. I stopped making any attempts to hook up or connect with anyone. I took a man break and decided not to be the initiator. But here I was again, putting myself out there. I had asked him to spend the night, not the other way around, and at that moment I had second thoughts.

Why was he so fine? Why was he so sexy? Why did he have to be so charming, so athletic? And he was the only man I've ever dated that could sing me to sleep. I hadn't even given him any and I was like totally taken by him. Just hearing his voice made me smile. Seeing his smile made my insides warm.

I told myself to hurry up and shower and let him have me. I went out to check on him one more time before I undressed.

"Do you need anything?" I asked.

"I'm good. I thought you went to shower?"

"I was … I mean, I'm about to. I just wanted to make sure you were okay first," I said, staring at him. His eyes were so intoxicating and I loved looking into them.

"I'm fine, you can go do your thang," he said.

I nodded and went into my bedroom. Opening my lingerie drawer, I pulled out a short purple nightgown with spaghetti straps and a slit on each side. I undressed and went into my master bathroom, started the water, and stepped in. I wanted to take my time, but I was anxious to be with Tony, I made myself squeaky clean as fast as I could. When I got out, I grabbed my smell goods and applied them to my skin. I brushed my teeth and decided put on a little makeup. I pulled my hair back and put it into a loose ponytail hanging over my shoulder and I was ready. I slid my feet into my slippers and headed out to join him on the sofa.

He looked me up and down. "You look…" I could tell he like what he saw.

"Thank you," I said and sat down.

"No, really, Joss, you look sexy."

I smiled. "So do you."

We sat looking at each other for a few moments until he said, "Do you want to take this to your bedroom?"

"Yes," I whispered.

We got up and he followed me to my room. I lit a couple candles and put on Pandora. I got into my bed and lay on top of my comforter and watched him undress. When he was down to his boxers, I made my way to the edge of the bed and sat up. He stood in front of me, caressing my shoulders and arms, and I planted soft kisses on his stomach. He lifted my chin and leaned in to kiss me. His lips and tongue felt and tasted so good. I couldn't help myself; I reached for his erection. He pulled his boxers away to release the magic.

He was packing, and I will admit my mouth watered, but I told myself, Calm down, Joss, it's just a dick. You don't have to suck it. I repeated this in my head over and over as I traced my tongue around his rippled stomach. He stroked himself and I knew he was telling me to trace his head with my tongue, so I did what he wanted me to do. He started breathing hard and playing with my hair. That encouraged me to please him more, so I let him enter my mouth. I grabbed hold of the base to have a little control and then I began to give him the Jocelyn special—yes, the head with slurping and loud sucking sounds. I could do it quietly, but when I was feeling someone, they got the head that let them know that I enjoyed pleasing them orally.

He moaned and groaned and called out my name several times before pulling back. When he took two steps back and I saw his dick jump a couple times in his hand, I knew he had to hold back his nut. I wiped the corner of my mouth and then licked my finger and his eyes widened. "Damn, baby, that's all you?" he asked as if I had a fake mouth and tongue.

"Can you handle that?" I asked seductively.

"Shit, I don't know," he said walking back up on me.

I pulled his dick back to my face. After a couple slurps, he was done and we had to change positions.

"Take this off," he said. He helped me lift my gown over my head. I went to pulled my purple lace thong off, but he stopped me. "No, baby, leave those on," he said, nudging me to lie down on my back.

He climbed on top of me and kissed my forehead, my eyelids, and then my nose. He got to my lips and planted a couple soft kisses and then moved down to my chin. He used his tongue to draw a line and a few circles on my neck before going to my nipples.

It was so intense and felt so good, I told him, "Bite it, baby. Please bite it."

He gently took my nipple between his teeth and my pussy went crazy. I took his hand away from my other tit and pushed it down to my clit. He massaged my pussy and continued to pleasure my breast, giving me buckets of pleasure. I moaned loudly, grabbed the back of his head, and told him how good he was.

"Can I have you?" he whispered in my ear as he kissed my earlobe.

I wondered if he just meant for the moment or if he wanted me for himself, but I whispered, "Yes."

I opened my legs and he climbed back on top of me, reached up and grabbed a condom from by my pillow. I briefly wondered when he put it there, but I didn't say anything. He had it on within seconds and I welcomed him inside of me.

If I tried to describe the feelings that Tony gave me, I couldn't because there are no words. All I know is I didn't want that feeling to end. If I could work, shop, and carry on with my day with his dick inside of me, I would have because it felt better than any encounter that I had ever experienced before him. He had a way of positioning my body that made me climax multiple times, and I never had multiples in my life. He turned my body over, and when he slid in from behind, I honestly thought I was going to cry. I knew Tony was it. I didn't want to see, touch, hold, talk to, or even smell another man. He was all I wanted. I lay on my stomach, closed my eyes, and let him ride me until he was satisfied.

After he climaxed the first time, I thought we were done, but after a brief recess he asked for more. There was no way could I deny him. Tony fucked me harder, longer, and stronger than any man that I've had before and my body was exhausted from the pure pleasure that he gave me that night.

Once we collapsed, there were no words to be said. We just looked at each other. I got up and went into the kitchen and he went to flush the condom. When I came back, he was already in bed under the covers. I eased into bed with him and he welcomed me into his arms and held me tight. It didn't take long for me to drift off to sleep. The next morning, the alarm on his phone blared and he had to go.

"No, boo, don't get up. I'll let myself out," he said. He kissed me and I looked up. He was fully dressed. I was going to walk him to the door, but truthfully, I was too tired to move.

"Are you sure, baby," I said in my raspy morning voice.

"I'm good. I'll lock the bottom lock, you get some sleep."

"Will I see you later?"

"Yeah, I'll call you," he said, bending to kiss my cheek. I smiled. "See ya' later," he said and gave me another soft kiss.

"Oh and Tony," I called out.

"Yeah," he stopped.

"You have to leave out the side door. The front entrance doesn't have a knob lock."

"Okay, get some sleep," he whispered.

"Okay," I said. I fell back into a deep sleep and when I woke up, I was already two hours late for work. I wasn't worried though. I was the boss, I could go in late. I got into the shower, on cloud nine and my brain in Tony-overload. I couldn't wait to see him again, and I definitely couldn't wait until I had him in my bed again.

I dressed and went into the office. When I gave Bailey a play-by-play of the night before, she confessed she went back to Dez's place and they'd burned a hole in his sheets too. She was so high off her night she didn't have time to scold me for saying how much I was in love with Tony. I assumed she didn't feel the need to lecture because she had something that I could have gotten on her about. We decided to leave work early and head to the spa, both of us basking in our newfound relationships. At least, that was what I hoped I had with Tony.

# The Pressure

"BABY, COME on," Jocelyn moaned. "You're at my place like five nights a week, and the other two I'm at yours. So what sense does it make to keep living apart?"

I truly didn't want to have this conversation again. We had been going strong for three months and I loved her—don't get me wrong, she was my heart—but I wasn't ready to give up my space.

"Babe, come on now," I said, "not this again. Tonight, we are going to have a marvelous time with our friends with some spades, domino's, food, and drinks. I am not in the mood to have this conversation again. I love you, Joss, but I just don't think we are ready to live together."

"But why?" She pouted. "This is stupid, Tony. We are together every moment, and it makes no sense for us to keep living apart. I miss you when you're not around," she whined, giving me puppy dog eyes.

"Okay, boo, look… Let me think about it, okay? I will think about it. I love you, girl. You are the best woman I've ever had. You are independent, you are self-sufficient, you are sexy and smart. And the head, baby, if I could bottle it up and sell it, we'd be billionaires," I teased. She slapped my arm. "No, seriously, Joss, I hear you babe, and I'll think about it. For now, let's just have fun with our friends. We can discuss moving in together later, okay?"

She smiled. "Okay, okay, Tony. As long as you think about it. I love you and I want to be with you every day."

Just then, my bell rang and I thought, Saved by the bell. It was our turn to host game night and I was glad I'd have a few hours of fun and games and not talk of living together. After Jocelyn and I made love, we became a couple. I got the boyfriend status quickly and I wasn't mad because I was feeling Jocelyn. But things kind of moved fast and after I got comfortable being in a monogamous relationship, she went into this living together mode and I'm thinking, Hey pump your brakes. I mean, I love Joss, I have strong feelings for her, but not on that live together level. I don't want any other women and I'm not on any BS, but I like having my own space. Even if Jocelyn is in it, it's still my space. Since I was renting, I knew I'd be the one to move with her and I wasn't too crazy about that idea. But, I said I'd give it some thought because Jocelyn was remarkable to me and she was the only one for me.

"Baby, these fools don't know how to bid their hands," I yelled. "Y'all are fucking set again." I slapped the big joker, little joker and the deuce of spades on the table.

"Man, that's some bullshit," Sean yelled. His girl, Penny, just got up.

"Come on, baby. I told you that I only had one and a possible and you were like 'Let's go seven,'" she said, mocking him. She grabbed her drink. "Now we done lost."

Sean got up, but he wouldn't stop talking shit.

"Yeah, whatever, dude, y'all lost," I said.

Bailey and Dez took their vacant seats. We played a few more games and then we all settled in the living room just to talk and drink.

"Excuse me, y'all," Joss said. The guys were debating so loud they didn't hear her. She got up and went to the entryway and motioned for me to come here, so I got up and eased away, following her into my room. When I walked in, it was dark, so I hit the switch.

"No, baby, turn that off," she whispered. When I did, she came over to me and put her tongue in my mouth to kiss me. Of course, I kissed her back.

"Joss, what's up?" I asked. "We have a living room full of guests."

"I know, but I really wanna suck your dick," she said, undoing my jeans.

"Babe, right now?" I asked. I'm sure my dick was wondering why I asked.

"Yes, right now," she said.

She pulled my man out and went to work. She was sucking my dick so damn good I thought she'd suck the skin off. I was leaning against the wall and couldn't see what she was doing, but I could imagine what she looked like doing it because there were a few vivid scenes in my memory bank.

"Awwww, Joss, baby, that shit feels so good," I moaned. I reached down to grab her hair. She loved it when I gently pulled her hair while she pleased me.

"Ummp, ummmp, ummmp," were the sweet sounds she made as she took my dick in and out of her wet mouth. I wanted to pull her up and push my dick inside of her, but there was no time. We had a room full of people, but I couldn't resist her head.

"Joss, baby, that's so good." I pushed her head further down on my dick. I could feel the back of her throat and I was ready to explode. "Joss, ooooh, baby. I'm ready to nut, baby, I'm ready."

I tried to pull away, but she held on. I squirted my hot juices into my baby's mouth for the first time and she swallowed it. I know she did because she continued to drain me with her mouth and when I hit the switch, there was not a drop or trace of semen anywhere. "Baby, did you swallow," I asked. When she nodded, I grabbed her and kissed her deeply. The residue of my dick and nut was still in her mouth, but that was okay because this was between me and my woman. I was so turned on I wanted to kick every ass out and devour her.

"Baby, I want some pussy right now," I said.

"Later, baby, we have guests." She went into the master bath. She grabbed the mouthwash, and poured some into the cap and threw it back, then poured some more and handed it to me. We both did a quick gargle and rinse. I went back into the living room and left her combing her hair back into place and reapplying her lipstick. I re-joined my friends who were either too into whatever they were talking about to even notice our absence or they just decided not to comment. It was after two when they all left and even though it was late, Jocelyn still rode my dick until I was satisfied. She lay in my arms and her last words were "I love you" before she drifted off to sleep.

Damn, I thought. What was I to do? Jocelyn was the best thing to have happened to me in a long while and I didn't want to lose her, but I wasn't ready to move in. It had only been three months and, as well as I thought I knew her, that wasn't enough. I mean, people that live together eventually talk about marriage and kids and all that family stuff, and I honestly didn't know if I was up for all that. When I was with my son's mother, I thought that's what I wanted. I tried it and then she up and wanted to relocate. I tried so hard to convince her to stay, but it was no use. She was from Atlanta, but was here in school, and even after our son was born, she wanted to be near her family. I didn't blame her because my friends and family were my main reason for staying in Chicago, but at the same time, I didn't understand how she chose her family over me. And I guess she couldn't understand how I chose Chicago over her. I'm just glad she is now happy with her husband and that we get along.

Jocelyn is a lovely woman and she is a good woman. She is a bit extra, yes, but she does all that she does out of love. Like she will send lunch to my office because she knows I barely take a lunch. I got so consumed with work one week that she came into my office looking for something and didn't say a word. I wondered what she was doing, but she tossed me her keys and left with mine. When I got off work, her Lexus was parked in the same spot my Range Rover had been parked in, so I drove her car to my house. My truck had been detailed inside and out. She'd boxed all the junk and clutter that I had in my SUV and told me if I ever let my truck get that filthy again, she was going to break up with me.

Jocelyn was just sweet. She cleaned for me, cooked for me, and the lovemaking was outstanding. She catered to me, so why would I decline? Why would I not move in with her? She was perfect, even in all of her smothering. She loved me, so she won. All the begging and pleading and pouting and whining worked. And that swallowing thing she did when she took my dick to a level of unknown pleasure had a little to do with my decision. Yes, I decided to move in. I decided to give it a try.

The next morning, I got up and fixed her breakfast. That was a first and I was proud of myself because it turned out well.

She sat up in bed when I brought it in. "Wow, Tony, this looks delicious."

"I just wanted to do something to show you how much I appreciate you." I sat on the bed, ready to tell her my decision.

"Awww, baby, thank you. You didn't have to do all this. I would have cooked for you, Tony." She gave me that bright smile of hers and those dimples had me.

"I know, boo, but I wanted to do something for you. And I also wanted to tell you something."

She put her fork down with a look of panic on her face. "Tony, please tell me you're not dumping me. I will throw these pancakes and eggs across this damn room," she said holding her chest.

"No, no, no, boo. Damn, bring it down." I laughed.

She let out a sigh of relief, letting the air out of her chest. "I was gon' say. How is this fool gon' break up with me over breakfast?" she asked. She shook her head and put a fork full of food into her mouth.

"I wouldn't do that. First of all, I wouldn't give you something that you can throw. And secondly, I love you too much to break up with you." She stopped eating and looked at me. "Listen, Joss, this move in together thing is not easy for me, boo, okay? I am used to being solo, just me. I mean, after my son and his mother left, I just fell into Tony, and for a while it's been all about Tony. But now I have you and you are like my superstar. You eased in and stole my heart, and if you want to live together, I'm down with that."

Joss brought her hands to her chest again and smiled. "Oh, Tony, baby, that is the best news. I promise you won't regret it baby."

"I know, Joss. You are a good person and I want to be with you. But understand that my son is also a part of my life and he will have to come to our place on breaks and holidays. I need to know that you are okay with that."

"Tony, I love you and everything you love, I'm so okay with that." she said, beaming. "I honestly can't wait to meet him."

"Well, it won't be for a little while because school just started. The next break will be Thanksgiving and I have plans to go to Atlanta. Since we're going to do this, you should go with me."

"Are you serious?"

"Yeah, I mean, we are going to be living together. His mom should probably meet you."

She put the tray aside. "Tony, this means so much to me. I mean I've never been in love with a man like I am with you. I promise to make you happy, baby. If at any time you're not happy, please tell me and I will fix it." I knew she meant it.

She kissed me and finished her breakfast. Afterward, we dressed and I took her to meet my parents. Then we went to meet hers. I was a little intimidated because they definitely lived on what's considered "the other side of the tracks." I thought maybe Joss was a little out of my league. I mean, her house was beautiful and I knew she did well, but her parents had what looked like a mansion. They had gates with a code to get in. I was more nervous than I ever had been in my life.

"Baby, relax," Jocelyn said. "My folks are going to love you just like I do."

She was right. Even though they live on about forty acres and had staff on duty to serve us, her daddy was cool as hell. He took me down to his "Lion's Den" as he called it, and I wanted to move in. I left with an open invite to come back whenever I wanted.

"So what now?" I asked when we left.

"Home, sex, and sleep," was her response.

"Sounds good." I leaned over and kissed her. Jocelyn had me and I was honestly happy to be her man.

# Changes

"WHEN ARE you coming home Tony?" I barked into the phone. I know it was Thursday, and he went to Genesis, but I thought he'd scale back now that we were living together.

"Joss, you know I'm with the band on Thursday's, so why are you trippin'?" he yelled back.

"I'm not trippin', Tony, but damn. Why must you go every damn Thursday?"

"Again," he spat, "because that's what I do and have been doing for the longest. I knew you'd do this shit."

I snapped back at him. "Do what shit?"

"As soon as I move in, you think you can control my coming and going."

"That isn't true, Tony. I just don't understand why you can't skip one Thursday."

"Because I can't. Either you're coming or not. I gotta go." He hung up.

I wanted to call back, but what would be the point? To argue? I wasn't for that. I went into the bathroom and decided to dress and go see why my man couldn't miss one Thursday. I made up my face and put on a pair of cute jeans, a sweater, and my boots. It was getting cold and I was mad I couldn't show any skin. I was only five-three, but my size fourteen frame was eye-catching and right. I had the right amount of ass, hips, and thighs and looked good in everything. Mocha skin, two deep dimples and a head full of imported weave—yes, the good shit that could get wet and not mat up.

I grabbed my light leather jacket, purse, and keys and made my way to the club. Approaching the door, I could hear my baby's voice from outside. I smiled. That was all he did and I shouldn't have been tripping. I walked in and went over to his table. When he saw me, he smiled and winked. I winked back at him. He finished the song and they went into the next one, which was Usher's 'Climax.' I loved for Tony to sing that to me, but not at Genesis because the women in there were sometimes ghetto. I knew Tony could do so much when the women would get up and dance in front of him or behind him. I normally ignored it because he was going home with me, but that night it was different.

I was sitting there watching my baby do his thing, with his eye's locked on me, when this stank bitch gets up and stands in front of him. He continued to sing and she moved closer to him. He looked at me and I hunched my shoulders and smiled because it didn't bother me. She went behind him and started dancing on him and he kept singing. She went to touch him, but in a smooth move, he grabbed her hand and moved it away. Then she took her other hand and touched my man's dick.

Before I knew it, I was out of my chair. I ran up on that bitch and yanked her ass. The music stopped and they had to pull me off her. I don't know what got into me. And it didn't help matters when Tony snapped on me. He dragged me to a corner and I wondered why he turned on me.

"Joss, what the fuck!" he yelled in my face.

I yelled back at him. "Tony, are you fucking serious!"

"Yes, you know better than that. You can't be up in a club, fighting and shit. What the hell is wrong with you!"

"Oh, so it's cool for some bitch to touch your damn dick?"

"No, it's not, but I can handle these bitches. I don't want my woman acting like some jealous lunatic. You know I don't give a damn about these women up in here. You know it's all about you, so why would you bring this unnecessary drama up in here?" He looked at me like I was supposed to admit to being wrong for my actions.

"Move," I said with my teeth clenched.

"No."

"Tony, get the hell out of my way." My teeth were damn near grinding.

"Jocelyn, you are my woman, and you are going to act as such. You are going to go over to our table and sit your ass down and control yourself. These chicks up in here don't mean shit to me, and you are not going to embarrass me or yourself by acting an ass."

I was so mad I could have spit nails. He stepped aside, grabbed my hand, and escorted me back to the table.

When I sat down, he leaned over and whispered in my ear. "I'm yours, so act like it. If you keep acting like that, all of these bitches are going to make it a point to fuck with you. Now, hold your head high and give me a kiss," he demanded.

I did. He smiled and went to find the rest of the band members. I took two gulps of my wine and wondered what the hell I was doing still sitting there. About two minutes later, the DJ stopped the music and they were back on.

"We are back, y'all," Sean said, "and we want to apologize for that minor disturbance. For those of you that don't know, Mr.

Tony, here, is not a single man, so keep yo' hands to yo' self," he joked. The crowd laughed.

"No, I'm not," Tony said. "My lovely lady is sitting right over there." They put the spotlight on me. "Come on, Joss, give Daddy a big smile." he said. I let my anger subside and smiled for my man. "Now that y'all know my baby will whip some ass, I advise y'all to be respectful," he said.

They began to play Tony, Tone, Toni, "Just Me and You." My baby sang that song like he normally did and made sure I got all the eye contact and smiles I needed to know that he was singing to me and not the other chicks in the house. After they were done, he walked over to get me and said goodnight to everyone with a smile. I thought everything was good, but when he got outside to walk me to my car, he showed me the pissed-off Tony that I thought was gone.

"I'll see you at home," he said. He walked away before I got in my car. I got in and called him, but he didn't answer. When I got home, he hadn't arrived. He came in about thirty minutes later. I had already showered and was in bed waiting for him, but he never came into our bedroom. I got up to see what was keeping him and found him on the sofa.

"Babe, why are you out here?" I asked.

"Joss, not tonight. I don't want to be near you right now."

"Are you kidding me?"

"No, I'm not. You have to stop! I am your man, not your property, and all this bullshit you are doing is on my nerves."

"Tony, that bitch touched your dick!"

"And I am a grown ass man, Joss. I can handle the women at Genesis. I know I have a woman. I know we are involved and I don't need you acting like some ghetto project bitch. You are my woman and I want you to act like it. Ever since I moved in, you act as if you own me, Jocelyn, and that shit is getting old fast. I can't go here or there without you blowing up my damn phone. I'm your man, not your damn son, so you need to fall back!"

"Fine, Tony, do you. Let hoes feel on your damn dick."

"Dammit, Joss, are you fucking listening? It's not only about tonight. All this checking in shit and you tracking my every move is not cool and not what I signed up for, so I say again, I don't want to be on a leash. If I say I'm gonna hang out for a minute or two after work, stop calling my damn phone every twenty minutes. Stop showing up without warning like you want to walk up on me doing some shit. I tell you where I am and who I am with, but I don't like you trying to keep tabs on my every move."

I heard him and I didn't see my error, but I agreed. "Okay, baby, alright, I hear you. Now can you please come to bed? I don't like to sleep without you," I whined. He sat up on the couch, but didn't move right away, so I went over to him. "Tony I'm sorry if I embarrassed you tonight. I'm sorry, baby. I saw her touch you and I lost it. I'm sorry."

He put his arm around my shoulder. "I love you, Joss. I'm here because I love you."

"I know," I whispered.

We got up and went to bed. I knew it was late and we both had to work the next morning, but head always made him feel better. Even though he said he wasn't in the mood, his dick said otherwise. I let him cum in my face that time. He never asked, but I figured I had to do something extra for him since I made him angry earlier. When I got back from cleaning myself up and got back into bed, he pulled me close and kissed me on the head. I knew that I had to chill. Tony was sexy, smart, and a good man and I didn't want the old Jocelyn to run him off, so I told myself I'd ease up.

But the old Jocelyn was who I was and things didn't change. I drove him away just like I did to every man I had. The difference is I didn't want any of them back as much or as bad as I wanted Tony back. I told myself that I'd never love again because Tony was it.

## Present Day

### THE MORNING AFTER TONY LEFT

"JUST PUT everything on my desk and I'll review them in the morning," I told my assistant.

I woke up saying I could make it, but the truth was I couldn't. I missed him and wanted him home. I called him a million times the night before, but he didn't answer. I texted him over and over, asking what I could do to make it work and got no response. Not a word and I was feeling sick to my stomach. I was in so much pain and I didn't know how I was going to get over him, let alone get on with my life. Tony was it, the end of the Love Road. He was everything I wanted, everything I needed. I wanted him back, but I had no clue what I could do to get him back.

"Please call me, baby. I'm so sorry, Tony, for whatever I did, baby. I am suffocating without you. I can't breathe, baby. Please call me and just tell me how to fix it. I can change," I cried. The machine cut me off.

I didn't know what to do. I just lay in my bed and cried. I begged God to send him home, but by nightfall he hadn't returned. I got up to go to the bathroom and sat there in a daze. All I did was love him. I loved him. How can you love someone too much? How can you go wrong when you have good intentions and only want the best for someone? Why didn't he want me anymore? I wondered.

I got up after my legs began to go numb from sitting so long. I washed my hands and I looked at my bed. His side was still nicely made. I cried some more.

I went to the kitchen because I needed a drink. I know I hadn't eaten, but I just needed something to take my troubles away. I polished off an entire bottle of Merlot and climbed back into my bed.

The next four days were the same thing. By then, I needed a shower and fresh pajamas. I was on my way down to my basement to bring up a couple of bottles of wine when my doorbell rang. As terrible as I looked and smelled, I raced to the door, thinking he'd come to his senses and wanted to come back. It was Bailey. I hesitated, but I opened the door.

"Why are you here, Bailey? I told you I wanted to be alone," I said when she came in.

"First, I'm here because even though you have love issues, you still have a company to run. Now, I've tried to fill in for you, but some of these decisions have to be made by you." She put a stack of files on the dining room table. "Secondly, I know you are hurting and didn't want any visitors, but I'm your best friend. If I don't do anything else before I leave, I will get you into the tub. Baby, you have to brush your teeth."

I knew she was right, but I was in no mood to freshen up. "Bailey, thank you for bringing my work to me, but, right now, I just want to stay funky and cry, so please don't … don't try to make me feel better or convince me to bathe or comb my hair because I don't want to!" I cried. "He left me Bailey. I don't know how it's possible to love too much. I loved him away!"

Bailey came over to my funky-ass body and held me. She held me and rocked with me, and I decided to allow her to care for me. I knew I smelled rancid and looked a mess, and for her to endure that to be by my side was a sign of love and someone who wanted to help me.

"Listen, Joss, I know you're hurting, and I'm sorry Tony left. You are an extraordinary woman and you love hard. You need a man in your life who loves you just as hard. Tony loved you, yes, but not hard as you love him. I know it is going to be a mother-fucker to get over him, but I'll be by your side to help you."

I sobbed, but agreed that I needed her help so I followed her into the bathroom. I was in my tub soaking and Bailey was right there. "Thank you, Bailey. Thank you, my friend. I just want to die," I said, being honest.

"Well, Ms. Jocelyn, if you die, you still won't get Tony back" she said. "We just have to keep living and keep it moving."

She washed my back and after I got out, brushed my teeth, and lotioned up, she brushed all the tangles out of my weave. She made me eat and sat with me until after three in the morning, going through days' worth of work that I had to finish. I promised her I'd be in the office the next morning and she went home.

I was about to get into bed, but I decided to go through my place and take down all the pictures and memories of me and Tony. It hurt to see so many captured moments of us that I thought made him happy and I started to feel like it was a lie because he'd left me. He just left me with no warning and no good enough explanation. He just packed up and left.

When I woke up, I was tired. Even though I promised Bailey I'd be in, I couldn't make it that morning. I stepped in around two that afternoon, looking like nothing ever happened. Bailey was happy to see me looking well. She told me her job was to help me get over Tony, and the first step for that was a hook up. Even though I knew that was the wrong answer, I gave in after she insisted her cousin, Marlin, was my perfect match. We went out and he was sweet, but my mind was on Tony. Everything reminded me of Tony, and after I talked about him the entire night, Marlin was more than happy to drop me off at home. After that, it was Keith, Stephen, Travis, Derrick, Jerome, and so on. It was two months after the breakup and still no Tony and no prospects because nobody measured up or compared to Tony. I thought of him morning, noon, and night and still wanted him back. I still prayed to God to bring him back.

I still called him and he still never picked up. I still texted him and he still never replied. I emailed telling him that I would take him back, but he never replied. A week after he left, he went in while I was at work and got all the things he left behind. He put my key in my mailbox. I think I cried the hardest that night. I missed him with everything. Even though my sister and Bailey told me not to, I dressed that Thursday night and headed to Genesis. I just had to see him. I knew there was a chance that he wouldn't talk to me, but I just needed see him. It had been two long months and had been hard to stay away that long. I couldn't make it another day without seeing his face.

I walked inside and looked over at the table where I normally sat when I was his girl. It was empty. I secretly thanked God that it was and went to sit at the bar. "Nina," I said when I saw her.

"Hey, Joss, how you been baby?" She greeted me with a kiss and hug.

"I'm okay, missing Tony like crazy," I confessed and wished I hadn't.

"You? Girl, we ain't seen him in weeks." I was shocked. He never missed Thursdays. "I'm hoping he comes through tonight because my birthday is coming up and I want him to sing with the band," she said.

"Well, I hope so too. I haven't seen him since the breakup."

"I heard, are you okay?"

"No, but I will be." I gave her a smile. I sat there for a couple hours, but he was a no-show. I left sad and tried again the following Thursday. He didn't show. The third week, I started not to show my face, but something told me to go again, so I dressed and went to see if he would come that night.

"Back again?" Nina asked when I took my seat at the bar.

"Yes. I can't give up. I just have to see him Nina."

"I know that's right. Let me get you a drink, Ma. Sit tight and I'll be right back."

I sat there hoping he'd come that night.

"Alright, ladies and gents, we are back," Sean said. I turned to the stage. "I am so happy to be back here at Genesis for your listening pleasure." The crowd applauded. "I am also happy to announce that my boy, Tony, is back in the house tonight to do a couple songs with us." The ladies went wild again. I scanned the room and spotted him at our table. I almost hit the floor when I saw a woman sitting in my seat. Well, the seat I use to occupy. My face became hot and I turned back to the bar quickly.

Breathe, I told myself. Nina put my drink down in front of me and I gulped it down and asked for another. I turned to make sure my eyes were not playing tricks on me, and, yes, there was a beautiful sister sitting in the spot I once occupied. I decided to chill. It was what it was. I downed the next drink, and when they called Tony up, I turned around. In a matter of seconds, his eyes were on me. I realized Nina had told him I was there because she was handing his new woman her drink.

"'Loose Control,'" some of the female patron's yelled out. I just stared at him.

"I know y'all love 'Loose Control,'" Tony said. "So do I, but tonight we are not going to do that one."

Sean looked at him. "Tony P, 'Lose Control' is what the ladies want." I remembered that was the first song I ever heard him sing.

"I know, but tonight we're gonna try something a little different," he said. The music went low. "Come and talk to me, I really wanna meet you girl. I really wanna know your name," he sang while the band played Jodeci's "Come and Talk to Me."

I tried to keep my eyes off him, but it was impossible and he failed at it too. Eventually, the woman he was with glanced in my direction to see who he was looking at during his performance. She looked at me and gave me a displeasing look. When he went back to the table, I witnessed some neck twisting and words exchanging. She then got up and made her exit. I turned back around and asked Nina for my final drink. I refused to turn in his direction. I turned back to the stage and listened to the band as I finished my drink and told myself not to look his way. I said goodnight to Nina and grabbed my purse and jacket to leave. Heading toward my car, I heard him call my name. I turned around.

"I'm sorry," he said.

I turned toward my car. Sorry didn't mean shit to me.

"Joss, hold up," he said when he made it to my car.

"Tony, I shouldn't have come. I was thinking I'd come and you'd see me and realize how much you miss me and beg me to take you back, but you know what? It's cool. You may want to find your girl and tell her you're sorry." I pushed the automatic start on my car.

"Listen, Joss, I am sorry for hurting you. You may think that I'm a major asshole, and I can't change that, but I love you," he said.

My hands trembled, and my eyes welled. "Love me?" I yelled looking at him like he was crazy. "Love me? Is that what you just said?"

"Yes, I love you."

"Well, you have a funny way of showing it." I snatched my car door open and got in.

He was talking and saying something at my window, but I drove off. How could he say love and he left me and wasn't trying to come back to me? I drove home trying to fight the tears, but they kept flowing. By the time I made it inside, Tony had called fifteen times, but I didn't answer. When I got in, I took off my clothes. The doorbell rang. I knew it wasn't Bailey and the only other person it could be was him. I hesitated, but opened the door for him.

"I miss you," he said. He stepped inside, grabbed my face, and pushed his tongue into my mouth. He pushed the door with his foot and closed it, then pushed me towards my room.

"Tony, no, please … no, wait, please."

But he wouldn't let me go. I became blinded by my heart and lust for him. I gave him my body over and over and over again that night. The next morning, I lay there with my eyes open and didn't ask him any questions when he kissed me goodbye. It didn't matter what he wanted or why he came, I missed him too much to deny him. My heart would have been free to love and move on if it wasn't for him. He was my lifeline and I wanted whatever he wanted. I was willing to do whatever he wanted me to do because he had possession of my heart and my body. Only a love exorcism was going to free me from him.

# Three Days Later

"HELLO."

I finally took Jocelyn's call. She'd called me several times after I left that morning, but since I didn't plan to say we were getting back together, I had no idea what to say to her.

"Hi," she said.

"Listen, I know you want answers, and I know you want to talk about the other night, Joss, but I can't do this right now." I hoped it wouldn't turn into a fight.

"So when will it be a better time, Tony?"

"Joss, I'll call you," I said.

"Just tell me, are you coming home or not? I need to know."

"No, I'm sorry, I'm not moving back in."

"Are we back together? I need to know something, Tony. I mean, you said you loved me; that has to count for something."

"I do love you, Jocelyn, and there is a chance for us to work it out, but it has to be on my terms."

"What terms, Tony? Why can't you just come home and we work this out. I miss you and I want you home with me," she cried.

"I gotta call you later," I said and hung up. My other line was ringing. It was Rameeka, the woman I'd decided to take to Genesis with me the other night. I hooked up with her a couple days before that, even though I knew I shouldn't have. She was cool, but she didn't help me forget about Jocelyn. I called her the day after the club episode and she accepted my apology and wanted to see me that evening.

"Yeah, what's going on?" I asked when I answered.

"Nothing much, trying to see what you're getting into tonight," she said.

"Well, I'm going by a friend's house. We do this monthly game night at each other's houses, and tonight my boy, Dez, is hosting it."

"Ooooh, sounds like fun, do you mind if I tag along?"

Why not? I thought. "That's cool, but I must warn you, they are all fans of Jocelyn's and they may be a tough crowd."

"I'm good, I've handled worse," she said.

I gave her the address. Jocelyn and I were over, so I could date if I wanted. I was back to being a free man. Back to being on my own and doing what I wanted to do, not what we wanted to do. I still loved Jocelyn and missed her, but I didn't miss the "couples only" all the time. No matter how I tried to have some Tony time, Jocelyn would somehow turn it into our time. It got to the point where I wouldn't disclose my true location because I'd get tired of her just popping up and thinking I was wrong for not wanting her there. When I'd lie about where I was going, it would cause an argument, and that got old too. I loved Jocelyn and I wanted her, but I had to move on to something else because part of me wasn't entirely happy.

Jocelyn was perfect in everything else. She was sexy with a plump ass and thick frame. She could cook her ass off and she kept the house spotless. She made not good, but serious money and the sex was, hands down, the best. Her head was top shelf and she never let me down. She spoiled the hell out of me, but I felt like I was in prison. It was a million and one questions when I walked through the door about where I was and who I was with. She wanted to know details of every moment of my day. It was cute at first, but it became so damn annoying.

If I said, "Baby, I'm leaving now," she called me five minutes later and asked, "Have you left yet?" One night, I was out with the guys up at this new spot that they wanted me to sit in with them on and she was with me, but she had a severe headache and wanted to leave. I told the guys I'd run her home and be back before the second set. When I got to the house to drop her off, she went off because I wanted to head back to the club.

"But, babe, you heard me tell Sean that I'd be right back," I said, waiting for her to get out.

"But I'm not feeling well, Tony. How you gon' run back to them and not stay here and take care of me?"

"Joss, you said you wanted to go home and I said I need to stay. You are the one who said take me home and come back, now you expect me to stay?"

"Tony, the band will be just fine without you. I need you here with me!" she said, raising her voice.

"Joss, get out the truck and go in the house," I ordered.

"Excuse me?"

"You heard me. Now, I told Sean I'd be back before the next set and that is what I plan to do, so get your ass out of the truck so I can go."

"Fine, Negro, don't bring your ass back to my house tonight." She got out and slammed the door.

I got out and went after her. "Your house? Now this is your house!" I yelled.

She turned around and shot me a look. "Yes, my house," she yelled.

I went back to the truck, turned off the ignition, and snatched the keys out. I took her key off my ring and threw it on the porch.

"Fuck you and your house!" I barked. I got into my truck and headed back to the club and did my thing. After it was over, she had texted and called me a million times, saying how sorry she was and for me to please come home. I didn't want to put my guys in my business, so, like a fool, I went home and let her fuck me to sleep like she always did after she pissed me off. The next morning, I woke up to breakfast and a side order of ass before she left to shop with Bailey.

She came home and vowed never to throw those words in my face again. And she never did again, but her controlling and smothering behavior stayed the same. I had to leave because I was tired of begging her to change. I was tired of telling her how she made me feel when she didn't give me space. Even though I've left, she hasn't once asked me just to be with her and we live apart. Her only plea was for me to come home, and that wasn't an option.

"So are you going to go back?" Dez, asked me, adding another bag of ice to the ice chest for our beers.

"Man, I'm not sure. I mean, I want to be with Jocelyn, man, I do. But it's like all or nothing with her. And I don't know, living together is not the move."

"Listen, talk to her man. Jocelyn loves you, and I'm sure if you tell her how you feel, she'll understand. Just tell her you want to be with her, but you think you guys should live apart."

But I knew Jocelyn. Once we got back together, she'd start hinting or suggesting, and I didn't want to be under her thumb anymore. I didn't want that kind of pressure anymore.

"Dez, if I go back to Joss and I don't want to do it how she wants it, she is not going to be happy or satisfied."

"Well, if you love her and you don't want her to slip away, you'd better do something. Jocelyn is smart, gorgeous, and she's got loot. She is not going to stay on the market long."

"I know," I said.

Guests started to arrive and game night was on. Since I invited Rameeka, imagine the look on my face when Jocelyn walked in with Bailey. The last couple of game nights she hadn't come, so I wondered why she showed up when I invited someone. I didn't want things to get ugly. Rameeka didn't know who Jocelyn was because she didn't recognize her from the other night, but it didn't take long for her to figure it out because Jocelyn didn't hesitate to make it known.

"Ummm, Tony, can I speak to you alone for a moment," she asked. The room got quiet.

"Can it wait?" I asked.

The look on her face, said "Get your black ass up, Negro, before I make a scene," but she said, "No, it can't."

I got up. "Give me a moment," I said to Rameeka and followed Jocelyn into the other room.

"What's going on, Tony? You see me the other night—come to my house and lay with me—and then no words from you for three days. You rush me off the phone today and then I walk in to see you with the same bitch that you were with the other night."

I knew I deserved to be punched in the face. "Look, Joss, I had no idea you were coming, for one. And the other night shouldn't have happened. I don't want to lead you on or make you think that we are getting back together." I tried to be honest as possible.

"Tony, what in the hell is wrong with you?" she yelled. "You can't fuck with my heart and head like that. You came to me and said you loved me and you missed me, you screw me and then get ghost. That is not how you treat someone that you love." She looked ready to cry.

"Listen, Jocelyn, I know and I'm sorry." I tried to hold her.

"Don't fucking touch me, Tony," she said and stepped back. "It's cool alright. You love me, yet you don't want to be with me. Okay." She tried to walk away, but I grabbed her arm and she yanked away.

"Jocelyn, wait a minute," I said. She stopped. "I want to be with you, baby, and I do love you, but you can't make all the rules. If we get back together, we cannot live together. I want and need my own place." She turned and walked into my chest and I put my arms around her.

"If that's what you want, Tony, I'm okay with that. I just want you back," she cried.

"I want you back too," I said and kissed her. Then I remember Rameeka. "Can you give me a second to walk Rameeka out to her car?" I hoped she'd be civil.

"Yeah, go ahead."

We went back into the living room. I didn't have to walk Rameeka out because she had taken the liberty of leaving without saying goodbye. We rejoined the party and our friends knew that we had worked things out and gotten back together.

The night ended well and the next day, when I got off work, I headed to Jocelyn's. I told her I wasn't going to stay all night and she said okay without dispute, but I ended up staying anyway. We were good after that for about five months and then we were right back to square one. She was back to asking me to move in and back to showing up to wherever I said I'd be. She went back to trying to control my coming and goings and I was done this time. I didn't want to do it, but I did. I told her it was over and then I truly moved on.

# All Tried Out

I STARED at his picture and wiped my last tear. I was done and over it. I decided it was time to find someone new who would appreciate me for who I was and not think that I was an overbearing nut job. All I wanted was something solid, someone to be all in and want to spend the rest of their life with me. As bad as I wanted it to be Tony, it wasn't. He'd left me again because he was too afraid of a solid commitment. How was it so hard to plant roots with me? I just wanted something guaranteed and he just wanted something pleasing until he didn't want it anymore. That bastard.

Everything I said to him concerning commitment and our future was always a smothering gesture or he'd say, "Baby, chill, slow down, we have plenty of time for that."

I'd be like, "Tony, if I'm what you want, let's make it official, let's get engaged. You can move back in; let's work on us and our future." Ha that wasn't what he wanted to hear. No, no, that was just too much of me trying to dominate his life.

"Fuck you, Tony," I yelled in my empty house. "Fuck you. It's not about your ass anymore." I ended up crying. I didn't want to, but I was confused and didn't understand how he didn't want a future with me. I sat on the floor and got myself together and then I called Bailey.

"I need to get out," I told her. "This Tony shit is too depressing. Let's hit up a few clubs."

"Wow, Joss, I'd love to, but Dez and I already have plans to go out. You're more than welcome to roll with us," she offered.

I didn't want to be out by myself, so I decided to go. "Okay, where are you guys going?" I asked.

"Well, there is this boat party at Navy Pier, a white party. The tickets are like a hundred a pop. Dez's friend, Will, still has a couple; I can call him for you."

"That's cool. I have something in white that's sexy to wear. Get me a ticket and I'll pay you back tonight." I hung up and then called her right back. "Please tell me Tony is not attending, he is the last person I want to see."

"Joss, I don't know. I didn't ask," she said.

"You know what? So-fucking-what if he is. We are done." I hit the end button and went into my walk-in and pulled out five different choices. I scrolled through my phone and landed on Porsha's number. I called and told her I needed an emergency overhaul. She was a stylist and makeup artist who worked for my mother's company. She dropped everything and showed up at my house in an hour. After she made my face beautiful, I dressed in a pair of white trousers and a cute white, backless, low-cut halter with my tits taped to the fabric to keep them in place.

I was looking like a sexy voluptuous model. Deep down inside, I hoped to see Tony to ignore his stupid ass. I wasn't conceited, not one bit, but I knew I was a good woman with a big heart and I knew how to please a man in the sheets. If all that didn't make him see the light, what would? I asked myself. Then I quickly said I didn't care because I wanted him out of my system.

"Girl, look at you, you are gorgeous," Bailey complimented me when I got out of my car.

"Thank you, and so are you," I said. She had on a long, white, backless dress with a slit all the way up to her right thigh. If I wasn't mistaken, she looked like she had a little bump in her stomach area. She was slim and petite and I didn't remember her having a little stomach, but she still looked beautiful. We went inside and I headed straight for the bar. I decided on white wine because the last thing I needed was a drink of red spilled on my outfit when we were out in the middle of the lake with no escape. After the boat couldn't wait anymore for the sisters and brothers on CP time, we finally began to move. There were three levels and it was packed, so I tried to stay close to Bailey and Dez.

"So why aren't you drinking?" I asked Bailey again because she declined earlier when I asked her what she wanted. .

"Okay, okay," she said and looked at me. "I wanted to wait until my second trimester, but you are my best friend and I have to tell you.

"You are not pregnant," I said, happy and shocked.

"I am, and Dez and I are moving in together," she said softly.

"Why didn't you tell me, Bailey? Oh, my gosh, I'm so happy for you." I gave her a loving squeeze.

"I wanted to tell you, but you and Tony were going through and then he left again. I didn't want to throw my good news in your face."

"Bailey Marie Washington, give me a break. We have been friends since we were kids and I'd never shit on your good news because I'm going through. You know me better than that," I said and hugged her again.

"I know, and I'm sorry. I just know how much you love Tony and how hard you tried to make it work with him. I'm sorry things went the way they did for you, Jocelyn."

"Hey, it is what it is, Bailey. I'm not bitter anymore, girl. I'll just have to find a way to get over it."

Then I saw him. I froze.

"What is it?" Bailey asked.

"Tony, he is on this boat. He is on this damn boat." I wished I'd stayed my black ass at home. No matter how I wanted to be, I wasn't strong enough yet.

"Where?" she asked.

"Nine o'clock," I said and downed the rest of my drink. "I gotta go."

"Ummm, Joss, baby, we are in the middle of the lake. Do you plan on swimming?"

My eyes welled. "Oh, my God, Bailey, I'm not ready. I thought I was, but I'm not fucking ready," I cried.

"Come on, let's go up top," she suggested.

I tried to move quickly, but he saw me. We locked eyes and then I saw her walk up. It was Rameeka. He was back with her. 'I'll be damned,' I thought. I went up the steps as fast as I could. I found a waiter, grabbed another white, and asked Bailey for some space. She refused to leave me alone at first, but I insisted.

"Okay," she said. "But I'll be right back at the table if you need me." I nodded.

I sat there wondering why I fell so in love with that man. Why did I want him more than I wanted any other man in my life? Why, when I knew he didn't want me, I still wanted him. I looked at the tall buildings and lights of this gorgeous city they called Chicago and wondered if I needed a change of scenery. Maybe moving would help me to get over him.

"Is this seat taken," a baritone voice asked. I looked up at the most decadent piece of chocolate on the planet. He was unbelievably sexy and I had to turn back to the city lights to keep from staring. "It's a beautiful night, isn't it?" he asked.

I answered without looking at him. "It is, and the weather is perfect." I added.

"So are you."

In my head, I was like, Please. Get on up from here and leave me be.

"I'm Brian," he said and extended his hand.

"I'm, Jocelyn. Nice to meet you." I shook his hand.

"Are you enjoying your evening?" he asked.

"I am now. I wasn't a little while ago, but being up here and taking in the view, I'm having a better time."

"So are you with someone?"

"No, just a friend and her guy. I'm solo," I confessed.

"So am I and I'd love it if you saved a dance for me."

I smiled. "Okay, Brian, I'll do that," I said.

He left and I continued to look out at the city lights. After getting myself together, I went back down to join Bailey. To my unpleasant surprise, Tony and his date were at our table. I sat near Bailey anyway and refused to give Tony any eye contact. Shortly after, Brian came over and asked for that dance and I quickly accepted. We stayed on the floor for a few songs. When we got back to the table, he asked if he could sit with us and I let him. Tony didn't like it at all and I didn't give a shit. After a few moments of eyeing me and Brian, he grabbed Rameeka and they vacated their seats. I got back to Brian. I learned he was a surgeon and he was divorced with no kids. We had endless conversation and I gave in and gave him my number.

When we docked, I allowed Dr. Payne to escort me to my car. He wanted to spend more time with me, so I agreed to go to a twenty-four hour coffee shop for some more conversation.

"So tell me more about your company," he asked when we were seated.

"Well, there isn't much more to tell. My mom was a chemist and her dad, my grandfather, owned a few hair care factories in the seventies and eighties. When he died, he left the business to my mom because she was an only child. She wasn't too enthused with hair products—although we still distribute hair care solutions—so she got into cosmetics. My mom had me late, fifteen years after my sister, Joanna, and she was just tired and ready to retire. I studied science and planned to be a professor one day, but my mom didn't want anyone other than blood to run her business. Since Joanna refused to move back, my mom asked me. I wanted to say no so bad, but my mother gave her all to her company and worked until she turned sixty-eight and I couldn't do what Jo did. I just said, 'Yes, Mother, when do you want me to start?'

"I tell you, my mother was so happy that day, and after everything, I am more than happy with my decision. The company is doing remarkably well. My job is more than easy; I can say out of a forty-hour workweek, I physically work twenty. I can travel, shop when I want, and live where I want. My life has been privileged because of my parents. My dad retired too, but he supported my mom and had her back every step of the way. I live well because of them and I can't complain."

"So what do you not have?" he asked.

I sipped my coffee. "Honest?"

"Yes, honest."

"The love of my life," I said. The gloss in my eyes was because of Tony. I'd be okay if it wasn't for Tony. "He was on the boat, with another woman. He was sitting on the other side of my girlfriend."

"The one that gave you that look before walking away?"

"Yep, that was him."

"So why don't you have him?"

"Because I guess I loved him too hard. Too much, you know. My love became uncomfortable for him. I don't know, I just loved being with him," I said and laughed a little.

"He must have been a helluva guy," he said.

"He was, but enough about him. Let's talk about you. What are you looking for?"

"Happiness and love, what we're all looking for."

"Why did you divorce?"

"Because I've traveled a lot and my wife was a momma's girl. She loved her momma and she let her momma into our marriage. I traveled because my main focus was to help folks and to find a place I wanted to call home. I found it in Chicago, but Regan didn't see it the same way. She decided to do her own thing and asked me for a divorce. It was hard in the beginning, but I'm a man, so I dealt with it and moved on."

"Wow, you seem like a great brother. And a doctor. I must say, I've never dated a doctor before."

"Well, we're not all dull," he said and I laughed.

We continued our conversation and I smiled more than I had in days. He finally walked me to my car, and when he asked me out again I said yes. He kissed the back of my hand and told me that he thought I was beautiful and that Tony had given up too easily. I smiled because I agreed, but I still really missed Tony.

I got in my car and drove home smiling, hoping that I could be happy one day and eventually get over Tony. After my pep talk to myself, I felt like Dr. Payne would prescribe the right get-over-Tony remedy and I felt better. I pulled into my drive and got out of my car to find Tony on my porch.

Lord, why the hell was he there?

# Reality Check

"WHERE THE hell have you been," he shouted when I approached.

"Uh-uh, no, baby. Get the hell off my porch and gon' wit dat," I said and proceeded to unlock my door.

"Joss, don't play with me. Where have you been? The boat docked hours ago."

"Tony, go home." I went inside and tried to close the door, but he wouldn't let it close. "Are you serious right now, Tony?"

"Baby, were you with him?" he asked.

I wanted to laugh in his face. "Tony, go home!"

He still refused to let me shut my door. It was after four a.m. and I was too exhausted to fight with him, so I let him in. I went into my room and started to undress and he came in.

"Did you fuck him?" he asked. I laughed. "Did you?" he yelled.

"Did you fuck Rameeka, Tony?" I retorted.

"Joss, this is not about me. I asked you a question dammit!" He yelled louder and I laughed harder.

"You have gotta be joking me, Tony. I mean, are you fucking

serious right now?" I took off my halter and stood there in only a thong and the tape over my nipples.

"Yes, I'm dead-fucking-serious, Jocelyn, so tell me the fucking truth! "His temples flared.

"Get out!" I yelled, pointing at the door. He didn't move. "Tony, get out of my fucking house right now!" He stood there looking at me like he wanted to say more, but no words came out of his mouth.

I walked by him and went into my master bathroom and removed the tape from my tits. "Please go," I whispered when he came in and stood behind me. He pulled his white button down over his head without unbuttoning the buttons. "Tony, no, I'm serious. I can't do this with you. You gotta go," I said firmly.

But it was like I hadn't said a word. He turned me to face him and lifted me up onto the vanity. He looked me in my eyes and kissed me, holding me under the chin in a firm grip.

"Baby, please let me go," I cried. He continued to lick me down my neck. "Tony please, you are killing me. You are killing me, baby."

He pulled his erection out, pulled my ass forward, and pushed his dick inside of me. He began to pump me as he moved his mouth to my erect nipple. He sucked on it like he was trying to suck a melon out of a lemon.

I closed my eyes and moaned. "Awww, aaaahhhh, Tony, please baby," I begged.

He continued to please my pussy like he had always done. His stroke was steady and hard. He knew that was what I loved. He pulled out and stroked himself with his hand. I wanted to give him what I always gave him, so I slid down onto my knees. He pushed himself into my mouth. I took control and after a couple minutes he couldn't take it.

"No, babe, come here," he said and pulled me up. We went over to the toilet and he sat on the closed seat with me straddling him.

I found the right rhythm and it was feeling so damn good I was ready to cum. "Tony, Tony, Tony," I moaned.

He pushed his tongue back into my mouth as my body jerked. My clit tingled as he pushed his dick up, deeper inside my body and I spread my legs wider and went onto my toes and began to bounce up and down on him. I felt his dick punch my cervix, and I began to scream. It was love, passion, and pain.

He let out a sound of pleasure and followed it with the words, "I love you, Jocelyn. You are mine, mine. You hear me?" I didn't reply. "Jocelyn, do you hear me?" he said again and looked me in my eyes. I nodded.

After a couple soft kisses and sighs, I got up and he walked into my bedroom. He pulled the covers back and got into my bed. I stood there with no words. He had done it again and I let him.

If it wasn't for Tony, I'd be a stronger me.

# Silly Me

TWO NIGHTS ago, he was here. Telling me how I was his and how I belong to him and all that jazz. Now, it's back to ignoring my calls and texts. He had the nerve to get up and fix me breakfast the morning after I allowed him access to my pussy and oral honors, just to do me the way he had done me before. Silly me, always falling into his arms, I mean traps, and letting him get the best of me. How crazy in love can one be to put up with such foolishness? I had to be the dumbest, most clueless and impractical bitch on this planet. I was so disappointed with myself for allowing my love for this man to destroy me. He was tearing me down, body part by body part, organ by organ. If it wasn't for Tony, I'd be a stable bitch. I'd be smarter, I'd be stronger, I'd be invincible, but he had me by my female balls.

He had the control. The ball was always in his court because whenever I had possession of the ball, I foolishly fouled out like a fool with no game. How was I supposed to get over him? The Tony drug was stronger than any other drug on this earth and it had kicked rehab's ass several times. There was no escape from his devices. I was stuck. I didn't know what to do. I was a mess. My phone rang and I rolled over to answer it. It was the doctor. Dr. Payne. I laughed at that. A doctor with the last name of pain had me rolling so hard I missed his call.

I waited until I could get over my own inside joke and then I called him back.

"Dr. Payne sorry I missed you. How are you?" I asked when he picked up.

"Great to finally hear back from you."

"I know, and I'm sorry. Things have been overwhelming lately, so forgive me."

"Of course. I'm not trippin,' just glad you finally returned a brother's call," he said.

"Again, Brian, I'm sorry," I said sincerely.

"So the big question is when can I see you? I'd love to take you out."

"Well, I'm free all weekend. Just say when."

"That's great, Saturday evening will be perfect," he said. I gave him my address.

A couple days later, it was date night. I was anxious to see Brian because Tony had gone back to ignoring me. I was looking and smelling good, and I said I was going to keep an open mind and try to forget about Mr. Tony.

"Wow, you look fantastic," Brian said when I opened the door.

"Thank you, so do you." And he was looking good. He wasn't Tony's height, but at five-nine, he was taller than me. He was dark like a Hershey bar and had the sexiest slanted eyes I'd ever seen on a man other than that model, Tyson Beckford.

"Thanks," he said and came in.

"I'll be ready in a sec." I went to put the finishing touches on my face. I sprayed on some smell good and grabbed my purse, and we left.

He took me downtown and we ate an exquisite meal and drank wine. We left and went to hear a little jazz. When our date was about to come to an end, Bailey texted and said to meet them if I was free. I asked Brian and he was game. When we walked in, I heard his voice, but I acted as if I didn't. Her inviting me to hang where Tony would be singing was crazy, but I had a date, and I had told myself earlier that day that it was time to let it go.

"Hey, you made it," she yelled and jumped up to hug me.

"Yes and why is your pregnant ass out in the club?"

"Because Dez asked me to marry him!" She flashed the bling.

"Get out!" I yelled in excitement with her.

"Yes, and this was so unexpected and you are my best friend, so I had to call you." We hugged tight. I caught Tony's eye during our embrace and I let go.

"You remember Brian," I asked and grabbed his hand.

"Yes, hi," Bailey said, smiling brightly.

We took the vacant seats by her and the bartender came over. We ordered a drink and Brian noticed Tony singing.

"That's him, isn't it?"

"Him who?" I said, pretending I had no clue what he meant.

"Your guy. I remember him from the boat," he said.

"Yes, and I don't want to talk about him or even acknowledge him." I leaned in and gave Brian our first kiss.

"Are you sure?"

"Yes, now come on, be my date and stop asking so many questions about my ex."

"Okay."

We drank, danced, and spent time being close. After a few glasses of wine, my focus was on Brian and it was as if Tony didn't exist. I went to the bathroom and when I came out, I ran into Tony. Literally.

"Joss," he said as he caught me.

"Tony," I said. I tried to move on quickly, but he grabbed me.

I yanked away and narrowed my eyes. "Not tonight," I hissed. I moved past him and went back to my date. "Hey," I said standing in front of Brian, dancing in place. "Let's dance."

We went out on the dance floor and I didn't hold back because I was tipsy, horny, and feeling good. I turned around and worked my ass on him to the music and felt him grab my hips. I turned to face him and it was over. I wrapped my arms around him and jerked my body like I was in a dance competition. I turned my back to him again and rolled my ass into him. When I saw Tony watching, I went down and started to sweep the floor with my ass. I was out of control and when the song ended, I was hot, sweaty, and ready for another drink.

After I cooled off, the club was winding down. They began the slow jams.

"Come on, Doc, one more dance and we can go," I whispered in his ear.

He took me by the hand and we went to the floor and swayed to Ohio Player's "Heaven Must Be Like This" and I wished my heart felt for Brian what it felt for Tony. I wanted to make love, but I didn't know Brian like I knew Tony. I knew our night had to end with that dance because my heart was stuck on Tony.

After the song ended, the DJ played Enchantment's "It's You That I Need" and I hurried off the dance floor because I knew Tony had something to do with it. That was our song.

"Can we go?" I said. I didn't want to hear the words of that song.

"Sure," Brian said.

I went over to Bailey and told her goodnight and congrats again. I hurried over to Brian, and we walked out a hand and hand. We got into his Jag without Tony stopping me. I just wanted to pull away. As soon as we exited the parking lot, I let out a sigh of relief.

"Is everything okay," he asked.

"Yes, everything is fine," I said and held his hand. We rode to my place and I told him to park in my driveway. I figured if Tony came and saw his car, he would leave and not ring my bell. We went inside and I knew I shouldn't have, but I asked him to stay.

"Are you sure, Jocelyn? We don't have to rush into anything."

"I know, I just want you to stay with me." I said.

He smiled. We went into my bedroom, undressed, and got into my bed in our undies. I drifted off to sleep quickly. My phone rang and, of course, it was Tony, so I powered it off. When I eased back under the covers, I felt Brian's erection. I grabbed his hand and put it on my breast. He began to massage me and it felt nice. I turned over and looked at him and he planted a kiss on my lips. I let him kiss me passionately and it was so good. He kissed so sensually I wanted his mouth all over my body.

I let him kiss my neck and move lower. When he landed on my nipples, I let out loud moans because he was incredible. I wondered how someone else could feel this good to my body because I thought Tony was it. When he made it to my stomach, I thought for sure this doctor wasn't going to take a chance on licking my clit, but I was so wrong. He went down to my pussy and ate like he had been there before. He ate me so well, I screamed when I climaxed.

"Condoms?" he asked. "Do you have rubbers?"

"Yes ... yes ... top left drawer," I said, trying to catch my breath. What the fuck just happened? Did someone top Tony? Did someone just put the love of my life to shame.

"No, baby, let me do you," I said when he opened the condom. I wasn't going to be defeated. He was a doctor, yes, but I was the head doctor and I had to leave the same impression on him that he left on me. I took his massive instrument into my mouth. Tony was bigger, yes, but there was something about Brian that made me want to make him pull away like I had made Tony do in the past.

"Ooooh, baby, yes. That's good, baby," he moaned. Instead of him pulling my hair, he put his hand on the back of my head and began to massage it. It felt so good to feel his strong hands and that made me want give him even more pleasure. "Baby, I don't wanna nut," he said and pulled back. I cut him some slack because I knew my head game was dangerous.

He rolled the condom on and positioned himself over me. I held my breath and received him inside of my body. He began to stroke my pussy like his dick was a paint brush and my pussy was his clean canvas. The angle his dick went in and out of my body gave me an orgasm that made me holler. I squirted liquid for the first time and thought I pissed on myself.

"Ooooh, baby, your shit is hot," he moaned. He pumped my body a couple more times and then released.

Tony who? I thought. I curled up close to Brian and wondered what in the hell just happened.

#  I Gotta Man

I LEFT my office beaming because Brian and I had gone out every night that week and I thought less and less about Tony. He'd try to creep up now and then, but a text or call from the doctor always rained on that fire. I was in good hands. He was kind, sweet, and he knew how to spoil a woman. Flowers, yes, he sent them. Dinner, always fancy. And even though we hadn't been dating long, he gave me a charm bracelet from Pandora with charms of all the things he noted that I liked because I said how bad I wanted one. He was romantic and charming, and he did have the prescription I needed to get over Tony. I was feeling free.

"I was thinking we should go out of town," he said.

"Out of town like where?"

"Okay, there is a medical convention coming up in two weeks and it is going to be in Vegas, and I thought I'd ask," he said.

I smiled. "Vegas? I'd love to go with you. Are you sure you want me to tag along?"

"Yes, it would be lovely if I had a date this time. Last time I went, I was solo and … let's just say, my downtime was truly downtime. I didn't have much fun alone," he confessed.

"Well, just let me know the dates, so I can get my ticket."

"Jocelyn, must you insult me to my face?"

"What?" I said, smiling.

"No, you will not purchase a ticket to accompany me. I invited you, so I'll be taking care of that."

I gave him a nod of approval. A girl couldn't argue that. "Well, I'll rephrase. Let me know the dates, so I can be packed and ready."

"That's more like it. And pack light, there is plenty of shopping that can be done while I'm in my conference. Again, my treat," he said.

I thought I'd melt. How did I find someone so damn sweet? "I shall keep that in mind," I said.

We finished dinner, went back to my place, and got cozy on the sofa. We were talking and the mood was nice. Then my doorbell rang. I looked at the clock; it was after eleven and I knew it was Tony. I started not to answer, but he began to ring my bell like he was insane.

"Excuse me," I told Brian and went to the door. "Tony, why are you here? I know you see there is a car parked in my drive and I know you know it's Brian's car."

"I know, but I really need to talk to you, Joss."

"Well, now is not a good time," I said, ready to shut the door in his face.

"One of my teens killed herself today," he said, his eyes watering.

I had never seen him this upset, so I stepped out the door, and we sat on the porch. "Tell me what happened, Tony?"

"Her name was Trina and I thought she was getting better, you know? I thought she'd be okay if she returned home to her family because she was doing well. I released her a couple days ago and I got a call saying she shot herself." He lowered his head and cried into his hands. "What if I made the wrong call?" I knew this conversation wasn't going to be short.

I took his hand and held it. "Hey, Tony, no, baby, don't do that. Don't go blaming yourself or trying to figure out what would have happened if you did something different."

After an hour, my impatient doctor came out the front door.

"Look, Jocelyn, I'm going to head home."

"No, wait," I said. I got up, but he continued to head for his car. "Tony, hold on." I hurried to catch Brian. "Brian, wait please," I said. He stood at his car. "One of his patients killed herself," I explained.

"You don't have to explain, Jocelyn. I'm not trippin' on that. Just call me tomorrow." He opened the car door.

"Are you sure, Brian?" I asked.

"Yeah, goodnight, Jocelyn," he said and gave me a quick kiss. He got in and drove off and I went back to the porch with Tony.

"Is everything okay?" he asked.

"Yeah, Brian is one of the good ones."

"So are you guys an item now or what?"

"We are dating, Tony, and things are going well."

"I bet," he mumbled.

"That's not fair," I said, looking at him.

"What?"

"Nothing, Tony. Are you going to be okay?"

"Yeah and I'm sorry I came by, but you're the only one I could talk to. You know how I feel about my job and these teens. No one other than you would have been able to make me feel better."

"Well, everything is cool," I said.

We sat in silence until he spoke again. "Can I come in?" he asked.

"No," I said quickly, because I knew him.

"Why, your boyfriend said you can't have company?"

"Tony, come on, be real. I can't keep doing this dance with you. We are no longer together and you cannot come into my house. You are not going to Tony me tonight," I declared.

"Tony you?" He laughed. "What the hell does that mean?"

"You know, Tony me out of my clothes and Tony me into my bed."

"Oh, so that's what you call it," he said, touching my back.

"Stop," I warned.

"Stop what?" He slid closer to me.

"Okay, that's it. You gotta go." I stood up.

He stood up and got in my face. "Let me in," he whispered, rubbing his fingertips on my collarbone.

"Tony, I seriously need you to leave. I have a man now."

"I will after I make you cum," he said.

I let him Tony me again.

I had a new man that was doing all he could to make me happy and I was too foolishly stuck on the old one to act right.

# I'm Getting Married Y'all

SIX MONTHS had gone by, and Brian and I were in couple heaven. I managed to keep my distance from Tony after that last night with him when we sat on my porch. I managed to keep my legs closed—to Tony of course, because Brian was putting it on a sister. I had met Brian's mom and he had long since met my parents. I was finally in love again. He was more than a woman could ask for and he managed to put a smile on my face every single day. I had no complaints when it came to him. I was now the person I was meant to be, one who was sane and happy.

"Remember, dinner starts at seven sharp," he reminded me for the tenth time.

"Brian, baby, I remember. I promise you I will not be late," I assured him.

"Okay, just make sure you're looking lovely and be on time," he said again.

"Baby, if you mention time again, I will be late on purposed," I joked.

We got off the phone and I hurried to my spa treatments to make sure I was on time because if I was late I knew I wouldn't hear the end of it. Brian was up to something, but I didn't know what and I couldn't wait to find out. I made it on time, and I was thanking God I did because traffic was a beast. I walked in and he met me and led me to our table. Shortly after, my family and friends started to arrive.

"Okay, Brian, what's going on, baby?" I asked.

He smiled. "Nothing, I just wanted to celebrate our love with a few of our friends and family."

I was still suspicious, but I enjoyed my evening and the meal was excellent.

"May I have everyone's attention please." Brian stood after we finished eating and everyone got quiet. "I want first to thank everyone for joining us tonight as we celebrate love. Now, Jocelyn and I have been together for a little over six months, but I can say from the moment I met her, I just knew she was the one." I blushed. "Jocelyn, you are like a breath of fresh air. When I'm not in the same room with you, you are the only thing on my mind, and I want to make our thing permanent." He went down on one knee, pulled out a ring box, and opened it up to show a diamond larger than my pupils. "Will you marry me?" he asked.

I jumped up and almost knocked him over when I grabbed him in a hug. "Yes! Are you serious, yes," I screamed. That was the proposal all women waited for their entire lives, and I'd just gotten it from the perfect man who bought the perfect ring. "I'm getting married," I screamed and held up my finger.

Not long after that evening, news made it to Tony and I wasn't surprised at all to see him on my porch when I got in from work one day. He tried to corner me and tried to Tony me, but my engagement ring was my shield to fight off evildoers. I stayed in my lane with no swerving and eight months later I was happily married and living in the doctor's house. I was happy and Tony was no longer a thorn in my heart. Me and my new husband were in marital bliss, working on a baby.

"SO you are going to be okay seeing Tony? He is Dez's best man," Bailey said.

"I'm okay, I'm just glad you two are finally getting married. Y'all had the longest engagement in the history of mankind."

"It did seem like forever, but you know Dez. He never wanted to set a date. When you got married before me, and I was engaged first, I told him to set a date or I'm leaving," she said. We both laughed.

"Well, it worked because tomorrow you will be a Mrs.," I teased.

People started to arrive for the rehearsal and we got busy. Seeing Tony wasn't as difficult as I thought it would be. He still looked sexy as hell, but I kept a safe distance. When we were done, he tried to talk to me, but I shut him down. When I got outside, I realized I forgot my shoes. I hurried back in and before I could leave again, he walked in.

"Jocelyn," he said.

"Goodnight, Tony," I said. I tried to hurry by him, but he stood in my path.

"Why are you treating me so mean?"

"Tony, my husband is expecting me and I have to go." He still blocked my path. Why was this fool in my face when he knew we were never going to be together again? Here we go again, I said to myself and prepared to go back and forth with him.

# All I Want is the Truth

"IT'S POSITIVE," I screamed.

Brian took a look at the stick. "Baby this is fantastic," he said and squeezed me tight. "I will get you in with Dr. Gordon, he's the best."

I was elated. We were having our first baby, and there were no words to describe the joy I felt. Everything was so good in my life, and I was more than grateful.

I saw the doctor and everything looked good. My husband was the best. He took extra good care of me and my entire pregnancy was worry and stress free. When we found out we were having a girl, we went all out and she had pink everything. I'd never hired a designer do a room before. Imagine my surprise when my husband told me that he was going to hire someone to do our daughter's nursery.

"You are too good to me," I told him. He kissed me and then my belly. Tony was now a thing of the past. After I got pregnant, I never saw him again because I never went into his circles.

He heard the news and sent congratulations by Bailey. It was pointless to send a thank you back to him, so I just looked at her like she was crazy when she said it. I didn't care to hear about him anymore and if his name came up, I'd quickly change the subject. I didn't need or want any drama or stress during my pregnancy and Tony's name normally caused one or the other.

I honestly thought he would be forever history until the day I delivered my first baby. Brian proudly coached me through a horrific drug-free labor and after fourteen brutal hours of pain, she was here. I was so out of breath and exhausted that they handed her to him first. He passed her to me and walked out of the room with no words. I looked down at her and immediately knew why my husband had cleared the room. She was undeniably mine, but she was not his.

"ALL I want is the truth, Jocelyn," Brian said. "I want to know what really happened that night."

I swallowed hard. I sat there wishing I could just disappear because I didn't want to tell him the horrible details of that night. How I betrayed him and let Tony bend me over in a maid's closet at a hotel. I thought I could carry that night to my grave, but the proof of that night was lying in her bassinet beside my hospital bed in my private room. A room fit for a surgeon's wife and their child. Sadly, I was his wife, but she wasn't his child.

There was no denying who her father was. Her honey-colored complexion and round hazel eyes was the baby girl version of his, the face that I never wanted to see again.

"Brian, please, you don't want to know what happened and I'm so ashamed. I swear on my life that I didn't know. I thought I was one hundred and ten percent sure that I was carrying your child," I cried, hoping he'd change his mind about wanting the details.

"Jocelyn, I am your husband, and for nine months, I looked forward to my wife delivering my first child. Imagine my surprise when I held her and looked at her face and saw him. When she opened her little eyes and looked up at me, I could have died. So, yes, I want to know how you conceived a child with a man you promised me you were done with. You married me, took vows with me, and yet, somehow, you bore a child that isn't mine. So, please, tell me how, dammit!" He yelled, and I and the baby both jumped. His eyes welled and I gave him what he wanted.

"We were at the hotel for Bailey's wedding rehearsal," I said, looking down at my wedding rings. I couldn't look him in the eyes and tell him the story. "I tried to keep my distance from him, but it was difficult you know? After everything was done, we were all getting ready to leave, but I went back in to look for my shoes. We had to rehearse in our wedding shoes and when I changed back into my shoes, I forgot my bag. Before I made my exit, he came back in and he cornered me and then he kissed me. And then he and I went into this little closet or supply room and it happened. He used a condom, Brian, and I swear that was the last time I was with him. I told him that it was a mistake and it could never happen again. I left and came home. I felt horrible, Brian, and I wished I could take it back. Seven weeks later, we when took the test, I didn't think twice about it being him because we used a condom. I don't know how this could have happened."

"It happened because you cheated on me. It happened because you allowed a man to enter your body other than your husband. Jocelyn, I can't see us coming back from this. You and the baby can come home until you find a place, and then I want you out of my house." He stood up. "I want a divorce."

"Brian, baby, please, don't do this. I know this is a hard pill to swallow, but I love you so much. I made a huge mistake and I am so sorry, but, please, let's work this out."

"Work it out?" he asked. He chuckled and looked down at Brianna. "I'm not going to sign your daughter's birth certificate, and she will not get my last name. You and I are done," he avowed and left.

I sat there and cried my eyes out. I could not believe what was happening to me. I could not believe that I just had a baby that wasn't my husband's. What was I going to do? I had to start all over again and find a place for me and my baby to live. I was going to be a single mother and the man I now loved didn't want me anymore. In that instant, I hated Tony and wondered how I was going to tell that bastard that he was my child's father. I sobbed until it was time to nurse my baby.

I looked down at her beautiful face, and as sad as I was, she made me smile. This was supposed to be the happiest day of me and my husband's life, but it was the worst day ever. I hoped to God that Brian would change his mind about leaving me. I fell in love with him and even though I still carried a small torch for Tony, I didn't want him more than I wanted Brian. I prayed that Brian would find it in his heart to forgive me.

# *What the Fuck Tony*

A WEEK later, I was home. Brian decided to move into a hotel. He told me to take my time, but don't take forever getting out of his house. That was his last words to me. He refused to talk to me, and I didn't blame him because it was painful for me too. All I could do was hope that he would forgive me. God knows my sin was the adultery because I had no idea Tony was even a possibility. I drove toward his place to tell him the news face to face, my stomach in knots.

"Hey, Joss, congrats, I heard you had a girl," he said. I was surprised that was all he heard. Bailey and my folks were the only people other than Brian who saw my baby and I had begged Bailey not to tell Dez.

"Thank you. Can I come in?" I said.

He looked shocked, but let me in.

"What brings you by, and how is your baby. I bet she's beautiful."

"Yes, she is." I decided to get straight to the point. "Listen, Tony, this is not a social or friendly visit."

"Okay. Have a seat," he offered. "What's going on?"

"There is no easy way to say this, so I'll just come right out and say it." I wanted to get it over with.

"Talk to me, Joss," he said with his brow raised.

"Brian left me." I started with that.

"Are you serious? You just had a baby and he left you? Jocelyn what happened?" He sounded concerned.

"Brian is not the father of my baby, Tony. You are."

He froze. His eyes opened like saucers. "Come again," he asked, now blinking a dozen times a second.

I pulled out my phone. I went to her pictures and handed it to him.

He looked at one and covered his mouth with one hand. "Joss, wait, I –I—I," he stuttered.

"I know, right? I'm as shocked as you. I mean, I had no idea, Tony, and I didn't try and hide this, I promise."

He stared at her picture. "I know, Jocelyn, and I have something I need to tell you."

I wondered what could be more important than what I just told him. "You're not upset?"

"No, and I am sorry. I—I," He stood up.

"What, Tony? What's wrong with you?"

"I knew there was a chance that I was the father," he said.

I was confused. "What, how, or why would you think that? We used protection."

"We did, but the condom broke," he confessed.

My eyes and mouth shot wide open. "What the fuck did you just say?"

"When I pulled out, the condom was broke. You were in panic mode and acting all hysterical and making me vow not to tell, so I didn't say anything," he said nervously.

"WHHHHAAAAAATTTTT!" I yelled, moving close to him.

"Jocelyn, I'm sorry."

I started throwing punches at him. "What the fuck, Tony?" I yelled, breathing hard. "How on earth could you do that to me and not tell me? You had me walking around pregnant, thinking I was carrying my husband's child, and you knew all along!"

"I had a feeling, Jocelyn, but I didn't know you weren't on the pill anymore. I had no idea that you and Brian were trying to conceive. By the time I heard you were pregnant, I didn't know exactly how far you were or when your baby was due, so I didn't say anything. I'm sorry."

"I hate you, Tony. You have ruined my marriage. He left me, Tony! He is gone. My husband is putting me and my baby out of our house, Tony." I was shaking. I wanted to kill his ass.

"Jocelyn, I am so sorry. I never meant for this to happen. I will help you." He tried to embrace me.

"Don't you dare touch me, you bastard! You are not sorry; you are selfish and you are an evil son of a bitch. I tried to give my life to you, but you didn't want it. I found someone to love me who wanted what I had to give because you didn't. All you did was use your Jocelyn's-stuck-on-me, card to have your way with me, when I should have been faithful to my husband. You knew I still had it bad for you every time you flashed your smile and cornered me, and I let you!

"You could have told me so I could have considered my options, or better yet told my husband months ago so I wouldn't have had to see the look on his face when I delivered a carbon copy of you. What else do you want from me, Tony, my blood? I have let you ruin everything for me. I would be at home with my husband, holding his baby and not yours, if it wasn't for you. I am standing here wondering how I let you put me under this Tony spell. I was a fool for you and I lost everything!" I shouted, tears drenching my face.

"Joss, I can be here for you now. Let me make it up to you. We can be together. I'll do whatever you want me to do, I swear I will, just say it. I love you, Jocelyn, and, yes, it was hard to lose you. When you moved on with Brian, it fucked me up inside that you got on with your life. Every time I could have you, it made me feel like he hadn't won, but please believe me, Jocelyn, I never intended for any of what I did to hurt you. I never wanted to see you hurt and I am so sorry. I will do whatever it takes to make it up to you, just say it."

I just looked at him. I wanted to choke the life out of him. "Whatever I want huh?" I asked and wiped my tears.

"Yes, whatever," he said, moving close to me.

"First, I would like to say thank you for giving me a beautiful baby. She is my only peace of mind in this world right now, so I thank you. And as far as making it up to me…" I paused. "You will never be able to make it up to me. You've taken too much already and the one thing you can do for me," I said getting in his face, "is stay away. I never want to see you or hear your name or be in the same room with you." I grabbed my purse and phone.

"You can't mean that. I am her father and I will not allow you to take her away from me," he said.

"Well, I'll see you in court," I spat and walked out.

I got into my car and drove off, but had to pull over a few blocks away. All I could do was cry.

Tony, Tony, Tony … Goodbye Tony.

# One Year Later

"DO YOU need anything else," Tony asked.

He'd stayed behind after my guests left to help me clean up. It was Tianna's first birthday. Yes, Tianna. We changed her name on her birth certificate from Brianna when Tony went down to sign it a few days after I confronted him. I figured it was better to do it then because she hadn't turned two weeks old yet and Brian didn't care one way or the other.

I found a house and moved out before she was a month old. I only saw Brian at the courthouse when the judge declared our divorce. He didn't even look my way, and when I offered my apologies to him, he walked away as if I hadn't said anything. Tony and I came to an agreement without going to court and by the time Tianna was six months, I was able to be in the same room with him without fussing and cussing.

"No, I'm good." I took her out of her high chair because she was falling asleep.

"I'll take her," he offered.

I handed her over. "Thanks." I went to finish loading the dishwasher and he left the kitchen with her. After a few minutes, he came back.

"Well, I changed her and put her into her night clothes, and she is knocked out."

"She played hard today." I said. "And the party was good. No fatalities and no major spills." I grabbed a wine glass. I was exhausted and had been waiting all day to have a glass of wine.

"Well, there was one, but I cleaned it quickly," he said. We laughed. "Thank you, Jocelyn," he said.

I took a sip of my wine. "For?"

"For allowing me to be a father to my daughter and for not hating me."

"Well, she deserves to have a father in her life, but you're wrong … I still hate you," I teased. We laughed again.

"And if you do, that's okay. You have every right," he said sadly. "I'm going to head home," he said, patting his pockets.

"Okay, and thank you for helping me today. It would have been a disaster if you hadn't come," I said, being honest. Tony was my lousy ex, but he was a devoted dad.

"It was my pleasure," he said. I walked him to the door. He paused before leaving. "Jocelyn, I still love you," he said and I looked away.

"Please, Tony, don't do that. I told you months ago that you and I will never, be an option."

"I know, but I had to tell you how I feel. I regret so many things, Joss, and I know I can't go back and change our past, but I wish I would have realized what I had with you instead of running away like a scared-ass little boy."

I appreciated it, but didn't want to hear it. "Okay, Tony. I heard you, now you should go." I opened the door and he walked out. I shut it behind him and hated that he still made my heart beat fast. Stop it, Jocelyn, don't let him back in. You are better off without him, I told myself. The next couple days dragged by. I was bored and needed a mommy break. I called my mother and she was more than happy to watch her grandbaby. I felt a sense of relief when I dropped her off. Since I had been out of the loop, I called Bailey to see what was going on that night. She said they were going out to listen to Sean's band. I wanted to decline, but I needed to do something.

I got fancy and felt sexy, something I hadn't felt in a while since I became a mom. I was a little excited to be stepping out that night. When I got there, I found Bailey and took a seat. The whole gang was there. I saw Tony and he greeted me with a quick kiss on the cheek. I gave him a look and he held up his hands, telling me not to act up, but I let it go.

The show got under way and I shook my head when they did that damn song. Why do they always sing "Loose Control"? I remembered when that song gave me chills and wondered why was I getting them same old damn goose bumps? And why was my baby daddy still so damn fine and why was he looking at me like that?

When the song was finally over, I needed a fan. I hadn't had any in over a year, and it was happening. I was falling full speed for him again, and I didn't want to. I got up and went to the bathroom because I had to have a talk with myself. Tony didn't deserve my love. Tony wasn't worthy enough to have me and I could not let him back into my life. He was a great dad and we got along, but when he was in my life, I went through too many emotions. Stop it, Jocelyn. We've been over this. He is like crack in the flesh, I told myself. But my heart wanted to debate what my mind was saying.

But he's changed and we have forgiven him. We know that he loves us, the man tells us every day. We are stronger now and we can handle him. We can give him a chance.

My mind wasn't buying it though. What if he hurts us again?

And what if he doesn't? my heart said.

What if he doesn't want to fully commit? my mind asked.

Then that's a deal breaker. Just talk to him and tell him our conditions. If he doesn't accept, we move on for good, my heart said.

I went back to the table. Tony was singing, "Lost Without You," and when I took my seat, his eyes were right back on me.

Finally, they took a break and he came over and sat beside me. "I didn't get a chance to tell you that you look really lovely. It's nice to see you in regular clothes for a change," he said.

"Come on, Tony, I wear regular clothes."

"Not since the baby. By the time I come over, it's sweats or loose-fitting granny clothes," he joked.

"Well, I dress up for work."

"Well, you dress down for me," he teased.

I smiled. "Can we go," I said, surprising him and myself.

"Are you serious?" he asked.

"Yes. We should talk before you do something stupid to make me hate you again."

"So you don't hate me right now?"

"Not at this moment," I said and gave him another smile.

"Hold on, let me holla at Sean," he said.

I got my purse and said bye to everyone and waited for him by the door. "My place or yours," he asked when we walked out.

"Since we are closer to yours, let's go there," I said.

I got into my car and followed him, going over and over all the things I wanted to say. Once we were inside, I felt a lot more nervous than I thought I would be.

"Have a seat," he said and went to the kitchen. He returned with a glass of white for me and a beer for himself and sat down.

"Am I in trouble?" he asked.

"No, not this time," I said. He let out a sigh. "I am going to be direct and I'm not going to beat around the bush. I still love you, Tony, a lot more than I wanted to admit and a lot more than just because you're Tianna's dad. The other night, when you said you still loved me, I wanted not to believe you, but I feel that you are sincere and I'm willing to give us another try if that's what you want." I stopped talking and held my breath.

"Of course that's what I want, Jocelyn. I was a fool, a dumbass back then, and I'm ready to be all in. It's all on your terms."

"Well, I want to get married." I waited for his reaction.

"Me too," he countered.

"I want us to live under the same roof." I waited for him to fold like a chair.

"Done. We can start packing tonight."

I smiled. "Tony there is one more thing."

He looked deeply into my eyes. "What is it, baby?"

"This is your last and final chance," I said seriously. "If I give you my heart again and you break it, you and I will have nothing, not even a friendship. I mean, everything will go through the courts and lawyers, and your pickups and drop offs will be done with my mom because I would literally never want to see you again."

"Damn, Jocelyn, it's like that?" he asked. I just looked at him. "Listen," he said, taking my hand. "You have absolutely nothing to worry about. You can trust me with your heart again and I will never ever hurt you again."

I believed him. We sat and talked until the sun came up. We got into his bed and he just held me. I slept like a baby in his arms.

Within a week, he was all moved in with me and Tianna, and three months later, we were husband and wife. I gave him another baby, a boy, and Tony did what he promised me he'd do. He loved me.

I learned to love without smothering and controlling him. He learned to appreciate me for the woman I am. We are now happy and none of this would have happened to me, or for me, if it wasn't for Tony.

# Mr. Wrong

# Chapter One

BROOKE stared at her laptop screen wondering where time went. She had gotten an invitation from Carver Military Academy, formerly known as George Washington Carver High School, to attend her ten year reunion. She had always gotten invites to something or another because she was a part of her school's alumni social network, but she never could attend because she no longer resided in Chicago. She had moved to Arizona right after high school to attend Arizona State University. After getting her BS in nursing, she went on and got her Family Nurse Practitioner's Certificate and landed a job in private practice in Phoenix. She'd tell her mother that she would consider moving back to the windy city and fours year later she was still considering it.

She didn't have any attachments in Arizona other than her beautiful home, but she still wasn't motivated to move back. She loved to visit, enjoyed seeing her family and eating at all of her favorite restaurants during her visit, but she was always just as excited to get back home to her own things. She'd miss her momma's cooking, but not enough to stay longer than her two week-long visits every year. She and her best friend, Rochelle, managed to stay close and maintained contact over their ten year separation and Rochelle visited Arizona at least twice a year to get away from her husband and two kids.

Rochelle said she was envious of Brooke's great career, beautiful home, and luxurious ride. She told Brooke she was lucky not to have to wash a man's drawers. Brooke disagreed. She wanted a husband and a couple kids. She just hadn't known it would be this difficult to find love. She would be twenty-eight on her next birthday and still wondered when she'd meet Mr. Right instead of Mr. In-Between-Jobs, Mr. Got-Money-But-Cheap-As-Hell, Mr. I-Don't-Do-Romance, and the worst, her last boyfriend, Mr. Beg-And-Borrow. That was her history with men—horrible.

The phone rang, jolting her from her trance. She looked at the caller ID. It was Rochelle.

"Hey, Chelle, what's up, girl?" Brooke asked, exiting out of the email invite.

"Nothing much, girl, cooking dinner and calling to see if you got the reunion invite. Can you believe it has been ten years since we graduated?"

"Yes, I got it, and, no, I can't believe it's been ten years. I mean, it seems like it was yesterday." She got up from her desk and headed for her bedroom to get comfortable because she and Rochelle never had a short conversation.

"I know, girl, and I am so glad they are giving me enough advance notice to hit the treadmill. I ain't trying to see everyone looking like I had ten kids instead of two. Hell, I've thought about getting a tummy tuck for this reunion. Mike looks exactly the same, but I done had two of his big-headed kids and my body went from p-h-a-t to f-a-t," she said, spelling out the words.

Brooke laughed. "Girl, you are crazy. It is definitely not that serious and you are not fat, Chelle. Granted, you don't have the same waistline you had in school, but who does?" While she spoke, she grabbed the remote for her drapes to open them. The sun was setting and she liked to watch its waning rays dance on top of the water in her pool as it disappeared behind the trees in the horizon.

"You," Rochelle blurted. Brooke could hear what sounded like dishes clattering.

"Girl, I don't anymore. I'm on my way to a twelve. I can barely zip some of my tens now," Brooke confessed.

"Well, I haven't owned a pair of tens since I had Tiara six years ago, and after having M.J., I can barely fit my fourteens. But that's okay though, I've got five months to hit the gym hard."

Brooke shook her head. "Well, I have five months to find a man to bring home with me because I refuse to go to this reunion dateless. I mean, every time I go on Facebook or Twitter, someone's announcing a damn engagement or marriage, or they're having a baby. All I have to brag about is my career, and that's not the most interesting subject in the world."

"Brooke, you don't need a man on your arm. You are smart, gorgeous, and you own a friggin' house with a pool. Hell, talk about your custom drapes. That'll shut some of the heifers up. Half of the baby announcements need not to be announced because they don't know who the daddy is and the engagements are their fancy way of saying they're living together, not a true union. And don't get me started on the wild and crazy marriages. Being single isn't the worst thing. Being married to a down low brother is worse than that," she joked.

Brooke knew what Rochelle was doing. She'd always find a way to make things humorous so Brooke wouldn't feel so bad about whatever subject she was complaining about. "Fake, bogus or whatever, I don't have a man, child, or prospect," she said and they both laughed.

"Okay, I get that. But please don't let this not having a man situation keep you from coming home, Brooke. I mean, you never know what's in store for you. You may see Wade."

Brooke almost choked on her saliva. Why, oh why, did she have to bring him up? Wade was her first and only love, who'd gone to Morehouse in Atlanta. At the end of winter break, he'd told her that he wanted to see other people. He said the distance was too much, but he didn't want them to break up. That wasn't going to fly with Brooke. It was either her and only her or no her. He'd had the nerve to ask if she would have preferred him to lie and cheat or be honest. Her reply had been, "I thank you for your honesty. Take care."

"Shame on you!" she yelled into the phone, hopping up from her chair. "We agreed on December 30, 2003 that we would never utter his name again." Still holding the phone, she raced to her kitchen. She snatched the fridge open and grabbed the open bottle of Pinot. "Why did you just dishonor our allegiance?" She got a wine glass from the cabinet and poured until the liquid hit the brim.

Rochelle giggled. "Brooke, my goodness, girl, that was ten years ago. I didn't know it was still unsafe to mention his name."

"It's not funny, Dr. Giggles. I told you to never mention or talk about that heartbreaking bastard, and I meant forever." She took a huge swallow of wine. Wade was the one, the ultimate one, the one she could never erase from her memory bank no matter how hard she tried or who she dated. She still thought of him often and that bothered her. She didn't want to still have feelings for him after so long.

She still pulled out her box of memories of them from time to time and would cry like the break just happened instead of a decade ago. His name hadn't parted her lips since the day she'd made Rochelle promise not to say his name again. She'd thought of him, but hadn't uttered his name once since that day.

"Brooke, that was so ten years ago," Rochelle said. "I just assumed you got over him long ago. Hold on, girl." Brooke heard her call her family for dinner. Brooke assumed she'd get off to have dinner, but no way was she going to let her off after mentioning the big W.

"I am over him, Rochelle!" Brooke spat. Rochelle knew that was definitely a lie. Brooke only got defensive like that when she was lying.

"Brooke Whitmore, I've known you since the sixth grade and I know when you're lying. No way do you still have the hots for Wade Harris after all this time."

"Rochelle Damesha Evans-Gardner, if you say his name one more time, on pralines and cream ice cream, I will hang up on you," Brooke said.

"Oooooooooh, you do still carry a flame for him!" Rochelle yelled.

"I don't. Now drop it. And I know for sure I'm not going to that stupid reunion," she declared. She took another huge swallow and decided to refill her glass before she exited the kitchen.

"You just proved my point," Rochelle said. "I need a drink now. My best friend is still carrying feelings for her first love and has never said a word or made a comment about him in ten years."

"Drop it, Chelle, or I'm hanging up." Brooke opened her French doors and went and sat out by her pool.

"Okay, okay, I'll drop it. But you are going to the reunion, so don't even think you're not. You've done well for yourself and even if you don't have a man by then, you are going."

"I don't know, Rochelle, I may sit this one out." She got up and move to the side of the pool. She went down two steps into the water and kicked her feet around.

"You will not. And please tell me you are not outside in your pool?"

"I am. I just wanted to get my feet wet." Brooke breathed a sigh of relief at the subject change.

"See, I hate you. It's is freaking freezing here and you're splashing water in your damn pool. Why did I stay here after we graduated? Why didn't I go away like you?"

"Because you wanted to do hair and Pivot Point is a great school. And … as soon as you got the results that you passed the board, you got the results that you were pregnant."

"Yes, Mike and I would have three kids if I hadn't lost that baby."

"Yeah, well, God knows best. You have two healthy brats now."

"And they are a handful," Rochelle said. Brooke could hear a smile in her voice. "Look, we'll continue this reunion subject later. I'm getting off now so I can eat dinner with my family."

"See, that's why I hate you. I ate dinner out of a delivery container, not with my family." Brooke stopped splashing and sat on the edge of the pool.

"Well, one day, you will have a family and I will have a pool," Rochelle joked and they laughed.

They said their goodbyes and Brooke sat and finished her wine before heading back inside. She went into her office, opened the closet door, and stared at the box that she'd labeled 'Lost in Love.' She hadn't pulled it out in a couple years.

Grabbing the box and taking it over to her desk, she took a couple of deep, cleansing breaths, snatched the lid off, and began to finger through the items in the box. There were love letters, notes that they'd passed when they were in high school, and memorabilia from concerts and movies they'd gone to together.

She dug deeper and revealed the most painful items in the box—the pictures. 'Wade and Brooke forever' one picture read. She held it close to her chest and wished that would have been true.

They met freshman year by the lockers on the fourth day of school after he'd almost crushed her. She was walking away from her locker when one of his football teammates tossed him the ball and he fell into her when he went to catch it. He caught the ball, but poor Brooke was trapped under his muscular frame. He quickly rolled off her and apologized over and over again. Not wanting to be late for class, once she was on her feet, she rushed away.

For two days, Wade stalked her locker area until he ran into her. "I'm so sorry about knocking you over the other day," he said, taking her by surprise when she closed her locker.

"It's okay," she said shyly. She wasn't too into boys back then. She was an honor roll student and boys were not at the top of her list of things to do.

"No, it's not. I could have seriously hurt you and I'm sorry," he said.

She gave him a little smile. "I'm fine. My brother has been tackling me all my life, so I'll live." She tried to walk away, but he stayed close.

"Your brother, huh? Is he a student here?"

"Yep, a junior. He's on the varsity team."

"That's crazy; I'm going to be on the varsity team. Skills. Just that good. Coach got me practicing with varsity. Who is he?"

"Brandon Whitmore," she replied.

"Word? I know him. He is a beast."

"Yeah, so I've heard over the years."

"So, what's your name?"

"Brooke."

"Brooke. That's nice. I'm Wade, Wade Harris."

"Okay, Wade, this is my class," she said, stopping outside the art room. "Shouldn't you be going to class?"

"Nah, sixth period is my lunch. I was just hanging around hoping to catch you."

The bell rang and she smiled. "I gotta get inside."

"Okay, can I meet you at your locker after school?"

"Sure," she said and hurried inside.

Nothing else mattered after that moment. All she could think about for the rest of the day was Wade Harris. He was fine, tall, mocha-skinned, and had an easy smile. She couldn't wait for the final bell. She stood by her locker and waited for ten minutes when school was over, but he didn't come. Just when she was about to leave, he ran her down.

"Brooke, Brooke!" he yelled.

She turned to see him running toward her wearing his uniform. She smiled. "You forgot about me?"

"No, I didn't. I suited up and tried to get to your locker, but Coach stopped me and he tends to be a little long winded, so I'm sorry."

"No apologies needed." She looked at the floor.

"Listen, I gotta get to practice, but I want to talk to you. If I give you my number, will you call me?" he asked.

She looked up at his beautiful face. "What do you want to talk about?"

"I don't know... You just seem cool and I'd like to hang out with you sometime."

"Okay," she said shyly.

She went into her backpack for a pen and paper and he gave her his number before he hurried back to practice. She got on the bus wondering if she should call him. He was a jock and she wasn't mature enough to handle a boyfriend, but she liked him. When she got home, she waited until Brandon came in and asked him about Wade. He told her not to call him and to stay clear of him, but that only motivated her to do the opposite.

Sitting there looking at all the memories made her wish she had listened.

# Chapter Two

"HEY, Dr. Z, what's going on?" Brooke asked. Dr. Zachary Jennings was the owner of the family medical clinic that she worked in.

"Hey, Whit," he said, shortening her last name as his late wife had. "Don't even ask what's going on. Mrs. Ella is here today and I think I need a couple shots of something before I go in to see her. That woman drives me nuts," he complained. "She over-talks me like she is the physician and she went to medical school half of her adult life like I did."

"Didn't she just come in two days ago?"

"Yes, but she swears the meds are making her dream unusual dreams. You know, the X-rated kind," he whispered.

Brooke laughed. "Mrs. Ella is eighty-four, Dr. Z."

"I know, and last time, I swear she tried to touch my no-no special place. After, she tried to convince me she had a lump in her breast and insisted I keep looking. There was nothing there. I think she's trying to trap me."

Brooke knew where this was going. "Okay, I'll take Mrs. Ella, but this is gonna cost you," she said.

He moved in closer. "Name your price," he whispered.

Brooke had a feeling he liked her in more than a work-appropriate way, but since she had been his wife's closest friend and was now his employee, they had to remain professional.

"I'll get back to you," she said.

They exchanged charts and he went to her patient and she went to Mrs. Ella.

After the day was done, Brooke was ready to leave, but she saw Zachary's office light on, so she approached and tapped on the door.

"Come in," he said.

"Still here, I see," she said, dropping her bag into the vacant chair near to the door.

"Yeah, got a few test results that I have to get to."

"Need some help?"

"Nah, I don't want to keep you. I know you probably got a hot date," he teased.

"Yes, with my Roku and white wine." She moved closer to his desk.

"What happen to Duncan, Dyson, or whatever dude's name is?"

"Dyson is a done deal," she said. Dr. Z had been there for her through her break-ups, just like she'd been there for him when his wife died. Over the years, they had become really good friends.

"Really? He didn't last long," he commented. "In that case, yes," he said, sliding a few charts her way.

She sat down in the chair in front of his desk and got to work. They worked diligently and without a lot of talk so they could finish quickly. When they were done, it was little after eight.

"Thanks so much, Whit."

"No worries, I didn't have anything big going on," she said, standing to leave.

"How about we grab a bite? Your choice because I know I owe you big time for taking Mrs. Ella today."

"Yes, you do," she agreed.

They locked up the office and walked to their cars parked in adjacent spaces.

"Anything Italian," she said and he didn't argue.

They got to the restaurant he chose, but didn't have a reservation. Luckily, it wasn't busy and they were seated.

"Wow, this is nice. I've never been here before," she said as the waiter poured them both a glass of aged red.

"I love this place. Angela and I used to come here a lot," he said. "I'm sure she told you about this place."

Brooke took a sip of wine. "No, she never mentioned it. But she was a lucky woman to be treated to a place like this. This is really nice."

"Yeah, she was." He laughed. "But I, too, was a lucky man to have her," he said.

"Yes, you were. Angela was an awesome person and she was the only one that I ever allowed to be close to me other than my homegirl, Rochelle." She tried not to get sad. His wife had suffered from mental illness and depression and no matter how hard he and Brooke tried to help her, nothing worked. When Angela became too ill to work, Brooke stood in to help Zachary out, and when she committed suicide a couple years later, Brooke took her place permanently. "But she was a lucky gal because you, Dr. Z, are a catch," she joked.

After the server took their orders, Zachary asked, "I know you've had a few heartbreaks, but why are you still single, Whit? I mean, you're intelligent, independent, successful, and not to mention gorgeous, yet there have been no successful love stories for you."

Brooke decided to be honest. After all, besides Rochelle in Chicago, she didn't talk to anyone else about personal stuff. She had a couple of colleagues she got together with from time to time and a couple nurses she kept in touch with from school, but she and Dr. Z had become tight. After Angela was gone, they kind of only had each other, so they'd grown close.

"Well, Doc, it's not my lack of trying, as you very well know," she said, giving him a little smile. "I've just had a list of not-for-mes."

He laughed. "Not-for-mes? Explain that one, Whit."

"Meaning they are for someone in this world, but definitely not for me." She took another sip from her glass.

"Well, what's for you?"

"I don't know, honestly. I'm still looking." She was quiet for a moment. "So when are you going to get back out there? It's been a couple years since Angela died and you're a young, successful doctor with your own practice. And, if I may add, you're gorgeous."

Zachary Jennings was the ideal man for all women. Six feet tall, medium brown chocolate skin, broad shoulders, and washboard abs were never a thumbs down in the history of fineness. He had perfect teeth and a full beard and mustache that lay so nicely above his lips and over his defined jaw line. There was not a female patient who had eyes and could see who didn't lust after him. And half of them came in even when there was absolutely nothing wrong just to be seen by him.

"I don't know, Whit. At times, I think I'm good and I'm ready to find someone new, then there are times when I just don't think about love, like it's not something that exists."

"Well, from experience, I get that way when I'm in denial. It's like, I don't have love, so why bother trying to get it." She paused when the server returned with a basket of bread and refilled their glasses. "I think that's just our way of dealing with having no love in our lives," she said after the man left.

They scanned the room and made small talk about the other patrons until the food came out. While eating, they talked about patients and work.

Afterward, while waiting for the valet to bring the cars around, Brooke smiled warmly. "Thanks for dinner, Dr. Z."

"You can call me Zachary, Whit," he said. "We are friends outside of the office."

She laughed. "And you can call me Brooke, but you never do," she retorted and they both laughed.

"Okay, I'll call you Brooke when there are no patients around and you call me Zachary when there are no patients around. Deal?"

"Deal." Her car pulled up first. "Thanks for dinner Dr.— I mean Zachary," she said, going to the driver's side.

"You are most welcome, Brooke. I'll see you in the morning," he said.

She smiled, gave a wave, and got in the car. Zachary was cool, but she didn't dare start to like him. He was her boss and her late friend's husband, so, no matter how sweet he was, he was just simply off limits. When she got in, she knew it was late in Chicago, but she called Rochelle anyway. She was happy to find her friend was up and she hadn't awakened her.

"I've decided not to go," she said, being blunt. She just didn't have the courage to face Wade. She wanted to let sleeping dogs lie.

"You are such a wimp, Brooke. I knew you'd be a pussy about it."

"Heeeeyyyy, Rochelle, that's harsh."

"Yeah, it's the truth and the truth hurts, doesn't it? Better yet, I'll call you what you really are. You are a punk-ass, bitch-ass pussy." Brooke knew Rochelle was going to get worse. She was the female Richard Pryor.

"Whatever, Chelle. Call me what you want, but I'm not going to change my mind."

"Fine, punk-ass. I gotta early client. I'll call you tomorrow." She hung up before Brooke could say goodbye.

Brooke knew she thought she was a punk for deciding not to go, but she didn't want to see Wade. Not as a single woman. What if he's married with kids and living the life? she thought. Going would be a terrible idea. The last thing she needed was to be in a room with her ex-love and his wife showing up looking like a dime after having his four kids. She didn't want to look like a loser who couldn't get a man. Maybe I'll go to the one ten years from this one, she told herself on the way to the shower. She had to be up early and she didn't want to think about the reunion and Wade and his fine-ass wife.

Climbing into her king-sized bed later, she looked over at the empty side. It had been occupied on a few occasions with men she wanted to forget because nothing came out of the relationships but lies, lies and more lies, with a sprinkle of heartbreak. She had become the mean bitch that men thought was an off-limit piece. She sometimes wore her bitterness on her sleeve, challenging everything a guy told her. For example, if he swore he didn't live with his momma, she'd demand he take her to his place immediately. If he gave her an excuse or hesitated, she walked away. If a man said he didn't have kids, she demanded a number to a close friend who could verify that on the spot. She ran a lot of men off that way, but she was okay with that because they turned out to be liars and she was tired and done with those types.

She snuggled under her covers and then double checked her alarm. She didn't fight the sleep that came too easy, and before she had enough rest, her alarm sounded off. She hit the snooze twice and thanked God that she'd showered the night before. Since she wasn't getting any and hadn't had any action for months, her night shower was enough to get her through the day. She hit her iPod and brushed her teeth listening to Jill Scott before dressing in her scrubs and heading out.

When walked into her office, she was greeted with a bag on her desk. She opened it to find an egg and cheese croissant, hash browns, and a little note from Zachary thanking her for joining him for dinner the previous night. She smiled and made a mental note to order lunch for him that afternoon. She ate quickly while she went over her morning appointments and reviewed test results.

On the way to the nurse's station, she saw him talking to one of the RNs. She didn't want to interrupt, so she went to pull the chart for her first patient. When he saw her, he cut his conversation short with that nurse.

"Brooke, good morning. I hope you enjoyed your breakfast."

"I did, Dr. Z," she said. "Thank you so much. And lunch is on me today; don't even think of disputing."

"Okay, Whit, I'm free at one," he said.

"One is cool. Next door?" she asked, referring to a little pub next to their office.

"Next door at one. If I run over, don't leave. I'll be there."

"Well, don't be too late, I have a two o'clock." She turned to the nurse, letting her know she was ready.

"I won't be," he replied, heading toward his office.

# Chapter Three

FIVE months later, Brooke was still not sure if she was really going to the reunion that was only three weeks away. She was tempted and had gone online several times to price tickets, but was still debating if she should go or not.

"So what do you think, Zachary?" she asked. "Should I go solo and risk seeing him with his wife or significant other, or should I just sit it out?"

"I think you should go, Whit. I mean, you don't have to have a man to be important or, as you say, 'the bomb.' This cat could be a crack head, who knows? It's been a while. I think you're putting too much thought into it."

"I know, Dr. Z, and I don't want to over analyze this, but I just don't want to look like a lonely cat lady," she cried.

"Okay, how about you go and take me? I can pretend to be your boyfriend and you'll save face. I am a doctor and I'm quite a catch," he teased with a smirk.

"You'd do that for me?" she asked, surprised.

"Whit, you are my best friend and I know how important this is to you. And I don't want you to look like a lonely cat lady either because you're not."

Brooke smiled. "That would be perfect. You can come with me and then I won't look like a total loser." He took a bite of his sandwich and nodded in agreement. "I'll get the tickets tonight and I can get you a room if you like or you can stay at my mom's with me." She stopped and waited for him to stop chewing.

"First, I will get the tickets because I have a zillion flyer miles. You just book a hotel room at a nice, luxurious spot with a pool and room service. I don't think meeting your mom on this pretend couple bit is a good idea, so I'll have a room and you can hang at your mom's if you like." He looked down. "Or with me."

She stopped chewing her food. "Come again?"

"I'm just saying … If you can get a nice suite, we can share a room and I'll behave. If you choose to stay at your mom's, I'll still be your pretend boyfriend." He smiled.

"Okay. I'll work on the room and you get the tickets."

WHEN she got home that evening, she called Rochelle and let her know that she'd decided to come home and would be bringing Dr. Z as her pretend date. Rochelle lectured her about pretending for about an hour before finally giving in to the idea and letting it be.

THE day of their flight came quickly and Brooke had second thoughts. She wondered why she had to front about her situation. She was single and happy. At least most of the time. She had her lonely moments, but, for the most part, she was good. Hell, she was doing well financially and success wasn't determined by marriage or relationship, she tried to convince herself. But it was important not to go to her reunion alone, so she finished packing, thinking Zachary going with her was the perfect lie to ensure no one would think she was a successful loser.

"Are you okay?" Zachary asked Brooke.

"I'm sorry, what did you say?" she asked, coming back from her journey in Brooke Land. They were at baggage claim, waiting for their luggage.

"I asked if you were okay."

"I'm fine," she said with a faint smile. "I'm good."

"Listen, Brooke," he said. "If this is making you uncomfortable, I won't go. I'll hang out in the hotel. You don't have to go through with this."

She thought for a second. Maybe it was a stupid idea to bring him along. She wished she hadn't agreed to it.

"I don't know, Doc. I mean, the initial plan sounded great, but I'm thinking I shouldn't have to lie, you know?"

"Brooke, I don't have to go," he said, taking his suitcase from the revolving belt.

"Don't hate me," she said, feeling bad for bringing him.

"Never." He winked. "But since I'm here, you're going to have to show me around and let me try this famous Italian Beef you're always bragging about.

"Most definitely, but since you came all this way, you're definitely going to the reunion." She gave him a bright smile.

"Most definitely," he agreed.

Her luggage finally came around and he got it for her. They picked up their rental car and went to the hotel. Exhausted from their early flight, they decided to order room service. Talking while enjoying their fabulous meal, they lost track of time. When Brooke looked at her watch, she knew going to her mom's wasn't going to happen because it was so late.

"So are you staying or going to your mom's?" Zachary asked.

"I was, but it's late and I'm exhausted," she said, stepping out of her shoes.

"Well, I got dibs on the bed." He dived onto it.

"Really? You gonna make me hit the couch?"

"Hey, this is my room." He sat up and removed his shirt.

When she saw his chiseled his chest in his tank, her mind went south. "You know what, you're right, Doc. I'll take the couch."

"Whit, I'm joking." He smiled. "The bed is yours."

"Really, I can take the couch." she said and headed for the desk phone. Her luggage was still in the trunk of the rental. She'd have to have the valet bring the car around so she could get it. She was pleased to hear that the valet would send her suitcases up by the bellhop.

She watched Zachary strip down to his boxers and the tank and stood staring at him, wondering how she hadn't known he was that defined under his clothes. She wanted her pussy to stop contracting at the sight of him.

"Whit, it is too late to argue and I'm tired." He grabbed a pillow from the bed and went over to the sofa.

Brooke felt bad. "Listen, the bed is big and we can share. That couch looks like a backache waiting to happen."

"Are you sure?"

"Yeah, yeah, of course. Sleeping together doesn't mean sleeping together. We're mature adults and we're just friends."

Zachary went back to the bed and she went to the bathroom to change. When she came back, he was knocked out. She crawled into bed, pulled the covers up, and closed her eyes. As the night progressed, their bodies behaved like magnets and before sunrise, she was in his arms.

Brooke opened her eyes and blinked a few times, trying to remember where she was and who was lying next to her smelling so damn good. Then she remembered she'd okayed Zachary to share the big bed with her. Why he was holding her was another story. He didn't budge when she eased out of his embrace. She hurried to the bathroom to release her full bladder. She washed her hands and grabbed one of the plush face towels from the towel bar and washed her face.

After retrieving her toiletry bag from her suitcase, she went into the bathroom to brush her teeth and shower. She put on the soft robe that she had been eyeing since the night before and was pleased with how soft it was against her skin. Going back into the bedroom, she walked over to the bed and stared at Zachary for a few moments, wondering if she should wake him. He looked so fine and his skin was so smooth and sexy. She had never seen him without a shirt and his tank looked as if it was painted on his body.

He opened his eyes and caught her checking him out. "Whit, what are you doing?" he asked.

"Huh?" She said, embarrassed that he woke up and caught her damn near drooling.

"What are you doing?" he repeated and sat up. "Are you sizing me up to kill me or something?"

"Yes, that is exactly what I was doing. Contemplating whether should I chop you up into little pieces or just roll your body up in the Oriental rug over there." She laughed and moved away quickly, ashamed of herself for staring at him. They were not romantically involved at all and she wanted to keep it that way.

"Well, I don't know how you were going to carry all of this perfectness out of here, lightweight," he teased, going into the bathroom.

"The bellhop would have handled that for me," she joked.

She opened her suitcase to find something to wear and he took his time in the bathroom. When he came out in the other robe, she was sitting watching the news.

"So, do you want to order room service or go out for breakfast?" he asked, joining her on the sofa.

"Well, I'd like to head out to the south side. We can go to this spot I know for breakfast and then head to my mom's."

"Cool." He got up and went to his suitcase. "What are you going to tell your mom about me?"

"What do you mean?"

"Well, Whit, you did bring a man from Arizona with you and you didn't show up there last night, so she's going to think something is going on," he said taking out his clothes.

"No, she isn't. I told her that I was bringing a good friend with me and so what if I didn't go there last night? That doesn't mean anything."

"Okay, Whit, if you say so."

"Hey, stop calling me Whit. We agreed that you'd call me Brooke, remember?"

"And we agreed you'd call me Zachary, yet you still seem to call me Dr. Z," he retorted.

"Okay, listen, if you are going to be my date for the reunion and events, you're going to have to make sure you call me Brooke or baby, or something that says we are not colleagues."

"Okay, baby," he teased.

She couldn't help but smile. Zachary was charming and he was a catch, but still off limits. She enjoyed him, but she wasn't interested in anything romantic with him.

"Whatever, Zachary. Just don't call me baby in front of my momma. That woman will start naming our children."

They both got dressed and left. After eating at The Original

House of Pancakes, they stopped by a flower shop to get Brooke's mom some flowers and headed over to her house. When they arrived, she wished she hadn't given her momma the heads up a couple hours before. The cars parked on her block meant her mom had invited folks over. At that moment, she wished she would have come alone because now everyone was going to think she'd finally brought a man home.

# Chapter Four

"OH, my goodness, Brooke, it's so good to see you." Brooke's mom squeezed her daughter tight. "I was wondering what was keeping you, and now I see." She released her and turned her attention to Zachary. "I'm Beverly, Brooke's mother." She held out her arms and he gave her a hug.

"Nice to meet you, Ms. Beverly, I'm Zachary," he said.

Brooke saw how long her mother held on to him and the son-in-law look in her eyes. "Momma, this is my boss, Dr. Z, remember? I told you he was coming with me. This is his first time in Chicago."

"Awww, Brooke, you don't have to be so secretive." Her mom took Zachary by the hand, pulling him toward the house.

He looked back and mouthed the words, "I told you," and Brooke hit him with the flowers.

"Everyone, this is Brooke's friend, Zachary," Beverly announced.

Everyone got up to greet them, exchanging hellos and hugs. After the fifteenth person asked Zachary how long they had been dating, Brooke was ready to make the announcement that they were just friends. Just as she stood, Rochelle and her children walked in. Brooke raced to hug her.

"Brooke, girl, look at you," Rochelle said, examining her best friend. "I've always said Arizona is good to you."

"No, girl, look at you. You finally stuck to your diet, I can tell. You look good." They hugged again.

"Now, where is this doctor? I'm dying to meet him." Everyone pointed and Zachary smiled. "Get over here, I've heard so much about you." Brooke wanted to slap her.

"Have you?" Zachary asked as he leaned in to hug her. He peered over her shoulder at Brooke.

"Yes, and you're even more good looking than Brooke described you."

This time, Brooke swatted her arm. "I did not tell her you were good looking," she said to Zachary.

He smiled. "Sure you didn't," he teased.

"I didn't," she said. She turned back to Rochelle. "Speaking of men, where is your man?"

"He's working. I told him that you and Zachary would come by later," she said.

Brooke could feel Zachary looking at her. "Well, listen, Momma has cooked up a storm, so help yourself. Me and my buddy, Zachary, here, need a moment." She pulled him toward her old room.

"So you think I'm good looking," he joked.

"Listen, Dr. Z, Rochelle is a shit-starter and I never told her you were good looking. And secondly, stop lying to my family about us." She punched him in the arm.

"Ouch," he said, rubbing his arm like it hurt. "What did I lie about?"

"When my cousin Charmaine asked you how long we've been together, you said a couple months. You know that's a lie." He laughed. "It's not funny. Now my folks are going to think we are a couple."

"And what's so wrong with that?"

"Because we are not," she cried.

"Come on, Whit, I'm just having a little fun. Don't be so uptight." He grabbed her by her waist. "All you have to do is wait until we get home and tell them we broke up."

"Are you crazy?"

"Nope, just having a little fun and putting smiles on your face. You know you want your family to think you have a man. And I'm a doctor." He laughed. "Do you know how many points you're racking up by bringing home a good-looking doctor?"

She wanted to punch him in the face, but he was right. Everyone was fawning over him. She frowned. "Look, you can pretend to be my boyfriend, but keep your hands to yourself."

"I'll try," he teased again. She gave him a look and he held up his hands. "Okay, Whit," he agreed.

They went back to join the family and it seemed as if the crowd had grown larger. Brooke didn't want to admit it, but it was cool to finally have people complimenting her for having such a good looking and intelligent man. She just hated it was pretend.

"Okay, Momma, we're leaving." She gave her a kiss. "We're going to go by Rochelle's and then to this mixer."

"Okay, baby, will you be by tomorrow?"

"I'll try to before the reunion tomorrow night. There's a picnic tomorrow afternoon, so after we do that, depending on how late it is, we'll come by. If not, definitely Sunday, okay?"

Beverly held out her arms to hug Zachary again. "It was nice meeting you, son. I hope my grandsons get your height and good looks." She winked.

"Well, I don't know, Ms. Beverly, we could end up with a couple of girls. And if they look anything like Brooke, I'm going to have to carry a loaded gun."

Brooke shook her head and pulled his hand. "Come on, we have to go." As soon as they got into the car, she let out a deep breath. "Oh, my goodness. I'm so glad that is over."

"Your family is great," he said.

"You think so, huh? Come around a few more times and let's see if you have that same opinion of them."

"And your cousin, Michelle, that one is … special."

Brooke knew her cousin was a ho. "What did she do, Dr. Z? Did she hit on you?"

"Did she?" He reached into his pocket and handed Brooke a piece of paper with three numbers on it.

"That ho gave you her number?"

"Yep and told me that she won't tell if I won't."

Brooke let down her window and tossed the paper. "She's still hoeing I see." They laughed.

"Yes, she's a piece of work."

"It's all good. Oh, I just realized I tossed her number as if you're really my man. Did you want that?" she asked.

"Whit, be serious," Zachary said.

She smiled. "I can get her number again. I mean if you really want it," she teased.

"Nope, not interested," he said.

She gave him directions to Rochelle's house. They went by and hung out for a little while then went back to the hotel to change.

When they got to the mixer, Brooke was nervous. It hit her that she had come home to reunite with her old classmates and possibly her first love. She wondered again if bringing Dr. Z was a good idea.

"Brooke Whitmore," she said to the person behind the sign-in desk.

"I know who you are, Brooke," the woman said.

Brooke tried to place her name. "I'm sorry, your face looks so familiar."

"Renee Washington," she said. Brooke couldn't believe her eyes. She was two persons less than she was in high school. The kids called her Rhino Renee.

"Oh, my goodness, look at you. You look great."

Renee stood and they exchanged a quick hug. "Thank you. So do you." She sat back down and handed Brooke a name tag. "And who is your plus one?" She gave Zachary a sexy smile.

"This is my boyfriend, Dr. Zachary Jennings." She hated bringing a fake boyfriend just so she wouldn't look like a lonely cat lady.

"Dr. Jennings, huh?" Renee said as she wrote Zachary's name down on a name tag.

Brooke smiled. "Yes, he's a doctor."

"And good looking," Renee added.

"So I've been told," Brooke said, taking his tag. She turned and put it on Zachary's chest, making sure she touched him a little longer than needed to let Renee know he was off limits.

"Are you ready, baby?" He took Brooke's hand and they went in.

Brooke enjoyed seeing all of her old classmates and wondered what was keeping Rochelle and Mike. She texted Rochelle asking where the hell she was and got a response that they were five minutes away.

She and Zachary were having a good time. It felt nice being close to him. Having all the women eyeing him didn't hurt either. He left to get them a drink and she stayed at their table to touch up her makeup.

"Brooke."

Hearing her name, she looked up and almost dropped her mirror. She'd been so busy with her lipstick, she hadn't noticed Wade approaching.

"You're still beautiful," he said.

She knew her mouth was open. He was deliciously handsome and she felt like she was fifteen all over again. She closed her mouth and snapped back into the present.

"Wade, what a surprise," was all she could come up with. "How are you?"

"I'm good, how are you?"

"Great, I mean I'm doing well," she replied, wondering why the sight of him was making her heart skip a beat. She had been over him, but seeing him again was like the wind of love blowing back her hair.

"You look well. Are you here with someone?" he asked

She had completely forgotten about Dr. Z. "Ummm, yes … Ummm, my boyfriend is—"

Zachary walked up. "Here you go, baby." He set her drink down in front of her and sat down next to her.

"Your boyfriend? Oh … okay. I'm Wade, Wade Harris." He extended a hand to Zachary and they shook.

"Dr. Zachary Jennings," Zachary said, putting an arm around Brooke.

"Wow, that's great. It was good seeing you, Brooke. Maybe we can sneak in a dance or two? Of course, if it's alright with you," he said to Zachary.

"No harm. A dance is a dance right?" Zachary replied.

"Yes … right," Wade said with his eyes locked on Brooke.

"Maybe later," Brooke said.

Wade smiled and walked away.

"So that's him? The notorious Wade Harris?" Zachary said, taking a drink from his cup.

"Yep, that's him." She downed her drink. She hadn't expected to get chills from seeing Wade and she hated he was even finer as an adult than he had been as a teen.

"Are you okay?"

"I'm good. I just need another drink, maybe two, and to talk to Rochelle."

"You still got it for this guy?"

"What? No, no, I don't. Just seeing him was a shock and I didn't expect for him to look so damn fine." She took a swallow of Zachary's drink.

"Need I remind you who you're talking to? I am your boy-friend," he joked.

"Ha, ha, Doc," she said. She looked around and was relieved to see Rochelle and Mike walk in. She hopped up. "Dr. Z, please get me another drink. I've gotta to talk to Rochelle." She dashed over to her friend. "He's here, Chelle. He. Is. Here."

Mike excused himself and went over to the table with Zachary.

"Where?" Rochelle asked. "Did he see you yet?"

"Yes. He came over to my table and he asked me to dance, even after I told him I was with Zachary." Brooke looked around to see if she could spot him.

"And did you say you would?"

"I said maybe. But the awful part is he is fine as hell now, Rochelle. He looks like he just stepped out of a modeling ad. It took every muscle in my body to sit still and not jump across the table and hug his neck."

"Wait a minute. Didn't we say that we were over him and didn't want to have shit to do with him?" Rochelle asked, quoting the words that came out of Brooke's mouth several hours prior.

"Yes, but that was before. I have to talk to him, Chelle. I have to see if he's with someone or alone. I need to know if he has kids and what's going on with him, but I don't want Zachary to know that I'm off trying to catch up with him."

"Why? The doctor knows he isn't your real boyfriend. And I didn't get a chance to ask earlier because we never got a minute alone, but why the hell is he not your man? He is successful, tall, and gorgeous. And did I mention gorgeous?"

"You did, but Zachary and I are friends and I don't want to mess that up. We get along so well and if we date and I ruin it, it'll turn awkward, you know? We work together and I just don't want to go messing up what we have because of a failed relationship."

"Well, I say forget about Wade and get with the doctor. Plus, I can tell he's feeling you," Rochelle said.

"No he isn't, that's just how we are. Its innocent flirting; that's what keeps us happy and safe from hurt." Brooke scanned the room again. "Listen, Wade is right over there. Come over with me and say hello and then pretend you have to get Mike a drink, so I can talk with him."

She led Rochelle to him "Wade, you remember Rochelle," she said, getting his attention.

"Of course I remember your best friend. How are you, Rochelle? You're also looking great. I mean, you two have blossomed into something spectacular." He gave Rochelle a quick hug.

"Thank you, Wade. You have certainly grown into your body," Rochelle said.

"Thank you," he said. His eyes locked on Brooke again.

Rochelle excused herself. "Listen, I have to grab Mike a drink."

"Mike? You and Mike are still together?"

"Yes, married with two kids," she said.

"Wow, that is amazing. I'll be over to holla at him," he said.

Rochelle made her exit and Brooke waited a moment before asking, "So what's your story, Wade? Are you married? Do you have kids?"

"Divorced and I now have a ten-year-old son. He lives with his mom in Louisiana. I've been divorced for four years and, as of two and a half weeks ago, I'm single."

"That's recent."

"Yeah. She wanted more than I wanted to give, so she finally told me to step off." Brooke didn't know what to say next. "So, you," he continued, "you brought your boyfriend, a doctor. How long have you two been together?"

"Yes, he's a doctor. We've been together a couple months."

"Is it serious?"

"Why do you want to know that?"

"Just curious. When I laid eyes on you, it brought back memories. If you and the doctor aren't serious, I think you should hang out with me a little while you're in town."

"Who told you I was in town?"

"Come on, Brooke, everyone knows you never came back after college," he said.

"Okay, that's true. What did you have in mind?"

"Nothing heavy, maybe you can come by and we can talk. You know, catch up and then whatever else you'd like to do." He moved closer to her and she stepped back.

"Well, I look forward to our dance and then we'll see if I can get out later, so we can." She paused. "Talk," she finished. She turned and went back to her table. When she sat, she could see Zachary wasn't too happy. "Are you okay?"

"I'm fine," he replied, looking away.

"Zachary, come on now. Are you tripping on me?" she asked.

"What? Naw, you straight," he said, straightening up.

"Okay then," she said and smiled.

The stayed until after one and then headed back to the hotel, but not before Wade and Brooke exchanged numbers. Back in the room, she and Zachary didn't talk much and she decided she'd wait until the next day to see Wade because she was too tired to go anywhere.

# Chapter Five

THE next morning, Brooke got up before Zachary. She tiptoed to her purse and took out her phone. Blushing, she scrolled through her contact list and stared at Wade's number. She sat down on the couch and took a couple deep breaths, asking herself why she'd even exchanged numbers with him. The scent of trouble hung in the air and the mental aroma of bad news reeked as she hit the button to dial, but that didn't stop her.

"Hey, good morning," she said softly, leaving him a voicemail. "This is Brooke. I just wanted to say it was good seeing you last night. When the automated recorder gave her edit options, she changed her mind and deleted it. "What is wrong with you, girl?" she said aloud. "It is eight a.m. and a woman with a fine-ass doctor boyfriend shouldn't be up this early calling her ex." She hit the end button, but then realized he'd see a missed call.

"Yeah, that would be a bad move, Whit," Zachary said.

She jumped. She'd been so busy looking at her phone, she didn't notice him. "Dr. Z, you scared me. And why are you eavesdropping?"

"First, I walked up on you talking to yourself and I'm just agreeing with you. If you want to get this ex of yours back, you need to chill and not be the initiator. You're in town with your man and as soon as your man turns his back, you're calling your ex. That's making it too easy." He joined her on the couch.

"Who said I wanted him back?"

"You didn't have to say it, Whit, it's written all over your face. I didn't come here to look like a clown, so before we go to all of your festivities today, are we a couple or do you want to go alone and get reacquainted with Wade?"

"Okay, okay, Doc," she said, resting her head on his shoulder. "You've got a point. I came to make him jealous and to show him that I'm happy. If he calls me back and says he missed my call, I'm going to tell him that I purse-dialed him."

"That's my girl. If you wanna rekindle this thing with him, at least play a little hard to get. Let him make all the moves and you shoot him down because of me. After two or three weeks, after we're home, return his call and tell him we broke up."

"You think that'll work?"

"Aha! So you do want to get back with him?"

"No … And why are you so concerned anyway?"

"I'm not. I'm just worried about you. I mean, you said he really hurt you, but as soon as you see him again, it's like you forgot about the breakup."

"Okay, listen." She sat up. "It was good seeing him last night. He looked good and, yes, my mind started to go there, okay, but you're here with me to keep me focused. I will not let Wade Harris just jump back into to my life because I'm not desperate. A little lonely, but definitely not desperate."

"That's what I'm talking about," Zachary said.

"Thank you, Doc." She rested her head back on his shoulder,

so she didn't see the disappointed look he had on his face.

"Anytime, Whit." They sat in silence for a few moments after that. "So, shall we go out for breakfast or order up some room service?" he asked, breaking the silence.

Brooke had closed her eyes and was telling herself to not think of Wade. "Ummm, what are you up for?"

"Well, it's early and we don't have to be at the picnic until two or so, so how about we go down and have something by the pool?"

She lifted her head. "That's sounds great, but I didn't pack a bathing suit."

"So I'll run down to the gift shop and get you one," he offered.

"Dr. Z, that's not necessary. Let's just order up room service." She got up and went to the menu on the desk by the phone.

"Listen, it's no bother. I want to take a quick swim while we wait for our food. Go shower and I'll be back," he said. He walked over and slid his feet into his Nike slippers and snatched a tee to put over his tank.

"A swim does sound good. Too bad I can't get my hair wet."

"Why not," he asked.

She gave him a look. "Dr. Z, you know damn well why I can't get my hair wet."

He burst into laughter. "Yeah, because you wanna look good for Wade," he teased.

She tossed a pen from the desk at him. "No, I wanna look good for my doctor boyfriend when he escorts me to the reunion later tonight." She smiled.

"Now that's more like it. I'll be back in a sec," he said, walking out the door.

Her cell rang. It was Wade calling her back. She contemplated whether or not she should answer, but before she made a decision, it stopped ringing. She got into the shower and lathered up, wondering what would be so bad about giving Wade another chance if he wanted one. She knew it was young love, but he was the only man she had ever actually loved.

They weren't teens anymore and it could actually work, she thought as she stepped out. She dried off with thoughts of Wade on her mind and started lotioning up. Before she could finish, there was a tap on the door.

"Hey, Whit," Zachary said through the door, "I gotta shower too."

"I'm almost done," she said. A couple moments later, she opened the door, wrapped in a towel. "I'm sorry, Doc, but lotioning is a regimen that I take seriously. I'm sorry I hogged the bathroom."

"No, no, no, you're fine," he stammered, looking at her.

"Oh, okay." She saw a gift bag on the bed. "What's this?"

"Your bathing suit. I told the clerk the gift bag wasn't necessary, but she insisted."

"Okay." She laughed, agreeing the bag was a bit much. "Let me see what you got for me." She removed the extra tissue paper from the top and pulled out a black and purple one piece suit with a sexy opening down the center. Definitely sexy, and definitely her style. "Wow, Doc, this is a nice swimsuit. You did well," she said admiring it.

"Well, it looks like something you'd wear," he said. She moved over to the mirror and held it up in front of her. "I'm glad you like," he said.

"Yes, I like this. I have to pay you back," she said, going for her purse. "How much do I owe you?"

"Whit, please. Come on now. Don't worry about it."

"Are you sure?"

"Positive. Now, I'm starving. I'm going to shower while you put on your suit." He went into the bathroom to shower.

As soon as he was on the other side of the bathroom door, she put it on. When he came out, she saw him in the mirror checking her out, but she didn't say anything. She knew she looked good and she didn't mind him admiring her.

"BROOKE, you look amazing," Wade said when he approached.

She felt Zachary's hand on the small of her back and smiled. "Thank you, Wade. You remember my boyfriend, Zachary right?" she said.

Wade reached out to shake his hand. "Of course. What's going on?"

"Nothing too much, just was about to get my lady a drink. How about you join me at the bar?" Zachary asked.

"Sure," Wade said. "It was nice seeing you, Brooke." He followed Zachary to the bar. "So, Dr. Jennings," he asked, "what type of doctor are you?"

"General practice. I take care of mostly anything."

"Is that right?" Wade paused to order his drink. "I'm not sure if Brooke told you, but we were a hot item back in the day," he said with a devilish grin.

"Yes, she did. I wanted you to join me to remind you that your thing with Brooke was back in the day, but I'm with her today. Now, I know high school crushes die hard, but I'd like you to respect my space and don't do anything to try to spark old flames. Brooke is with me."

"Oooooooh, it's like that, Doc, huh?" Wade flexed. "Look I'm not trying to come between you and Brooke's here and now, but seeing her brings back some old memories, and if she wants to act on them, that's on her, so you're talking to the wrong one." He gave Zachary the once over and then walked away.

Zachary took a couple deep breaths and turned to the bartender. He hated it, but if he didn't say something quick, Brooke would be back with her ex and the chances for him would go from slim to none.

# Chapter Six

"SO, do you wanna get out of here and go someplace quiet?" Wade asked Brooke.

She had excused herself to go to the ladies' room, but he'd stopped her before she could get back to her table. They had been making eye contact all night. She figured he didn't care that she was there with Zachary because he kept eyeing her down every other minute. "Wade, I can't leave with you. You know I'm with Zachary."

"Well, I see you're with him, but all eyes are on me."

"Look, I know I've been watching you and, yes, I want to sit and talk and catch up, but that's it. Me and Zackary got something good, okay? I should get back." She tried to walk away, but he blocked her path.

He looked into her eyes. "Listen, Brooke, we were kids back then, and breaking up with you was a mistake."

"Brooke, baby, there you are," Zachary interrupted. "Rochelle and Mike are ready to leave." He put an arm around her waist.

"I'm ready," she said nervously, giving Wade one last look. She took Zachary's hand and they walked away. "You came just in time." She let out a deep breath.

"Yeah, I guess I did," he said.

Brooke frowned at his tone. "What's wrong, Dr. Z? Why are you trippin' out on me?"

"Look, Whit, maybe this was a bad idea. I'm going back to the hotel. Are you coming?"

"Wait, wait, wait, Zachary. What's going on? What did I miss?"

He sighed. "Nothing. Are you ready?" he asked again.

"No, you go ahead. I'll get a ride with Rochelle," she said.

Zachary left and she stood wondering why he was so upset about her talking to Wade. She and he were pretending to be together and she knew better than to assume otherwise or cross any lines with him. She enjoyed their friendship and she didn't want to develop any type of feelings for him and things not work out and lose him as a friend. She wasn't willing to risk that.

"What happen to Dr. Z?" Rochelle asked.

"I don't know. He walked up and saw me talking to Wade and he just left."

"Well, I didn't want to say anything, but if you brought the doctor to make yourself look large and in charge, you eyeing Wade down all night right in front of Zachary's face didn't help. You would have been better off leaving him in Arizona. You said you were over Wade, but you come here and you're gazing at him every five seconds."

"I know and I didn't know that would bother him, Chelle. Dr. Z is like my best friend and I'm not trying to go there with him. Angela and I were good friends and I don't think dating him is appropriate. I've never had a successful relationship and Zachary is just different. He's too good of a guy for me to mess up with and entertain any thoughts of him and me romantically."

Wade walked up and Brooke gave Rochelle the I-need-a-moment look. Rochelle rolled her eyes and walked away.

"Hey, I didn't mean to get you in trouble with the doctor," Wade said, using air quotes on doctor.

"He'll be fine. He just needs a moment. He wasn't too happy with me eyeballing you all evening and he didn't believe me when I said nothing happened outside of the restroom."

"Well, since he's taking a break, how about we catch up a little?"

"Wade, I can't. I have to get back to Zachary." She wanted to hang with Wade, but she had to talk to her friend.

"Hey, I'll tell you what, go and deal with your man, and if you wanna meet me later for a drink, then just call me." He planted a soft kiss on her cheek.

Brooke wanted to leave with him, but she had to talk to Dr. Z. She pulled her phone out of her purse and called him.

"Yeah?" he said when he answered.

"Doc, I'm sorry, okay. I don't understand why you're so upset. Just come back and get me please, so we can talk. I'll meet you out front, okay?"

He sighed. "Okay. I'm on my way back."

"Hey, Chelle, I'm gonna go. Zachary is coming back for me. I'll see you tomorrow, okay?" she said. They hugged.

"Okay. And Brooke, don't step on Mr. Right, to get to Mr. Wrong. Wade and you are history, but you and Zachary have a chance. Like you said, he's different and his wife died. He's not messing around on her. It won't make you a bad person if you wanted to be with him."

"Goodnight, Chelle. Tell Mike I said bye."

Outside, she waited for Zachary to get back. When he pulled up, he got out to open her door for her.

"I could have gotten it," she said.

"Get in, Whit," he said sadly.

"Dr. Z, what did I do?" she asked when he got back in the car and pulled off. "Why are you so angry with me?"

"You didn't do anything, it's me. I foolishly got my black ass on the plane to come here with you to hold your hand to face the man you said broke your heart in two, but you didn't need me to do that. I didn't have to be your hero, so you didn't do anything, Whit."

"Listen," she said, reaching over and touching his arm. "I'm sorry for dragging you out here to be my support system, I just didn't know what to expect. I didn't know if I could handle seeing him after all these years by myself. The thing is, seeing him jolted all these feelings that I thought were gone. I'm sorry if you think I'm a loser for feeling like I do."

"I don't think you are a loser and I'm sorry for catching an atti- tude. You're a great person and I care about you. I've been there to nurse you back to normal a few times and I just don't want to see you hurt again."

"I know, Dr. Z, but I just want to talk to him, spend a little time with him. Maybe things will be different this time."

"You're absolutely right," Zachary said. "I think you should go for it."

"So you think I should go for it?"

"Yes. He seems to be interested, so call him, go out with him."

"Awww, thank you, Zachary. I knew Rochelle was wrong."

"About what?"

Brooke smiled. "Nothing. Thank you for being the best male friend on this planet. I've never been this close to someone who wasn't trying to get into my pants and I am so glad I have you in my life."

She pulled out her phone. First, she texted Rochelle to tell her that she was wrong about Dr. Z and then she texted Wade and asked where he wanted to meet. She and Zachary went up to their room and she changed clothes. He kissed her on the fore-head and wished her luck. Before she left, she saw Zachary open-ing up a bottle from the wet bar.

"Hey, take it easy on that bar. You know that mess is an arm and a leg."

"And I'm a doctor, I can handle it. Since I'm going hang alone, I might as well get wasted."

"Well, don't get too wasted because if things don't go well, I'm going to need an ear when I get back."

"Sorry. By the time you make it in, I plan to be in a deep, drunken sleep."

"Okay, Doc, if you wanna get lit, do your thang." She headed for door, wondering if she shouldn't go. She felt a little bad leav-ing him alone, but she had to see Wade and she was confident that Zachary understood.

# Chapter Seven

"IT was after four when Brooke finally walked in. Zachary was sitting on the sofa watching the news when she put her purse on the coffee table and flopped down next to him.

"How did it go?" he asked.

"It went really well," she lied.

She didn't want to tell him the truth about what went on that night. The only person she could tell that horrible story to was Rochelle, and since she was in church, she held it all inside, dying to get it out.

"So you're going to see him again?"

"We talked about it. He plans to come out to Arizona to visit in a couple weeks."

"Wow, that well, huh?" he asked, staring at the tube.

"Yes, and from there we'll see," she said, standing up. "I'm going to shower and dress so we can get to my mom's for dinner," she said.

"Okay," he said.

When they got to her mom's, Brooke smiled and tried to pretend everything was okay, but she knew her sadness must have been written all over her face because when they got back to the hotel he asked her again.

"Whit, what really happened last night?" Zachary asked.

"What do you mean?" she said.

"Whit, come on, talk to me. I know you and I know you aren't telling me something."

She shook her head. "Doc, I'm fine."

"No, you're not," he said, getting in her face. She looked up at him and her eyes welled. "Whit, baby, what's wrong? What happened?"

She covered her face. She wanted to talk to Rochelle and not him. "Awww, Dr. Z, I'm so fucking stupid," she blurted out.

He helped her to the sofa. "Whit, stop it, okay, and tell me what happened."

"Dr. Z, I'm so embarrassed about the entire episode."

"Whit, talk to me."

"Okay, first we met up at this lounge. It was really nice and I was impressed. We sat at the bar, conversation is good and all, we're drinking and catching up, and everything is cool. The attraction was there and I could feel us reconnecting. Before we were going to close out our tab, he asked if I was hungry. I told him no, I was good, and he says 'Well, I'm starving.' I noticed that other patrons had food, so I suggested he order something from there because I didn't want to drive to a new spot and start from scratch. He said, 'Cool,' and ordered. About twenty minutes later, the barmaid brought the food and the ticket and I didn't think anything of it when he looked at it and then put it on the bar." She sniffled.

Zachary got up and got her a tissue. "Go ahead, tell me the rest."

"So, it was getting later and I was ready to go. He asked me could I handle the bill. Initially, I was shocked and then I assumed he was joking, but he was dead serious. I picked it up and it was almost eighty bucks, which isn't a biggie for me, but I had no idea he wasn't in a position to take of it. I just smiled, pulled out my card, and took care of it. I was a little annoyed and turned off, but he said, 'Next time I got you, boo. It's just today I had to send my son's mom some cash that wasn't planned and it threw me off.'

Me being the understanding person that I am, said, 'Okay, unexpected things arrive. I have it, so no big deal.' We walk out and he walks me to the rental. He asked me to go home with him, and after a little persuading I go because, hey, this is Wade, the man who took my virginity, and I'm feeling him, so why not? We get to his place and it wasn't fully furnished, but it was clean and that was fine. So I asked, 'What do you do again?' And he was like 'I'm a repair tech at Verizon.'

He goes on to say he lost this high profile position at this major company about a year ago and things been rough with this economy. I was like okay, it's possible. We kissed and one thing led to another and we had sex," she confessed.

"And then what happened, Whit?"

"It was better than ever and I was lying there in the glorious aftermath and he gets up and fires up a blunt. Now, I know that was his place and all, but I was like, are you fucking kidding me? This old-ass, broke Negro got weed, but can't afford drinks? But I didn't say anything, I just let him do his thing. I finally fell asleep and at eight a.m., some woman starts banging on his door like the damn police. I jumped up in a panic, out of my sleep, and he literally begged me to be quiet. I was thinking 'You can't be serious.'

Then his phone began to ring over and over and over and over again. Zachary, I swore this had to be a prank because anything that could go wrong, went wrong. After two hours of her banging and me lying in his bed being silent, she finally stopped banging. I got up to leave and he begged me to wait. He told to me some bullshit about him just breaking up with her and she didn't want to let it go and some old tired-ass garbage. Bottom line and end of this sorry-ass story is I sat in this fucker's apartment until three this afternoon with four leftover dry-ass chicken wings and tap water because he was afraid for me to open the damn door.

"What the hell was I thinking? How could I sit there and take that? He kept saying she was crazy and he didn't want me to get hurt behind her crazy ass. It was just horrible. So I drove back here feeling like an even bigger loser than I already am." She sobbed and he held her.

"Whit, you are not a loser. As horrible as this whole thing sounds, at least you know now that you aren't missing out on anything. You're doing well and Wade is the one who missed out on a good thing," he said.

Brooke knew he was right, but she still didn't feel any better. She felt like a damn fool. They fell asleep on the sofa and both woke up with aches and pains, but they had to shower and get to O'Hare to make their flight.

When they got back to Arizona, Zachary invited her to stay and talk for a while.

"I guess so. My back is killing me. Can we sit in the hot tub for a while?"

"Sure. Let me go turn it on and it can warm up while we get changed. Oh, wait, you don't have a suit." He grinned devilishly. "We can skinny dip, of course."

Brooke laughed. "I have the suit you bought me, remember?"

Zachary laughed. "You can change in the guest room. Then meet me outside."

After changing, she went out and found him already in the tub.

"Ummm, this feels good," she moaned, stepping in and sitting down. She laid her head back, glad she'd decided to stay.

"It sure does," Zachary agreed.

"It feels good to be back."

"Yes. Hopefully, the next time we visit Chicago we can have some real fun."

"You'd be willing to visit that place again with me?" she asked, shocked.

"Of course. I mean, with the reunion and alumni activities, we didn't get a chance to do anything. And then you left me alone for hours without the rental, so I didn't get to see the city. Wait, from the window I did, but that was about it."

"Zachary, I'm sorry," she said.

"Hey, Whit, no apologies needed."

They relaxed in the hot tub a little while longer then she went home. As soon as she walked in, Wade called, but she didn't answer. He called right back and still she didn't answer. Then she got a text.

I'm so sorry bout everything. I miss u already, pls don't b mad call me gurl.

She read it and put her phone down. She was too exhausted to deal with him and wished he'd lose her number. He continued to call and text for the next week. Tired of playing games, she finally gave in and answered. She planned to tell him to stop calling her.

"What, Wade, what?" she spat.

"Hold on, Brooke. Relax, baby, and just hear me out."

"I'm listening."

"I know we got off to an awful start, and I'm sorry. It's just, since you left, I can't think of anyone else but you and I was hoping you'd reconsider your decision not to talk to me."

"Wade, you lied about not having anyone and you have a few habits that I don't like."

"I wasn't lying about me and Tenita. She and I are over, but she's crazy for real. I know you don't believe me when I tell you that, but she's a pain in my ass."

"And the weed?"

"Look, Brooke, you've always known me to smoke since high school. You and I have different views on it, but I'm not a weed head. I take care of my business, but, yes, I hit my blunt."

"Wade, what do you want from me? We're miles apart and I don't know what I can offer you or what you can offer me."

"Love, Brooke, I know damn well you felt those feelings because I know I did. We broke up way back then, yes, and that was fucked up, but I'd like to try again."

"I don't think that would be a good idea," she said.

"Why? Because of the doctor? I know you're not feeling him. If you were, you would have never got with me. What did you tell him anyway?"

"I just said I needed to help my mom," she lied.

"And he went for that? See, he don't deserve you, Brooke. All I'm asking is for a chance. I miss you, baby, and seeing you was like … I don't know. All I do know is I haven't been able to think of nobody but you."

Brooke was silent for a moment. "I don't know, Wade. I don't know. That night was terrible, and every time I think of it, I cringe."

"I know, baby. Me too and I'm sorry," he said.

She smiled and felt a little warm inside. She didn't like how their night went, but she did like him. "Listen, Wade, I'll call you when I leave the hospital. I can't do this with you right now."

"Fair enough, just please call me back."

"I will."

She got back to work and tried to not think of Wade, but thoughts of him wouldn't go away. When she got home, she called him back like she'd promised. And their long distance relationship began.

They texted and talked several times a day and within a month, she couldn't go a day without hearing his voice.

# Chapter Eight

"WHIT," Dr. Z, said, sticking his head in her office.

She was texting Wade and she looked up with a big smile on her face. "Yes?" she said, caught off guard.

"What are you up to? Why are you smiling like a fat kid in a candy store?"

"No reason," she lied. She hadn't told Zachary that she and Wade had been reconnecting and getting closer over the phone.

"You're lying, Whit. Let me see," he said, coming in and reaching for her phone.

"No. And what do you want?"

"You met someone, didn't you?"

"No … Why are you sweatin' me?"

He took a seat. "Because I know that look, Whit. Every time you're being wooed by some guy, you wear that grin and I've noticed it the last couple days."

"Well, nosey, there is someone, but I'd rather not share." She knew he would hit the ceiling.

"Oh, now we keeping secrets?" he teased.

"No, it's just still early, so I don't want to jinx it." She stood. "I have a patient to see, so I've gotta run." She grabbed a chart from her desk and walked toward the door.

"Okay, Whit, but you can't hide your secret forever," he said from behind her.

♥ ♥ ♥

"SO when are you going to come back and visit me? You know I am dying to see you."

"I don't know, Wade, I just took time off."

"But I need to see you."

"I wanna see you too, baby, but I have to clear my schedule. I can't leave Dr. Z without notice and I volunteer at the hospital one night a week."

"Dr. Z?" He paused. "Speaking of the doctor, did you break it off with him yet?"

"Wade, I asked you to give me a moment to do that," she said.

"A moment for what, Brooke? You said you still loved me."

"Okay, Wade, I'll tell him tomorrow," she lied. She and Wade had been getting cozy over the past few weeks and she really was dying to see him. She didn't want to tell Zachary, but she was back in love again. Even though they'd had a bad reunion when she was home, she was going to give him a chance.

"I hope you will. I need you to clear your schedule and come see me, baby, I miss you."

"I miss you too," she said. They talked for a little while longer then she got off the phone to shower and prepare for bed.

The next morning when she got to work, she looked over her schedule. Her weekend off was in two weeks. She went online and paid for a plane ticket and reserved a hotel room because she wanted to just spend the weekend with Wade and not alert her mom that she was in town.

She kept her arrangements a secret from Dr. Z, and two weeks later, she was in Chicago to see Mr. Wade Harris.

"BABY, right there," Brooke moaned. Wade was deep inside of her, making her pussy scream. "Deeper, baby, take this pussy." He was older, better, and his dick was surely better than the last encounter they had when she was home.

"Open up for me, baby. Spread 'em wider, baby." He pushed her thighs back further so he could push his big dick deeper.

Her clit tingling, she was glad she'd taken the time to fly out. "Baby, I'm there, I'm gonna cum," she moaned. He pulled out and went down and sucked her clit. Her orgasmic juices squirted into his mouth and on his face and he kept trying to get more. "No, no, no, baby, please. I can't take no more." She pushed at his head, but he refused to stop. "Wade, baby, no more … I can't take no more, baby."

She continued to push his head away from her hot spot. He finally let up and moved back up to her nipples, squeezing them and sucking on them hard. His dick stiffened even harder and he wanted to cum, so he slid back in. He pumped her hard and strong and when he was close, he pulled out and ripped the condom away. He stroked himself and squirted all of his hot juices on her stomach and tits.

He came down on top of her as if his nut wasn't all over her and pushed his tongue into her mouth. His kisses made Brooke want to cry. Wade was her heart from the very start and she hated she'd had others after him.

"Baby, your pussy is still good," he whispered, sucking on her earlobe.

"And your dick is even better."

"I love you."

"I love you too," she said.

He gave her a couple kisses and then got up. "Come and shower with me, baby."

She didn't want to move, but she followed him. After showering, they dressed and went out. She'd picked him up in her rental car when she got into town. He had a packed bag to stay with her. She'd booked a room at the same hotel she and Dr. Z stayed in when they were there.

"Let's go in there," she said. Wade had been driving around for an hour.

"Baby, that place is like mad expensive," he said.

"So what, babe? It's late and I want to have a drink."

"I do too, but I don't have it like that," he snapped.

"Listen, it's on me. Let's just go inside, baby," Brooke said.

Wade turned in and found a parking spot. When they got inside, they found standing room only. The club was super crowded. Brooke got a waitress and started a tab. Since the music was jamming, she wanted to dance.

"Baby, let's dance," she said.

"Naw baby, do your thing," he said.

Shocked, she frowned and turned her back to him and moved to the music until the waitress came back with their drinks. After the first one, she was feeling nice and wanted to get her party on. She texted Rochelle and invited her and Mike to meet them there. When they made it, Wade asked them what they wanted to drink and put it on their tab, but Brooke didn't mind. She would have offered herself, so she decided not to catch an attitude. After three drinks, she and Rochelle were on the floor tearing it up. Brooke begged Wade to dance with her, and she was more than disappointed when he refused her.

"Is there something wrong with me?" she asked Rochelle.

"No, baby, you look fab," she said.

"Wade won't dance with me."

"Girl, don't sweat that. He is the same old Wade. He didn't even dance at prom, remember?"

"I guess."

"Well, you got me, and Mike ain't dancing with me either, so let's hit it. Forget them."

They went back out on the floor for a while and then left the bar after Brooke signed a tab totaling one hundred and sixty-four dollars. Wade drank the good shit on her dime, but she didn't complain.

When they got back to the hotel, she didn't want to have sex, but he pushed her legs back and licked her pussy so good she had to finish him off. She opened wide and let him slide his dick in and he fucked the shit out of her. It was undeniably good, so she let the other issues with him subside and worked her pussy back on him, helping him to his nut. After he caught his breath, he got up and didn't come back. She got up, went into the bathroom to grab a robe, and found him on the terrace smoking a blunt.

She cringed, but was grateful he at least had sense to take that shit outside. "I thought you said you quit." During the weeks of their phone affair, he promised her he'd stop.

"I did for a minute, but you know how it goes, babe. I'm not a weed head, I just like to smoke, so please don't deny me and don't preach." He took a pull.

She stood next to him and decided to join him. She hadn't done it in years, but, what the hell, she was grown.

She reached for the blunt. "You gon' share," she said.

He looked at her for a moment. "Baby, I know you don't smoke, so you don't have to."

"Baby, I'm grown and I've had weed before. You're the one that taught me, remember?"

"You're right, baby, it was me, but let me give it to you like I did back then." He pulled and gave her the smoke. She sucked it in, inhaled it, and let it go. Surprisingly, she didn't choke. Ten minutes later, she was high as hell with him.

"Wade, baby, I want a double cheeseburger and some dick at the same time," she said. They both laughed.

"I wanna fuck you while you eat a double cheeseburger," he said. They laughed uncontrollably. "Let's order room service," he suggested. But the kitchen was closed.

"Okay, I'm too high to drive, baby." Brooke giggled.

"I'm never too high to get food," he said. They threw on something quick and drove around until they found the first open spot. They walked in laughing and got two jumbo gyros and fries. Brooke ordered mozzarella sticks and fried mushrooms too. She had to pay, but again she didn't say anything. When they got back to the room, they ate everything and fell out on the bed.

# Chapter Nine

THE next morning, Brooke woke up to find Wade fully dressed.

"Why are you dressed so early, baby?"

"I gotta go and help a friend move some stuff," he said.

That was new news to Brooke. "Oh. Is someone picking you up?"

"Naw, I was hoping I could use the rental. I won't be gone long."

Brooke wanted to say hell no, but she didn't. "Okay, well, what time will you be back? I thought we could go by Rochelle and Mike's and then maybe hit a couple clubs to listen to some jazz. You know my flight is kinda early tomorrow. We'll only have time for breakfast before I gotta head to the airport."

He came over to the bed and leaned in and kissed her. "Okay, babe, and I won't be long. When I'm done, we can do whatever you wanna do, just as long as you incorporate riding my dick."

That made her smile. She kissed him back and let him leave. She went back to sleep and when she woke up again, it was after two. Wade had left at ten that morning and she figured he'd be back by then. She called and he didn't answer, so she didn't leave a message. Figuring he'd walk in any minute, she decided to shower and dress.

By four, with still no Wade, she was starting to feel pissed. She was hungry, but didn't want to order anything because she planned to go to Rochelle's to eat. By six, she had lied to Rochelle twice, telling her they'd be coming soon. She didn't admit she hadn't seen or heard from him since ten that morning.

She started to blow up his phone. She texted and called and texted and call and nothing. When nine o'clock rolled around, she was mad as hell. At a quarter to ten, her phone finally rang. He had been gone for twelve hours and she was scheduled to leave the very next morning.

"What the fuck, Wade?" she yelled. "Where the hell are you?"

"Calm down, baby, for real. I locked the keys and my phone in the car hours ago and I'm just getting in," he said.

She could have punched him in the face. "Wade, are you fucking kidding me? You couldn't find a friend's phone to call me?"

"Yes, Brooke, but I don't know your number by heart."

"Okay, the hotel, Wade. Come on, you are a Morehouse-educated brother. And you know that this shit ain't cool." She fumed.

"Look, Brooke, I'm tired and I've been stressed about this car thing all day. I know this is a rental and I wasn't trying to make no issues for you. I finally got into the car and I'm headed back. I don't need to hear this shit," he spat.

She took the phone from her ear in disbelief. How was he going to hit her with an attitude when he'd been gone all damn day? She spoke through clenched teeth. "I'll see you when you get here."

She paced until she heard him he walk through the front door twenty minutes later. She was boiling and she wanted the car keys to go to Rochelle's alone. When he walked into the bedroom, she was dressed to kill, and as soon as he tossed the car key on to the table, she snatched it up.

He stopped her on her way to the door. "I know you're mad, and I'm sorry. Where are you going?"

"Move out of my way, Wade. Again, you've managed to ruin my time with you. When I go back to Arizona, I'm done," she declared.

"Because I got locked out the damn car and couldn't call you?" he protested.

She could tell he was high. "Locked out, Wade? Really? You really expect me to believe that bullshit!" she shouted. "You left over twelve hours ago. I flew from Arizona to see you and I spent my entire Saturday alone, so get the hell outta my way."

"Look, Brooke, I'm sorry. I didn't mean to lock the key in the fucking car and if you got a fucking attitude about it, just drop me by my place."

"Fine, get yo' shit."

"Listen baby, I'm sorry, okay? Please don't be mad at me," he pleaded. He moved close to her and put on the charm.

"Wade, I'm not feeling you right now. You are a liar," she said, standing her ground.

"You're right, babe, and I'm going to tell you the truth. I got to my man's place and his girl was trippin'. She didn't want to give my man his stuff, so after hours of waiting for her to leave, we broke in and got my man shit. By the time we were done, it was late, but to blow off steam, my man Harv wanted a drink. And since my boys were all going, I couldn't say no. We went by Mo's spot, had a few drinks and smoked. I'm sorry."

Brooke stood giving him a look and then she let the tension fade. She believed him, but she was still mad as hell. She got her phone and called Rochelle and told her she'd call her the next day when she landed. Her friend wanted to know details, but Brooke promised her she'd enlighten her the next day.

"Baby, come on," Wade said. "Please don't be mad. I wanna spend this last night with you. I can't let you leave tomorrow being mad at me, baby. Come on, I fucked up and I'm sorry. Don't be mad," he said planting gentle kisses on her neck. He caressed her and then gave her a sweet kiss.

She forgave him. She wanted to stay mad, but it was impossible because Wade was slick, fine, and convincing.

She ordered room service because she was starving and ordered double because Wade had weed. She wanted to make sure they had something to eat after they fucked and smoked.

They went at it and Wade did his duty, fucking Brooke senseless. Then they took a break and went out to the balcony to smoke. Brooke got so high she grabbed a piece of the ribeye from her plate before falling onto the bed. He made her get on her knees so he could hit it from the back, but he licked her first. She carefully held on to her piece of steak and devoured it while he devoured her pussy. He licked everything, including her asshole, before he invaded her pussy with his rock hard dick.

She was so high she giggled. She moaned because it felt good, but the idea of being fucked made her laugh. By the time she got down to her last piece of meat, he was slapping her ass cheek with his dick and then she felt hot droppings from his nut squirting on her ass. She popped the last piece of meat in her mouth and went down giggling. He dived onto the bed with her and they both laughed uncontrollably.

"I love you, baby, and I don't want you to leave," he said.

"Why don't you come to Arizona?"

"You would let me come stay with you?"

"Of course, baby."

"Okay then, I'll come," he said.

"Okay," she said, eyes heavy.

The next morning, her wakeup call was on time. She rolled over to answer it and realized they had slept on top of the covers. She looked at the brown stains on the pretty duvet and she knew it was from the steak she ate in bed. She dragged herself into the shower and it helped her to wake up. She came out and woke Wade. He didn't want to get up either.

"Baby, I gotta be on time to make my flight," she reminded him.

"I know, baby, but I need twenty more minutes."

"Wade, there are no more minutes. I wanna have breakfast before I drop you off, so chop-chop."

He finally sat up, stretched, and yawned. "Baby, last night was so good. I know you have a flight to catch, but I wanna fuck you one more time."

"As good as that sounds, Wade, it's not going to happen because we have to get going."

"What if we skipped breakfast?"

She thought about it. Wade had stamina and they didn't do quick rounds. She'd definitely have to have another shower, but what the hell. "Well, if we skipped breakfast and you can get a ride back to your place, we have time."

"Done." He held his enormous erection in one hand. "Now come and ride my dick."

Brooke, still in her panties and bra, went over and took him in her mouth. Then she took off her panties and slid down on him. She was close to orgasm when her phone rang. It was Dr. Z. She knew it was him because he had his own ring tone. She instantly she lost her rhythm.

"What's wrong, baby," Wade asked when she stopped riding.

She got up. "We need to go." The thought of lying to Zachary made her feel bad and she was no longer in the mood to finish.

"Come on, baby," he begged. "I need this last nut."

"Well, get on top," she said. Now, her mind was on Zachary back in Arizona, not in the room with her and Wade.

"Okay, turn over." He positioned himself and went back in. He pumped her right, but she was no longer into it. She faked it until he busted his nut.

"Now go shower, baby, because I can't miss my flight."

Wade pulled out of her and she turned over, thinking about Dr. Z. He was her friend, a good friend, and she'd lied and didn't tell him about Wade. Nor did she tell him about leaving town to visit him.

# Chapter Ten

THE next day at work, she tried to avoid him, but he was in her office after she was done for the day.

"Dr. Z," she said.

"Hey, Whit, what's up?" he asked.

"Nothing," she said, nervous. "Why are you in my office?"

"I'm here because I want answers. You're seeing someone and I know it, so spill."

"Wow, an ambush. Are you serious? You're in my office to interrogate me, Dr. Jennings?"

"Yes, I am. Now let me have it. Is he jobless, ugly, living with his momma, a drug addict, or better yet homeless? He's homeless right? You met him at the Circle K when he cleaned your windshield," he joked.

"First of all, nosey," Brooke said, walking around to her desk chair. "He is not homeless or living with his momma." She wanted to say that he might have a drug problem because he chain smoked weed, but she didn't. "And why are you so interested?"

"I am just curious. You've changed. We used to talk more and you'd text me here and there. Now, when I call you, I get your voicemail and the last text message I got from you was over a month ago, so he must be special." He shrugged. "I miss my friend, Whit, so I'm curious to know what lucky guy out there has your nose open."

"Okay, damn, Doc. It's Wade, okay. Wade and I have reconnected and we've been texting and talking. I flew to Chicago on Friday and spent the weekend with him." It all came out in one breath. She was relieved to have confessed.

"Wow. Now I hate that I asked." He stood. "Congratulations," he said, heading towards the door.

"Dr. Z, hold on. You don't have anything to say?" she asked.

"No, Whit, I don't. Have a good night." He turned and left.

Brooke sat and tried to take in what just happened. She knew he wouldn't approve, but not to wish her well wasn't like him. She shut down her computer and headed home. She called Wade on her ride home and didn't get him, so she left a message. A couple hours later, still no Wade. She texted that she was going to bed.

Over the next couple days, they barely talked, but then he started calling her a lot, trying to convince her to get him a ticket to come to Arizona.

"So what you're telling me is I can't see you for another two months? I told you that Lena is draining me with child support. I have two weeks' vacation that I can take now, but since I can't afford to buy a ticket, I can't come. I thought you had my back," he barked.

She could understand where he was coming from, but she felt like a fool. She wanted him to come, but couldn't understand why he couldn't sacrifice something in his life to buy a ticket. He didn't even offer to pay half. But she gave in.

"Fine, baby. I want to see you, so I will get the ticket. What dates can you come?"

"When I go in tomorrow, I'll put in for it and when I get approved I'll let you know," he said.

"Okay, baby, okay," she said.

"Thank you, boo. You know I'd handle it if I could."

"I know, Wade," she said sadly.

"So are you going to send me those pics?"

"No, baby. I told you I'm not sending you pics of my pussy."

"Come on, baby. I wanna look at it while I jack my dick. And I'd love a pic of them pretty titties. Your nipples are so fucking sexy." Within minutes, they were having phone sex. She was in her bed rubbing her clit and listening to him talk dirty and nasty enough to make her squirt. She had more than one orgasm, something uncommon with phone sex, but with Wade, it was possible.

"Okay, baby, call me in the morning," she said before hanging up.

When she got to work the next day, she wanted to talk to Dr. Z, but he acted as if he was too busy. At lunch, she found him next door at the pub, eating alone.

"Hey," she said.

"Hey." He didn't look up from his newspaper.

"Do you mind if I join you?"

He finally looked up at her. "No, have a seat." He closed his paper.

"So how are you?" she asked.

"Fine." He focused on his lunch.

"So you're really mad at me, Dr. Z?"

"No, I'm not mad, Whit." He bit his sandwich and she waited for him to swallow and say more. "I'm just disappointed. It's like, every time I think you've learned from a bad experience with a guy, you haven't. You're the type of woman who is drawn to heartbreak and I can't be there for you anymore when you know what you are getting into."

"Oh? So you think I have bad judgment?" she asked, twisting her neck.

"You know what, Whit?" He paused. "I gotta get back." He shook his head and left.

Brooke was no longer in the mood to eat. Dr. Z had a point, but she was a grown-ass woman and she could have as many failed relationships she wanted. Who was he? She got up and headed back into the office.

For the next few days, he avoided her. She brought him breakfast a couple mornings and all she got was a note on her door that said thank you.

She decided to just let him be disappointed because she wasn't going to break up with Wade. And in a few days, he'd be at her house for a visit.

# Chapter Eleven

"BABY, I missed you so much." She pushed her tongue into his mouth.

"I miss you too, baby, and I can't wait to eat your pussy," he teased. Her nipples got hard and she couldn't wait to get him home.

"Let's go and get it." She smiled. He grabbed his bag from the conveyor belt and they left the baggage claim area. "You wanna drive? I don't have any panties on and I'm sure you can steer with one hand and play with my pussy with the other." He quickly took her keys. "I'll tell you how to get there," she said seductively.

"I hope it's not far because all I thought about on my flight was bending that ass over," he said and popped the trunk of her car open. He threw his bag in and paused to kiss her again. "Damn, girl, you are sexy."

She smiled. "So are you, Daddy. Let's go."

When he got on the highway, she lifted her dress and he reached over to play with her clit. She slid forward and before long, her feet were on the dash and she was close to orgasm. When they go off the highway, she gave him a couple quick instructions and then her head was in his lap. He tried to stay focused on the road while she serviced his pipe with her wet tongue, but he had to stop her.

"Baby, I can't. I don't want to crash."

"Okay. Since you're a bitch about it," she joked.

"Brooke, baby, your head is too good and I can't take it while I'm driving."

"Well, that's cool because the next right will put you on my block. We'll be at my house and then I can take you inside and do your dick right."

"I'm for that, baby, and you know I'm gon' tear that pussy up. I hope you got my drink; I got some fire in my luggage," he said.

She was shocked he'd taken a chance on flying with that shit. "Baby, you got weed in your bag?"

"Yep, and it's that fire, baby, so I hope you got snacks," he said.

Her house was stocked with plenty of food; she just couldn't get past him flying with marijuana in his luggage. "What if you had gotten busted, baby?" she asked.

"Calm down, Brooke. It's not enough to get me locked up, so I'm good. Plus, I know how to pack right."

She let it go. "It's the red brick on the right."

As they were getting out of the car, her next door neighbor, Josie, happened to be on her porch.

"Hey, Brooke," she yelled when she saw them.

"Hey there, Josie," Brooke yelled back.

"And hey, you," she said. Wade gave her his winning smile with a nod. "Don't forget the block party next weekend. And you're welcome to bring your friend."

"I won't forget, Josie, and this is my man, Wade. He's in town from Chicago."

"Nice to meet you, Wade. Enjoy your visit," Josie said.

They hurried inside and went at it as soon as the door closed.

After a couple rounds, they were naked in Brooke's hot tub with drinks. Wade wanted to smoke and Brooke declined. She had work the next day.

"You don't wanna hit this?"

"Naw, baby, I'm good."

"You sure? I mean, you get loose when you hit it."

"Naw, baby, I'm good. I have work tomorrow. After this glass, I'm going to call it a night."

"Baby, it's only nine," he said.

"I know, Wade, but I work twelve hour days and trust, seven a.m. comes quickly."

"Can I at least hit it one more time?" He took another drag.

"Yes, but I'm not staying up all night with you, baby. The weekend will be here in a couple days. But for tonight and tomorrow night, I have to hit the bed on time."

She straddled him and his dick got hard. He pushed it inside of her and she rode him while he continued to smoke his blunt.

"Yes, baby, fuck that dick," he whispered. He took a hit and blew it into her mouth. She didn't want to smoke with him, but by the time he nutted, she felt a little buzz.

"I need to heat up that pasta, baby, you want some?" she asked, getting out of the water.

"Of course. And I need some of that garlic bread and salad too," he said.

"Grab my drink and follow me." She giggled.

"Right behind you."

They went inside and ate the rest of the pasta, salad, and garlic bread and then hit the bed hard.

The next day she went to work tired out of her mind.

# Chapter Twelve

"DR. Z?" Brooke tapped on his office door and went in.

"Yeah?" He looked up when she entered.

"I wanted to invite you over for dinner tomorrow night. I know you don't care for Wade, but I think you should try to get to know him. If you got to know him you'd see he's not a bad guy. I invited my neighbor, Josie. She's single, pretty, and successful. I think it would be nice if you two meet."

"Look, Whit, I'm not trying to get set up or be in the same room with Wade. No, thank you."

"Come on, Dr. Z. I told him the truth about you being my best friend and that you pretended to be my boyfriend. He won't be convinced that we're just friends unless you act like we are and not like you hate me."

"You know I don't hate you."

"No, I don't," she said sadly.

"Come on, Whit, be serious," he said.

"I am, Zachary." She sat down. "I mean, ever since I told you about being back with Wade, you've been treating me like a stepsister, and I don't want it to be like this with us anymore. You used to be my best friend, now you avoid me and don't talk to me anymore."

Zachary blew out a breath. "Okay, Whit. Listen, I'll come, and if Wade is the one, I'll be happy for you. I'll try to be nice." He got up. He leaned in and kissed her on the top of her head. "I'm happy for you and I'm sorry for being a jerk."

"Apology accepted." Brooke stood. "I miss your friendship and I know that episode back in Chicago with Wade was bad, but he is a great guy." She knew that wasn't completely true, but she was with him in spite of his flaws.

"Okay, tomorrow night I'm there. What time?"

"Eight and don't be late," she joked.

"I won't, but I will be honest with you, Whit, and this is because I want the best for you. Wade isn't the guy that is right for you, but, hey, that is just my opinion." He paused. "But it's not my choice, it's yours, and if he makes you happy, I'm happy for you."

"I am happy Doc, and I know you are not fond of Wade, but he makes me happy."

She waited for a rebuttal, but he just smiled. They both exited his office and she was happy he had cut her some slack.

THE next evening, Brooke hurried to get dinner ready while Wade continually tried to distract her. He wasn't too thrilled about her having Dr. Zachary over because he had a feeling that he had a thing for Brooke. The look he had on his face when he told him to stay away from Brooke was a little too convincing.

"Baby, can you just stop and give your man two minutes?" he said.

He was driving Brooke crazy. She was happy he came and happy he visited, but it had been a week of him eating her out of house and home and smoking blunts like they were cigarettes. She knew he smoked in her house even though she told him not to. He denied it of course. And she was getting tired of reminding him that she worked early and needed her sleep when he wanted to stay up fucking all night. She couldn't wait for the next week to be over so she could get back to her normal routine and get that weed smell that clung to him out of her house.

"Wade, two minutes? What do you need two minutes for? I'm trying to finish. It's almost eight. Zachary and Josie will be here any minute."

"Fine, whatever. Cook your damn food." He walked off, but she didn't go behind him.

He walked back into the kitchen. "As a matter of fact, let me help you so we can get this over with and get this dinner done. And I'm not taking no for an answer tonight, Brooke, believe that." He picked up a spoon to stir the soup.

"Don't start, Wade, damn." The last two nights she'd been too tired to give him ass and he acted as if he couldn't go even a day without it. "It's only been two days, so stop acting like you're starving for it," she said, tossing the salad.

He walked up behind her. "Two days too many," he said, embracing her. He gently kissed her neck and then the doorbell rang.

"I'll get that," she said, taking off her apron. She hurried to the door. It was Josie with a bottle of red in her hands. "Thank you," Brooke said and took the bottle. She invited her to join them in the kitchen. "Dinner is almost done and Zachary should be here soon."

"Hi there, Wade," Josie said.

"What's going on, Josie?" he said.

The bell chimed again and Brooke went for it. It was Zachary with another bottle of wine, this time white. "Another exquisite bottle," she commented. "Come on in, everyone is in the kitchen."

He followed her.

"Hey, Dr. Z," Wade said. He came over and extended a hand.

"Wade," Zachary said, shaking his hand.

"This is my neighbor, Josie," Brooke said. "Josie, this is Zachary."

"Hello." Josie walked over and extended her hand.

Dr. Z gave her a gentle handshake. "Nice to meet you," he said.

"Well, dinner is done, so you guys can have a seat. Pour some wine and I'll bring the food."

Her three guests moved into the dining room. Zachary came back to help her while Wade and Josie talked in the other room.

"So, what do you think about Josie?" Brooke asked, trying to keep her voice down.

"She's attractive, a little too provocative for my taste though. She definitely didn't leave anything to the imagination in that dress," he said filling his glass.

"Yes, she is sexy, but she's nice. She's divorced and looking." She winked and picked up two dishes of food. "Can you grab the rolls?" she asked. When they got to the table, Wade and Josie were laughing. "What's so funny?" she asked, putting the dishes down.

"Your man is hilarious," Josie said.

"Yeah, he's a comedian sometimes," Brooke said.

Brooke and Zachary took a seat across from each other, since Wade and Josie were already seated across from each other. During dinner, they talked and got acquainted. After they'd eaten, Dr. Z offered to help clear the table, while Josie and Wade went out to the pool.

"So, any sparks?"

"Nah, she is interesting, but not my type."

"Awww, that's too bad. I was sure you guys would hit it off."

"Well, she and Wade seemed to get along great."

"Yeah, well, Wade is charming."

"Yeah, he is definitely that. You want more wine?" he asked.

"Yes, I can have more since tomorrow is my night shift at the hospital."

"It's mine too. How did we get the same night?"

"I don't know," she said, opening the dishwasher.

Zachary grabbed another bottle and opened it to fill Brooke's glass. "Well, it'll be cool to have a night shift with you."

"Yeah, it will," she said.

They finished cleaning and went out to join Wade and Josie, who were giggling and having a great time.

"Brooke, I didn't know you had a hot tub. Even though I have a fabulous heated pool, I don't have a hot tub," Josie said.

"Well, you're welcome to use it, I don't mind," Brooke said.

She sat near Wade and Zachary sat on the other side of Josie. They chatted for a while, with Josie and Wade carrying most of the conversation. When Zachary was ready to go, Brooke walked him to the door and when she came back, Josie and Wade were smoking.

"I thought he'd never leave," Wade commented.

She wondered why he thought it was okay to light a blunt in front of Josie. "Wade, can I see you in private?" she asked.

He handed the blunt to Josie and got up. "What's up babe?"

"What in the hell are you doing?"

"What do you mean?

"You fire up a blunt in front of Josie?"

"Baby, Josie and I've smoked a couple times. She's the one who help me get more since I've been here. You thought I had enough weed with me to last two weeks?"

"When have y'all smoked together, Wade?"

"A couple days after I got here. She came over and asked to borrow some coffee one morning and I had just finished. She smelled it and asked could she have some. I told her I'd have to come over to her place because we couldn't smoke in the house, so I went over and we smoked. When I got low, she hooked me up."

"You know what," she yelled in his face, "go back to your new smoke buddy, I'm going to bed!"

"Why are you mad, baby?"

"Figure it out." She stormed off.

"Don't go to sleep because I want some pussy," he called after her.

She rolled her eyes and went into her bedroom, slamming the door. She could see them from the French doors in her room, so she snatched the remote from her nightstand and pressed the button to close the curtains. She took a shower and went to sleep. A couple hours later, Wade was in bed tugging on her nipples, trying to wake her.

"Get your hands off me, Wade," she snapped, pushing his arm hard.

"You gon' do this bullshit again?" he asked, sitting up.

"I'm tired, Wade, and I'm not in the mood to fuck."

"Just lift your leg, baby," he said, going under her nightgown, trying to rub her pussy from the back. He tried to play with her with his fingers, but she pushed him away again. "Come on, baby, let me in." He pushed his dick against her ass, trying to get it to her opening. He was rubbing himself against her pussy from the back and she started to get a little excited. He pulled the strap off her shoulder and went back to her nipples and she let him twist them. She lifted her leg slightly and let him in. He began to pump her hard and she started to moan. "It's good, baby, it's good," he moaned. She tried to continue to act mad, but soon he was on top of her, rolling deep inside.

"Ummmm, ummm, ummm." She didn't want to him to know she was enjoying it, but it felt too good to hold back her moans. "Yes baby, yesssssssss. Ooooh, yessssssss," she cried.

He pulled out and told her to get on her knees. He grabbed hold of her gown that was now around her waist and pumped her long and hard. He took it out, squirted his nut on her ass, and then slid it back in for a couple more strokes. She went down and he slapped her ass hard.

"Go clean up so I can get some more," he said.

She raised an eyebrow. Wrong answer, she thought, getting up. When she came back from the bathroom, he was lying there stroking himself. She rolled her eyes. "Wade, we're done. I'm going to sleep."

"Damn, Brooke, it's not like you have to work in the morning."

"That's not the point. I'm tired, and let me just be honest, I am pissed that you have been hanging with Josie and smoking with her and shit," she yelled. "Why didn't you tell me that you and her were cool like that?"

"Because I knew you'd trip," he yelled. He got up and threw on his boxers. "This shit is for the birds. I wish you would stop acting all up tight."

"Uptight? I wish you'd stop chain smoking blunts and eating up every damn thing in sight. I gave you two hundred dollars to get groceries and I see some of it went to weed because two days later I had to go to the grocery store again."

"What? I thought you said it was okay for me to smoke. And I did use some of the money because you knew before I came I was low on cash."

"Yes, Wade, I did. But I didn't know I'd have to not only buy your ticket, but pay your damn cell phone bill, hit you with three hundred to send your son's mother something, and pay for every dinner and drink we've had. You haven't spent a dime on me since we've been together and I'm starting to feel like you are just playing me. I'm not made of money, Wade, and I'm getting tired of picking up the tab for everything. You're supposed to be the man in this relationship."

"I am a man, dammit, and if you are tired, that's cool, I can go. I'll change my ticket first thing." He walked out.

Brooke was fine with that. She climbed back into her bed and lay there awake for what seemed like hours. Later, he got back in bed with her and turned his back to her. She felt bad, but it was true. She was tired of carrying him.

"I don't want you to leave," she said, giving in like a chump. She reached and touched his back when he didn't say anything. "Wade, I'm sorry," she said.

"I'm sorry too, and I'll pay you back everything when I get back on my feet."

"I don't want you to do that, it's okay."

"Well, I am. I didn't know you felt like you're carrying me. I just thought you had my back."

"I do, Wade, and I'm sorry," she said. "Will you stay?"

He didn't say anything for a few moments. "If you want me to," he finally said.

She slid over and held him from behind. "Yes, I want you to stay," she said and kissed his back.

The next morning, she got up and made him breakfast and they hung around the house until it was time for her twelve hour shift at the hospital.

"Can I drop you off and keep the car?" he asked.

"Sure, I don't mind."

# Chapter Thirteen

BY ten, Brooke wasn't feeling well. She had a terrible headache and went into the doctor's lounge to lie down after taking a couple aspirin. A couple hours later, she still didn't feel any better and Dr. Z suggested she go home. She agreed, but when she called Wade, she didn't get an answer. She texted him and told him she needed him to pick her up, but no reply. She called her house and there was no answer. Dr. Z offered to take her and she agreed. When she got home, Wade wasn't there, so she just went to her bed.

Around two, she heard him come in, but he wasn't alone. She heard talking and giggling and then she heard the same voices coming from her backyard by the pool. She was tired, but she eased out of her bed to see.

She peeped through the curtains and saw Josie and Wade. Clothes went flying and then they jumped into her pool. She stood watching as they swam close to each other and her mouth dropped when she saw Josie wrap her arms around Wade's neck and they kissed. He lifted her up out of the water to bring her tits to his mouth and he began to suck them. Brooke's eyes bulged.

She couldn't move, her feet felt as if they were stuck in cement. Josie got out of the pool and went over to the chaise lounge chair and Wade followed. When she bent over, he squatted, grabbed his dick, pushed it in, and started to pump.

When Brooke heard Josie moan, her eyes burned with tears and she suddenly remembered how to walk. She snatched the door open and ran out, charging at Wade.

"You motherfucker, how could you?" she yelled, punching him.

He and Josie both fell over, naked and wet.

"You bitch!" Brooke yelled, going for Josie. Wade got up and pulled Brooke off. She kicked as hard as she could and landed one in Josie's stomach. The other woman rolled over in pain. "Put me down, you asshole. Let me go this instant!" She struggled, trying to get away.

"Baby, I'm sorry, I'm sorry," he said. He held on to her for dear life.

"Wade, if you don't let me go right now!" She screamed and tried to break free, but it was no use. "Please let me go. Please," she said, now sobbing. Josie got up and started gathering her clothes. "This ain't over, you bitch!" she shot at Josie.

"Josie, just go," Wade said. "Baby, we need to talk, okay. I'm sorry you saw me like this. I swear it was a mistake. Please," he pleaded, not letting her go.

Brooke tried to wiggle away, but it was no use. She stopped struggling, hoping he'd let her go, but he didn't until Josie was gone and she'd stopped breathing hard.

"I'm going to let you go now, but please don't go crazy," he said before releasing her.

She was too weak to even swing at him. She had spent all of her energy trying to get away. "How could you?" she cried.

"Brooke, I'm sorry," he said, trying to hold her hands.

She snatched away. "I'm sorry? I'm sorry is all you have to say? You brought her into my house to fuck her. What is wrong with you? Her house is right next door, Wade. Not only are you cheating, but you do it here! Get your shit and leave right now!"

"Wait a minute, Brooke. You're going to just put me out?"

"Yes. How are you confused? Get out!" she shouted in his face.

"And go where?"

"To Josie's? I don't know, you just need to leave here right now."

"Come on, Brooke, just calm down," he begged.

"I will not calm down. Wade. In my house? In my fucking house? How many times?" she asked, not sure if she really wanted the answer.

"Brooke, that's not important."

"Dammit, how many times?" she yelled. "You've been here for a hot minute and you fuck my neighbor, Wade? And since you don't want to answer the question, my guess is tonight is not the first night."

"Brooke, the first time was the second day I got here," he confessed.

She wanted to throw up. "Get your sorry ass outta my fucking house this instant before I call Scottsdale's finest on yo' ass," she shot him stormed into the house.

She went into her room and started gathering his things for him. She began to throw all his stuff into the bag and when he walked in dressed, she pushed his bag into his chest. "Whatever I missed, I'll send it. Now leave."

"Just like that, we're done?"

"Yes, just like that. Now get your trifling ass out," she spat. He walked out of the room and headed for the door. "And I need my keys."

"They're on the counter," he said.

After confirming they were there, she opened the door for him to leave and slammed it as soon as he was on the other side. Then she broke down and cried. How could she be so stupid? She knew Wade was a freeloading ass, but she had excused everything she hated about him just to have him. She hated he was broke, hated he was a weed head and hated the way he talked to her at times, but she put up with it because when he was sweet, he was sweet. The sex was amazing and she did love him. It was close to three in the morning, but she called Rochelle. When she didn't answer after her third attempt, she had no one else to call but Dr. Z. She told him the entire story and by six-thirty that morning, after his shift was over, he was at her door.

# Chapter Fourteen

AS sleepy as Dr. Z was, he sat on the sofa and held Brooke while she cried. He never said 'I told you so,' he just assured her she'd be alright.

By noon, they were both knocked out on the couch and the uncomfortable position Brooke woke up in made her want to stretch out and sleep comfortable. "Zachary, come on. Let's go to the bed," she said, reaching out her hand for him.

"The bed? Are you sure?" he asked, taking her hand.

"Yes, this couch is uncomfortable and I don't want your neck to hurt because of me. We've slept in the same bed before, remember," she joked.

"Yes, we have." He stood and followed her to her room where he stepped out of his tennis shoes. He pulled her shirt over his head and tossed it on her ottoman.

"Jeans too, Doc," she suggested.

"You sure?"

"Doc, I've seen you in your shorts before, so quit being shy." She pulled back the covers and climbed in. When he was down to his boxers, he got in. They faced away from each other. "I'm so stupid," she said.

"You're not stupid, Whit."

"Yes, I am," she cried, wiping tears from her eyes.

"Listen, come here." He pulled her close. "Wade was just Mr. Wrong, you're not stupid."

"I know, but I let him just use me and play me. I knew he had issues, but I stayed, Dr. Z. Tell me that's not stupid. I just want my Mr. Right; I'm tired of Mr. All-Fucking-Wrong."

"He's out there, Whit." Zachary yawned. "You just gotta recognize him."

"I hope he comes soon," she said.

When he didn't say anything, she looked over her shoulder and saw he was asleep. She lay in his arms and dozed off. A couple hours later, she got up and left him sleep. She showered and dressed in comfy pajama pants and a t-shirt.

Putting her hair up, she decided she do a quick house sweep and get rid of all Wade's things. Once she put the couple items he'd left behind in the trash, she went back and looked in on Dr. Z. He looked so beautiful sleeping so peacefully in her bed. She wondered why she didn't just pursue him.

Rochelle was right, he was the one, but now she was too embarrassed to even go there. He already thought she was a bad decision maker and she didn't want him to feel like the rebound guy, so she shook it off and went to make them something to eat. After she was done, she went to wake him.

"Dr. Z," she whispered. She waited until he opened his eyes and looked up. "Hey, I made us some dinner. I know it's early, but I'm starving. Are you hungry?"

"Yes." He sat up. "Can you hand me my pants?"

She tossed him his jeans. "There's a new toothbrush and fresh towel on the vanity for you."

She went back into the kitchen. When he came out, he had on his jeans and a tank.

Sexy, she thought. "Have a seat," she said. When he sat down at the island, she put a plate of food in front of him.

"This looks good, Whit."

"It's my famous garlic chicken and pasta," she bragged, joining him.

Her phone rang. When she saw it was Wade, she hit ignore. After that, he began to blow up her phone, so she powered it off.

"How are you feeling," Zachary asked.

"Better," she said and smiled.

"That's good. I didn't want to say I told you so and I'm not, but I'm going to say you're better off without him. You are beautiful, Brooke, and smart and intelligent, and you are just too good to keep wasting all your time on these losers."

"I know, Dr. Z, but I just can't find the right man. I've tried, but they just end up being all wrong."

"Well, I suggest you stop looking over me," he said.

She dropped her fork and swallowed hard. "What do you mean," she whispered, wanting to be clear.

"Brooke, come on. Stop playing these games with me, okay. You know that I've got it bad for you. I mean, everybody can see it but you."

"I-I-I," she stuttered.

"Brooke, it's just me and you right now, baby. Look me in my eyes and tell me you didn't know."

"Dr. Z, I-I-" She just stared at him. She'd had a feeling, Rochelle had even told her, but she didn't want to ruin their friendship.

"Say it, Whit," he said, grabbing her hands.

"I knew, I mean I had a feeling, but wasn't absolutely sure," she confessed. "I just don't want us to not work out. You're a great man, Zachary, you are beautiful inside and out, and I don't think I'm ready for you."

"You are, so stop running and do something good for yourself. I'm good for you." He got up and came around to the other side of the island and lifted her chin and kissed her. She closed her eyes and let his tongue ravish her mouth. It felt good. "Still think you're not ready?" he asked softly after he stopped.

She blinked a couple times and closed her still open mouth, then smiled at him. "Is this real? Are we really going to do this?" she asked.

"Yes."

"Well then, I'm ready," she said.

"Wade is history?" he asked.

"Wade who?" she joked. He kissed her again.

"Finish your food, baby," he advised and went back to his seat and they smiled at each other while they ate. After they finished, they cleaned and enjoyed the rest of their evening on the sofa with a blanket, wine, popcorn, and movies.

That night, he stayed over and for the first time, she and Dr. Z saw each other naked. He made slow and sensual love to her and she enjoyed the way he made her body feel. It was romantic lovemaking, full of passion, not insane fucking just to get one off. She knew they shared something deeper than she'd had with Wade or any of the other Mr. Wrongs in her life.

THEY were happy and inseparable for the next year and when she and Zachary visited Chicago again, they were engaged. Brooke's mother was so happy that her daughter was getting married she wanted to plan the entire ceremony in one night. Brooke had to reel her back in. After they left, they went to Rochelle's. Since Rochelle was nine months pregnant, the guys went out for a drink and left the girls home. When they got to the bar, some of Mike's friends met up with them. Among them was the ex from hell, Wade Harris.

"Are you serious?" Zachary mumbled when he saw him.

"I had no idea he'd be hanging tonight," Mike said. "We can hit another spot."

"Naw, I'm cool." Zachary took a swallow of his beer.

"Mike, man what's up." Wade said. Then he noticed Zachary. "Dr. Z, is that you?" he asked. Zachary nodded. "What brings you to Chicago? Pretending to be Brooke's boyfriend again?" He laughed out loud.

"No, my fiancée and I are here for Rochelle and Mike's baby shower. Are you here scouting for a new sponsor to support your habit?" Zachary snapped back.

"Oh, you got jokes, huh? Sorry, not tonight. Brooke was my last sponsor and when I left, I didn't leave empty handed."

"Yeah, well, word on Brooke's block is you left just as broke as you came. Josie is the one who paid for you to change your flight and got you to the airport. At least that's what she told Brooke when she tried to give her weak-ass apology for hooking up with you. " Zachary got up. "I'm gon' hit the head."

"Speaking of head, is Brooke still good at it? I'm sure Harvard bitches don't get down like Morehouse dawgs." Wade looked at Zachary and took a swig of his beer.

Zachary stopped and turned to him. "Watch yourself, Wade Harris. Don't let the doctor's coat fool you."

"Whatever, old bitch-ass nigga. I can call Brooke now and still be able to hit that pussy."

Zachary turned around and punched him in the face. He flew back into some tables. "Harvard educated, Brooklyn raised, bitch!" He stood shaking right hand.

Mike stood up. It was definitely time to go, security was coming their way. When they got in Mike's truck, Zachary looked down at his swollen hand. When they got back, Brooke was shock to see his hand.

She rushed over. "Baby, what happened to your hand?"

"Wade is what happened to his hand," Mike said on his way to the kitchen for ice.

"Wade, baby? Wade? What in the hell?"

"He was running his mouth and got out of line, so I let him have it."

"Baby, why did you do that? Look at your hand," she said taking the towel-wrapped ice from Mike. "Thank you Mike," she said.

"I know, baby. I overreacted."

"You could have gotten hurt."

"I know, but I'm fine," he said.

"Look, Rochelle is already sleeping, so we're going to go, Mike."

"Okay. And, Zachary, he had it coming."

"Yeah, but I should have walked away."

"Well, it's done now, baby," Brooke said. "Let's go."

Back at the hotel, she made him put his hand in the bucket of ice.

"Easy, baby," he said.

"I'm sorry," she said, trying to be gentle. "You actually hit him in the face?" She laughed.

"Yep, knocked him into a few tables." Zachary laughed too.

"Wow, I wish I could have seen it. He deserved it, I know."

"He did, but I know better than that. I'm a grown ass man and that was stupid."

"It was, but I thank you for defending my honor, baby. I love you."

190

"I love you too, Brooke."

"After all this time, I finally have my Mr. Right." She smiled and gave him a soft kiss. They made love that night like it was going to be their last time.

EACH day with Zachary got better and better. When it was time to move into his house, she came across the love box that she'd had in her closet. She went over to her gas fireplace, turned it on, and tossed the box of memories of her and Wade Harris into the flames.

Not long after that, she and Zachary were married. They later had three beautiful children and never mentioned her Mr. Wrongs ever again.

# CHAPTER ONE

I stood and gave my dining room table another once over, making sure everything was in place. My son was coming home after being in Iraq for eighteen months and I was eager to see him. He was here for a visit a few months ago, when he came home on leave, but to me it felt like ages ago, and I couldn't wait to see him.

"Do you need anything else? I have to run home to shower and change before my favorite nephew gets here," my sister and best friend, Catherine, asked.

"No, no, no, I have it from here. I am going to head to the airport soon. Mo' is coming over to greet the guest and hold down the fort until I return."

"Are you sure, because I don't want to get down the street and have to turn around. And don't think I'm running into nobody's store in this heat to pick up anything, Miss Char."

"I have everything I need, Catherine, and if I don't, I will find somebody to get it for me. You've done enough, darling, and I thank you. Trey always said you're the only one on this planet who can cook better than me, and he is going to be so happy to see that his favorite auntie cooked all of his favorites."

"Well, Trey is the only son we both have, and I know we have spoiled him rotten. He turned out better than my baby girl, Mesha. She is a piece of work."

"I know that's right, but we still have to love our kids and have their backs no matter what, Cat."

"I know, I know." Catherine sighed.

"Go ahead and get out of here and go get dressed. I'm going to head to the airport."

Just as I said that, Mona walked in smiling brightly. "Divas... Hey!" she yelled.

"Hey, Mo'. You are right on time. I was just about to call you," I said.

"Well, you know me, baby. I'm always on time," she said and kissed and hugged us both.

Catherine sucked her teeth. "Hump, except for church. I get tired of holding your seat with my purse."

We laughed.

"Well, church starts too damn early. Hell, my husband died and left me a ton of money that allowed me to retire at forty-two, and I don't get up before ten," Mona proclaimed.

I had to go. "Well, I have to get to O'Hare and Catherine needs to run home and change. All the side dishes and desserts are done, and Bernie is handling all of the meat. All I need you to do is make your fabulous punch and greet anyone who arrives before we get back. And please, don't let Bernie open up one bottle of liquor. He should be here any minute to get started on the meat."

"Girl, go ahead. I got this. Bernard ain't no match for me. I will make my famous punch and make sure he gets started. Where is the meat, so I can show him when he gets here?"

196

"In the kitchen. There are four coolers near the French doors. Everything is seasoned and iced, so he can roll them out back. One has chicken, one has steaks, one has burgers and hot dogs, and that red one has kabobs. My dear sister, Catherine, turned me on to Ziploc bags, so it will be easier than coming in and out of the house. And there is a stack of aluminum pans on the island and like five gallons of sauce. Bernard travels with his own utensils, grills, and pine wood, so he knows what to do."

"Got you, love. Now tell me there is chilled wine, because y'all know Miss Mo' can't work sober."

We all laughed again.

"Girl, you know it. The wine fridge is full, so help yourself. We have to go," I said. Catherine and I both hurried out.

Before I could pull out of my circular drive, I noticed my brother, Bernard, was unloading his truck. He had brought two more grills with him. I smiled. Bernard had the best barbeque on the planet and never declined an opportunity to show off his skills.

"Hey, Bernie, I'm headed to the airport to get Trey. All the meat is ready for you!" I yelled.

"A'ight, lil' sis. I'm on it. Drive safe!"

"Mo' is inside. Gon' in!"

I drove off, anxious to see my baby. Trey was my heart. My grown-ass little man. I couldn't wait to see him.

He and I grew up together, to be honest. I was fifteen when I had him. By the time I was seventeen, I was enrolled in college, working two jobs, and living with my evil-ass mother. She kept him a lot for me back then, and by the time I got my associates degree, we moved out. I was able to afford a little townhouse because I managed to get a job working as a junior accountant. By the time I got my masters, things moved quickly, and after busting my ass, I was in charge of marketing.

By the time Trey was in the seventh grade, I purchased my thirty-five hundred square feet home that had an in-ground pool. Things were good.

Yes, I dated, of course I did. But I never had, or should I say found, the man who was quite right for me. I had brief engagements twice. Once to a man who I later found out was already married, and then to another who decided he like to put his hands on women. There was always a reason things just didn't work out, and now at forty, I was single, still dating, but definitely single.

I parked and hurried to get inside. Trey's flight had already landed and I wanted to be there at baggage claim when he made it. I walked over and read the digital boards and when I found the one with the correct flight number, I stood and waited. I kept looking around for him, but I didn't see him. As soon as I pulled out my phone again to call him, someone covered my eyes from behind.

"Guess who?"

I spun around and he lifted me up from the floor with a big hug. "Hey, son, how are you?"

"I'm good, Ma."

He continued to hold me tight, and even though I said I wouldn't cry, I couldn't hold back my tears. He put me down and I wiped my eyes.

"Ma, you promised."

I wiped more tears. "I know, son, but it is just so good to see you. Look at you, handsome." He had on his uniform and I thought he looked more and more like his absent father each time I saw him.

"Ma, stop it."

"You are," I said. We hugged again.

"Where is Auntie Cat— I mean Catherine? I thought she'd come too." My sister had gone by Cat her entire life, but after she became a judge, she told everyone to stop calling her that. I didn't care. She was my sister, so I still called her Cat.

"She had to go change. She and I were up all night fixing your favorites, and this morning we were up early to make desserts. She'll be at the house when we get back. And call her Auntie Cat, Trey."

"And catch a beat down? No, thank you. If she wants to be Auntie Catherine, she will be Auntie Catherine. Momma, you know she don't play."

"I know, but not like you, I ain't scared of her."

"Well, I am." We laughed. "Man, I can't wait to eat. That flight was long and all I could think about was your potato salad and Auntie Catherine's baked beans. And if Uncle Bernie ain't grilling, I ain't eating no meat," he joked.

"Well, you know your uncle got the grill, and Catherine put her foot in those baked beans. I tasted them this morning. A little spicier than usual, but still delicious."

"Well, I'm ready." The conveyer belt started to rotate. "Let me check for my bags, Ma. Hold this," he said and handed me what looked like a computer bag.

"I'm going to run and get the car, so meet me outside, son."

I hurried to the parking lot. By the time I made it around, he hadn't come out yet. I sat tapping the steering wheel to the beat of the song on the radio, hoping the officer would give me a break. But of course, he waved for me to move. I drove around once, praying I wouldn't have to circle again and was relieved to see Trey standing under the American Airlines sign. I pulled up to him and popped the trunk. After he loaded his things, he got in.

I reached over and rubbed his head. "Oh, son, it is so good to have you home safe and sound. You know, you being deployed turned your momma into a prayer warrior. If I didn't know God before, I found him when you boarded that plane to go over to that place."

"I know what you mean, Ma. I mean, I knew what I was signing up for when I joined, but I'm so glad to be back I don't know what to do."

"I heard that. Now will you please find a wife and give me some grandbabies? Hell, I'm single and lonely. My only son left me, so I'd like a grandbaby to spoil."

"Momma, I just got home. Let me at least shower first."

We laughed.

"Okay, but after your shower, get a wife and make me some grandkids."

"How about you date again? You are only forty and you're still fine, Momma. Every time I show someone your picture, they don't believe you're my mother."

"Well, son, your mother has tried dating. I've met some nice guys, but I don't know, son. It's like that spice, that wow factor, is missing. Most men I date have baggage and problems and alimony and kids in college and so on. I don't know, son. When that right one comes along, who sweeps me off my feet and makes me happy, I'll make it work. Until then, I work on making myself happy."

"He's out there, Ma, I know he is. You're too beautiful and smart. He'll come soon."

"I hope so, baby, but in the meantime, give me some grandbabies to spoil."

"I will, Ma, maybe sooner than you think."

I was shocked by his comment. "Tracy Keyshaun Jones, what are you trying to say?"

"I don't know yet, Ma, but La-La and I have gotten closer while I was away. I mean, she helped me get through some tough times over there, Ma, and I think she's the one."

"Lavitra from high school? I didn't know you and her were talking again, Trey. When did this happen?"

"Well, when I went back after my break. I checked my Facebook and she sent me a friend request. Now you know I was shocked, right, after how bad our break-up was."

I interrupted. "Yes. I don't know how that girl thought you'd give up your dreams of going into the military to stay here with her. Hell, I didn't want you to go into the military either, but it's your life."

"That wasn't exactly the reason, Ma. The problem was I didn't want to get married or at least engaged to her before I left. I was eighteen and I wasn't ready to make that kinda decision back then.

"So we started conversing by email and I told her she just missed me, that I had just left Chicago, and from there, we started emailing every day. And then I called her and we started talking on the phone, video chatting, and we just reconnected."

"So did you tell her you're only going to be in Chicago for two weeks before heading to Fort Hood?"

"Yeah, I told her and she isn't too happy about it, so I've decided to take her with me."

My heart stopped and I shot him a look. "Boy, what the hell? You know I'm not with that living together mess. And you have to find a place before taking on the responsibility of taking care of a woman."

"Momma, calm down. I didn't mean taking her with me in two weeks. I'm talking about asking her to marry me and then get the house and all. Marry her and then take her to Texas."

I let out a deep breath. "Well why you didn't say that? I almost crashed my Jag." I slapped his arm.

"Ma, you taught me better. You know I'm not the type to leap first. La-La has always been in my heart since high school and I've never been able to completely get over her, no matter how I've tried. Hopefully, these two weeks at home will be good, and if so, I'll pop the question before I leave."

I shook my head and smiled. "I knew my baby would grow up, but damn it's hard to swallow another woman being in your life. I know you and La-La have been in love for years, and that love you can't shake is the love that is meant, so I wish you two the best. I'm just scared that once you are married, I won't be number one anymore."

"Awww, Ma, you will always be my number one, just don't tell La-La."

"Okay, okay, son. I can live with that. You know I'll always have your back, baby, no matter what you decide. Plus, you need someone to care for you. Just let her know that she has to hang with me and your Auntie Cat to learn how to cook your favorites," I teased.

"I will, Ma, you know this."

We laughed. We continued endless conversation and when we got back to the house, there were five cars out front. Three I recognized and the other two I had no idea. "I wonder who those two cars belong to." I undid my seatbelt to get out.

He undid his. "I don't know, Ma. La-La is coming, I think that Infinity is hers."

"Well, let's get inside and find out."

We went inside and sure enough, La-La ran into Trey's arms. They held each other tight and I saw my son share a tongue kiss with a woman for the first time. I turned my head because it was apparent they missed each other, and then I noticed a young, handsome face.

He interrupted Trey and La-La's reunion. "A'ight, La-La, let me get a hug in too."

He looked vaguely familiar, but I couldn't place him. I had a very strong feeling I knew him, but I couldn't put my finger on from where. All I knew was he was fine as hell, young, but delicious.

"Hey, man, what's going on? It's been like forever. Man, you have changed," Trey said. He could barely hug this stranger because La-La wouldn't let him go.

"Welcome home, man. We have to definitely do better with keeping in touch. It's been far too long."

"I know. I mean, you went to college, I joined the army, and I did my best, man. I holla'd atcha when I could."

"I know ,Trey, man, same here. I ain't mad atcha. You're back now, and we gon' do it big."

"Hey, don't think y'all gon' kick it without me. Wrong answer!" La-La snapped.

"Hold on, hold on. Save the bickering. Come here, Lavitra, and give me a hug," I interrupted.

She released my son and gave me a tight hug. "Hey, Miss J. It's so good to see you." She smiled when she released her embrace.

"You too. You are just as pretty as you were back in high school."

"She sure is," Trey said and pulled her back into his arms.

I looked at the young man again. "I'm sorry, have we met? Do I know you?"

Trey tilted his head. "Ma, you don't know who this is?" he asked in disbelief.

Puzzled, I looked again, trying to figure out who this young, fine, sexy god was. "No, I can't remember. I mean there is familiarity, but I can't say. I'm afraid I'll say the wrong name."

"Miss J, you don't remember me?"

I did, but I didn't. Trey hung with a few guys because he played sports. However, the only face I'd never forget is his best friend Lil' Ricky. He was my baby, sort of like my young best friend. He hung around me more than he hung with Trey, and helped me way more than my son. Anything I'd asked that kid, he'd do, but I hadn't seen his little pimply face since he left to go off to college. I was surprised he never called or visited after he left. He was my best young buddy. I'd ask Trey had he heard from him and he'd say yes when he did.

I swallowed hard and tried not to look like a horny-ass old lady, because whoever this was, his woman was a lucky girl. "Come on, somebody tell me who this tall, handsome guy is."

Still trying to jolt my memory, "Two houses down," Trey said.

"No fucking way. Oh my goodness, Lil' Ricky? Get the hell out of here," I said and leaped into his arms. He had grown into a fine specimen. He looked like a completely different person.

"Yes, ma'am, it's me," Lil' Ricky said.

"Oh my goodness, you look so … so … different. I mean, I can't believe I didn't recognize you. Even your voice. You sound like a grown-ass man."

"I am a grown-ass man, Miss J," he returned.

I laughed. "Yes, you are. Where have you been? I mean, even when your father died, I don't remember seeing you at the funeral."

"I know, Miss J, I was overseas, and by the time I got the news, I couldn't get home in time. I moved back a couple years ago, and now that my stepmom is ill, she moved in with her daughter, so I'm going to do some upgrades and cleaning up the house so I can sell it."

"Oh my, this is, like, crazy. To see you and Miss La-La over here is great. You guys were like the Three Musketeers. When you graduated and went off to college, I never heard from you again. You know you were wrong for that, young man."

"Well, I didn't lose touch with Trey. We talked when we could, and every time I talked to him, I said to tell you I said hello."

"Well, he didn't tell me, and it's good to see you." I remember I had people coming so I had to cut our reunion short. "I need to get in this kitchen and make sure things are in order."

Trey picked up his duffle bag. "And I need to shower."

"Well, I can help you in the kitchen," La-La offered.

"Yes, baby, come on, and Lil' Ricky, you can go out with Uncle Bernie. I'm sure he needs help and I know he has a cold beer for you." I smiled.

La-La and I headed to the kitchen, Trey headed upstairs, and Ricky walked through the kitchen and went out the French doors.

Catherine hadn't made it back yet and Mona was bringing in a covered pan of meat.

"Char, you're back. Where is Trey?"

"He went up to shower. You remember La-La?"

"Child, of course I do. She and Lil' Ricky were the first ones here."

"So Pat and Gene and Mesha must be out back. I saw their cars."

"Yeah, they're out back. Why didn't you tell me Mesha was pregnant? When I saw her belly, my mouth dropped to the floor. Ain't she seventeen?"

I washed my hands. "Yes, girl, and she just turned seventeen a month ago. I told her how hard it was for me when I had Trey at fifteen too, too many times, but that didn't stop her from getting knocked up by that damn Sammy. His ass done left and went on to school on his football scholarship and she is still here looking crazy. Catherine fusses about it every single damn day."

"Well, she is going to have to learn the hard way, like we all did."

I laughed. "You sho' right."

Catherine walked in. "Hey, y'all. I saw your car, Char, where is my baby?"

I pulled out my fancy deviled egg dish to put some of the eggs on it. "He went to shower."

She put a bag on the counter. "Is that you, La-La?"

"Yes, ma'am."

"Girl, get over here and give me a hug. How you been?" Catherine asked and squeezed her tight.

"I'm fine, Miss Catherine. How are you?"

"I'm good, child. Look at you, just pretty as you want to be."

I spoke up because I wanted to brace Catherine for Lil' Ricky. "Here, La-La, take this out to Uncle Bernie for me." She grabbed the bowl of seasoned corn I handed her. "Tell him to put those on the grill for me." As soon as she was on the other side, I pulled Catherine's arm and told Mo' to come closer. "Girl, just wait until you see Lil' Ricky."

"Oh, yes," Mo' co-signed.

"What, girl?" Catherine asked wanting to know the juice.

I said. "He is fine as hell. Girl, when I saw him, my pussy clenched. When Trey told me who he was, I almost died."

"Me too. I didn't even recognize him at all," Mo' added. "All I knew is this chocolate, tall piece of art walked in with La-La. When she told me who he was, I was like 'no fucking way.' He has been drinking milk or fine juice."

Catherine got excited. "Where is he? I want to see him."

"Out back," I said.

She headed for the French doors. "Let me go see him."

She went out and Mo' and I continued to chat. "Girl, you better hold me back, because I'm a widow with money, and I ain't afraid to spend it. I can travel and be his sugar momma," Mo' said.

I burst into laughter.

"Girl, stop it, that boy is Trey's age."

"So, I'm not trying to get with Trey. That would be wrong, but Lil' Ricky can come tuck me in tonight."

Catherine walked back in. "Girl, pour a bucket of ice water on me. Hot damn! That boy is fine."

We laughed.

"I told you. I could not believe my eyes. And for a split moment, I wished I wasn't this old."

"And Trey's mother," Mo' added.

"That too."

We continued to laugh and joke. More guests arrived and, finally, Trey came down.

"Auntie Catherine!" he yelled.

"Trey!" She rushed over and hugged him tight. "Look at you, boy. You are looking so handsome, nephew, just like your daddy."

I threw the oven mit at her. "Hey, watch it, Cat." We never talked about Trey's father. I hadn't seen him since Trey was three, so she knew better.

"Thank you, Auntie, and Momma told me you were on this crazy diet. I see you stuck to it. You look gorgeous, Auntie," he teased as Catherine posed.

"I do, don't I?" She smiled.

"Yes, you do."

Mona cut in. "Well, I know I'm not your favorite auntie, but I missed you too, baby."

"Hey, Auntie Mo'," he said and lifted her little petite body from the floor when he hugged her. Mona was the smallest of the three of us. Not even five feet and maybe a size three on a good day.

"Hey, nephew. It's so good to have you home," she said.

The party got underway and I enjoyed my family and close

friends. It was after three in the morning when my house was almost clear, and I didn't argue when my son said he was going to La-La's for the night. I knew he was grown and had grown folk needs. Lil' Ricky assured him he'd help me and Catherine finish up. That was Lil' Ricky, always there to help me.

I walked Catherine to her car, while he put the last of the trash on the curb for me.

"Okay now, you call me when you make it, Catherine. You know you can stay another night."

"Char, I want to get home and sleep in my own bed. I don't want to have to get up for hours, so that needs to be done at home in my own bed."

"Okay. I'll call you tomorrow. We will probably eat leftovers and play some cards. I'm sure Trey and La-La will be back tomorrow to eat since we still have so much food."

"Okay, I'll come back tomorrow and I'll tell Mesha." She put her seatbelt on. "Goodnight, Lil' Ricky!" she yelled. He yelled goodnight back to her and I shut her door and watched her leave my drive.

"Are you leaving?" I asked Lil' Ricky.

"Yeah. I need to run in to get my plate," he replied.

We headed back in. In the kitchen, he reached for the foiled-covered plate.

"Did you get dessert?" I offered.

"No, ma'am. I was supposed to remind Miss Catherine."

I grabbed a knife. "Well, I can't let you leave without a slice of my lemon pound cake."

He sat down at the island. "I thought it was all gone."

"Yes, the two I put out are gone, but I always hide one for Trey." I went into my walk-in pantry, got the plastic cake container, and set it on the island. I opened it and cut him two slices and put them on a plate and then covered it with foil. "There you go," I said and slid it his way.

"Thank you." He smiled and gave me a look.

"You're welcome," I said, placing the lid back on. I felt a little vibe in the air.

He sat there and watched me. I rinsed the knife and added it to the dishwasher and turned back to him still watching me.

"You okay," I asked. It wasn't an uncomfortable stare down. It was more like a checking-me-out stare down.

"Yeah, yeah, I'm good. I guess it's time for me to head home." He stood.

I moved around the counter to head to the living room. "Yeah, it's pretty late. Let me walk you to the door."

He followed close behind me and I could feel his eyes on me. I welcomed it because he was young and I hadn't had much male attention lately. I opened the door and he paused.

"Thanks for having me, Miss J. I mean, it was so good seeing you again. I mean, you still look amazing, and Trey coming home is just great."

Paying attention to the fact that he said I still looked amazing and observing the way he was looking at me, I smiled. He was looking at me in the way a man would look at a woman he was interested in and I liked it. I knew him when he was a funny-looking kid, but he had grown into a man I'd be interested in. "Yes, it's good to have him home."

He flashed his beautiful smile again and I could see the braces he'd worn when he was younger had done him justice, because his teeth were perfect. "Yes it is. I'm going to go now." He turned to leave and something in me wanted to ask him to stay, but I knew that would be inappropriate. He was my son's best friend, and entertaining him like a man my age would be insane.

Being extremely attracted to this young man, I invited him to come back. "We are getting together tomorrow. We have a ton of leftovers. You should come."

"Okay, I'll be here. Do you need me to bring anything?"

"No, we have liquor, beer, food, you name it."

"What time is good?"

"I'd say six, maybe seven. I'm sure everybody wants to recoup from tonight," I said nervously. What was I doing? I wasn't supposed to be attracted to him. This was Lil' Ricky, the pimply-faced kid from two houses over.

"Okay, I'll be here." He smiled and turned to leave. He walked down the drive and passed the BMW that I thought was his that was parked a few feet away from my driveway.

"Isn't that your car?" I shouted.

"Yes, but I'm staying at my dad's house."

"Okay," I said and watched him proceed on his short trip home. I went back inside and let out a deep breath, happy everyone had chipped in and helped me clean. I turned out the lights and headed upstairs.

I asked myself why I was having sexual thoughts about Lil' Ricky. He and my son were best friends, why did I want to fuck him? The entire evening, we had exchanged glances. He had helped me in the kitchen and made it a point to check on me throughout the evening. When we danced in the backyard, my hands were the first hands he reached for to step. He was young, sexy, and oh my. "Stop it, Charlotte," I told myself. "You are too old and you can't go there. Trey would lose it!"

I tried to tell myself that I wasn't feeling him, but it was obvious that I wanted to do things to Lil' Ricky that someone closer to his age should be doing. "Oh my, Char, what has gotten into you? It is not right or natural," I said and got into bed.

I closed my eyes and he was back in my thoughts, so I decided to just go ahead and dream about him. Hell, no one had to know about my dreams.

# Chapter Two

When I walked into my dad's house, I took my plate into the kitchen. I put my food into the fridge and put my cake on the counter and went up to my old room. All of my old posters and high school memorabilia were gone, and now there was a full-sized bed. I had been in the house earlier that day, but I hadn't ventured upstairs, so I had no idea they had converted my room. Before I finally moved back to Chicago, I'd visit and stay in a hotel. I never thought to look into my old room when I'd come by for a visit.

I fell onto the bed, closed my eyes, and let the thoughts of Ms. J enter my head. I hated that she was still on my mind after all of these years. I was in grade school when I first met Trey and Ms. J. Things were normal until around fourteen. The summer before our freshman year, I saw her differently. I looked at her for the first time as a woman, not as Trey's mother.

Trey and I were out riding our bikes and she yelled for him, so we rode together to see what she wanted. She stood on the porch in a red halter and a pair of cut-off shorts and flip flops. She reminded Trey not to make her come looking for him when it was time to come in. He guaranteed her he'd be in on time for dinner and then asked, "Can Lil' Ricky join us?"

She looked me up and down and said, "Why can't Lil' Ricky eat at his own house?"

"He can, Momma, but you're cooking real food."

I tried not to stare at her breasts. They were sitting in her halter like a perfect set of cantaloupes. My little penis stiffened.

"Yo' momma didn't cook?" she snapped.

"I live with my dad, and he isn't home yet," I replied.

"Your daddy don't mind you being outside while he's gone?"

"My stepmom is there. She is sewing, and not cooking. She makes clothes."

"Well you can come this time, Lil' Ricky, I don't mind. But don't think you're going to eat here every night. I have one child to feed, not two."

"Yes, ma'am."

When she turned to go in, I got a peep at her ass. It was plump and I fell in love. Trey and I had already been friends since seventh grade, but I was always too shy to hang out. After some convincing and Trey saying he'd have my back, I got out more. He was my only friend, and even though I had seen his mother a few times, I didn't really look at her until that day. I joined them for dinner that night and somehow ended up eating with them four or five nights a week.

My father worked second shift and he had no idea that his wife, Darine, wasn't taking care of me properly. She couldn't care less whether I ate, came in late, or even if I did my homework. Trey's home became my second home and Ms. J took care of me just like she took care of Trey. When they went to the movies, I went. When they went to barbecues, I was in tow. During the summer, I was there every day in my trunks.

The first time I saw Ms. J in a bikini, I ran to the bathroom and squirted in the sink. I cleaned everything and owned up to the fact that I was in love with my best friend's mother. She was sexy then and even sexier now. She still had a banging body, and even though she had aged a bit, she was still sexy as hell to me. When I laid eyes on her, I wanted to grab her and hold her close. She had on a yellow strapless sundress and sandals, and her natural, curly, short hairdo look sexy as fuck. It wasn't a teen crush anymore for me, it was real attraction. She was my type and I wanted her.

But how? She was my best friend's mother, and I honestly didn't know how old she was. I just knew she was old enough to be my mother. I wanted to act on my feelings, but I was afraid to approach her.

How could I? What would she say? What would Trey say? How would he react if he knew I wanted to be with his mom? I wanted her back then, and after seeing her, I wanted her even more now. I wanted to take her tonight, but how could I? How could I just approach her? What would I say to her?" Those questions bounced around in my head until I finally fell into a deep sleep.

The next day, I didn't wake up until after one in the afternoon. I rushed to the bathroom, and after I dried my hands, I decided to explore. The house was still full of my dad and stepmother's things, and since my stepmother had stage-four cancer, I knew she wouldn't be back to get any of it. My stepsister was married and doing well, so I knew she didn't want the old furnishings from our parents' house. My dad's bedroom was still fully furnished, and the only thing that had changed was there was no more carpet or wallpaper. I noticed the French doors and wondered when Richard Sr. and Darine had added on a balcony.

I went over and opened the doors and it blew my mind how fabulous it was. It was spacious, large enough for a four-piece patio set, and when I looked to my right, I had a bird's-eye view of the Jones' backyard and pool. Are you serious? I asked myself and took a seat. The deck terrace was covered with a retractable awning, and since it was extended, it wasn't burning hot. I sat and looked at the back of Ms. J's house. A few moments later, she walked out in a two-piece, carrying a tray with a pitcher and glass on it. I immediately rose from the chair and went over to the cement rail and watched as she stepped out of her slippers and dived into the water.

I could barely see her body moving from one end to the other, but I saw when she came up. She flipped and did another lap and then another. She did two more and got out of the pool. She grabbed a towel and did a swipe of her hair and face and went over to the pitcher and poured herself a drink of whatever it was. I watched her take a couple swallows and then settle on one of the chaise lounges.

My dick stiffened and I took a couple steps back to sit. I hoped she didn't see me watching her. I questioned myself again and wondered if something was seriously wrong with me. I'd seen plenty of older gorgeous women, but none made me feel the way Ms. J made me feel, and I wondered why I was so caught up on her. I didn't want to be in love with Trey's mother, but I was, and I knew I had been in love with her for a very long time.

I had dated, even had a couple serious relationships, but as soon as Trey crossed my mind or if we spoke, it would jolt a memory of his mother. She was sexy all the time, even when she didn't want to be. I could remember seeing her in her nightgown with no panties and her tits with no bra and wanting to touch her the times I stayed over. I remember how she used to cook whatever we wanted and would load our plates, taking pleasure in how much we loved her cooking.

I had tasted her lemon pound cake years ago, and I used to try to get Trey to sneak me an extra slice when we were kids. She was smart and helped us with our homework, and when we turned it in, we got good grades.

I jumped when I saw her get up. I focused and watched her go for her phone. She talked with a smile on her face and I saw her laughing. I hoped it wasn't a man in her life making her smile so brightly.

I watched her the entire time she was out by the pool and I was a little disappointed when she went inside. It was close to three by the time I went down to my suitcase. I wanted six o'clock to come quickly.

Deciding to do something to occupy my mind, I started taking down the kitchen cabinets. The entire house was getting an overhaul, so I might as well work on something. The packers were coming on Monday to pack up the entire house, and my crew and I were going to get started Tuesday on the remodel.

Wanting to be close to Ms. J, I thought of remodeling the home for myself instead of putting it on the market. Since my father had the house before he married Darine, it had been left to me. It was paid for in full and had ample square footage, but I didn't want to live in Beverly; I had a loft in the city. But for Charlotte, I'd move.

At five-thirty, I stopped what I was doing and went to the shower. By five after six, I was on my way to Ms. J's house.

I rang the bell.

Trey opened it. "Hey, man, what's up?"

"Same ole same," I said going in.

"Well, I'm glad you are here. My momma talking shit about beating us in Spades, and since my Auntie Catherine isn't here, you need to sit so we can get this thing going."

I followed him into the dining room and saw La-La and Ms. J at the table laughing.

"Hey," I said.

"Heeeeyyyyyy, Lil' Ricky," Ms. J said. I hated that, but I didn't say anything.

"Hey, Ms. J."

"Hey, Lil' Ricky," La-La said, shuffling the deck.

"Hey," I replied and sat across from Charlotte.

She stood. "You want a drink, baby?"

The word baby was music to my ears. I wanted to say, "Yeah, baby, get Daddy a drink," but instead, I said, "Sure."

She headed to the kitchen and came back with me a mixed dark drink.

She handed me the glass. "Here you go, baby, and if you need another, let me know. Trey and La-La think they got skills, so I hope you got game, baby, because Catherine and I ain't no joke. We whip ass on this table!"

"Well, Ms. J, I'm ready to show them how to play," I said nervously. I knew how to play, and well, but the pressure was on to whip ass for Charlotte.

"Oh, okay, Ricky, we gon' see," Trey said and sat.

The game got under way and I was so glad we were winning. Trey and Ms. J talked the most shit, while me and La-La just laughed.

Trey looked at his watch. "Momma, call Auntie Catherine, she should have been here by now."

"You're right," Ms. J said and picked up her cell. She called and said. "Let me text her, because she's not answering. After her text attempt, she put her phone down, and a minute later picked it up when it rang. She read the text and smiled.

"Was that Auntie Catherine" Trey asked.

"Yep."

"What'd she say?"

"Boy, stay out of grown folks business," she said.

We all laughed.

"Some dude, I bet, but that's alright, Auntie Catherine. I'm going to remember that."

"Boy, please, let your auntie have some fun."

"Speaking of fun, Ma, when are you going to have some?" The room went quiet.

"Boy, didn't I just tell you to stay out of grown folks business?" she retorted.

We laughed. We played until after one and La-La kept fake yawning. She kicked me a few times under the table and I knew she was trying to give Trey the hint to leave.

Finally, he acknowledged her eagerness to go and stood. "Well, Mom, we are going to head out."

"Yeah, because if Lil' Ricky and I beat y'all again, Lavitra might cry," she teased. "Lavitra, I felt you kick me twice under this damn table." We all laughed.

"Oh, I'm so sorry, Ms. J, that was meant for Trey," she said and stood too.

"I know, but I almost kicked you back."

We said our goodbyes, and I decided to clear the table while she walked them to the door.

"You don't have to do that, Lil' Ricky, I got it," she said, taking a glass from my hand.

I stood over her and looked her in her eyes. "Please call me Rick. I'm not Lil' Ricky anymore."

"Okay." She smiled and headed towards the kitchen. "I won't call you Lil' Ricky. I know there is nothing little about you anymore," she murmured, but I heard her.

I followed her into the kitchen. "You're right. I'm a man now."
She laughed. "That you are."

Taking a chance, I stood in her path when she headed back for the dining room. "Listen, Ms. J, I may be way out of line, and if I am, I beg you not to hold it against me or tell Trey."

She took a step back and leaned against the wall, seeming interested in what I had to say. "Okay. What is it?" I could see nervousness on her face.

"I am in love with you," I confessed. She laughed. "I'm serious," I said.

When I didn't laugh with her, she stopped. "Say it again."

I stepped in her direction. "I'm in love with you, and I've been in love with you since I was fourteen years old. I've been hooked on you since then. You are sexy, and smart and, and I—"

She cut me off. Sternly, like a parent, she said. "Stop it, Lil' Ricky. You are confused. You can't be in love with me. I mean, I've treated you like a son. You're Trey's best friend and I-I-I-I'm … I'm old," she nervously stuttered. "I'm Trey's mother."

I was too terrified to continue, but I had to let it out.

"I know you're Trey's mom, but you are not old to me. I know it's unorthodox, but I can't help the way I feel about you." I moved in closer and she tried to back away, but her back was against the wall. She looked up at me and I caressed her cheek.

"I-I-I," she stuttered.

I went for it. I grabbed her face and pushed my tongue into her mouth. She welcomed me and kissed me back. My dick swelled instantly and I pulled her away from the wall and gently pushed her back to the dining room table. When I hoisted her up, she wrapped her legs around my waist. I kissed her deeply and sat her on the dining room table. When I touched her breasts, she didn't stop me.

I pushed her spaghetti straps down, and to my pleasant surprise, she was braless. I licked down her neck to her chest and landed on one of her erect nipples. She moaned when I sucked. I slid a hand under her sundress and went for her center. She opened wide for me. My dick was so hard I just wanted to get inside, but I wanted to please her first.

After teasing her hardened nipples, I said. "Lay back, baby." When she did, I pushed her legs up and moved her panties to the side. I gently licked her swollen clit before sucking on it. She came in a matter of minutes.

"Ah, ah, ah, ah, ah," she moaned. She squirted a little and her thighs trembled. "Ricky," she panted, "what are we doing? What are we doing?"

My dick was harder than the pipes in the drains and all I wanted to do was push it inside of her. I didn't want to discuss what we were doing or rationalize our actions.

"Shhhh, baby, just relax," I said, probing her opening with my finger. She was good and wet. I undid my jeans. She looked scared, so I grabbed her hand and kissed her fingers. "Just relax and don't think about anything other than me, okay?"

She nodded. I pulled my erection out and rubbed my head against her wetness. My dick throbbed. I was so ready for this moment. It seemed unreal or like a dream.

I whispered. "Can I feel you, please?"

She nodded, so I opened her legs a little wider and slid inside of her. Yes, I did it without a condom. No, I had no fear. She was a woman whom I loved and respected for longer than I could remember, and I felt safe. I felt she'd do me no harm.

"Ahhhhh, baby, you feel so good," I moaned. Getting over the initial shock of being inside her, I began to pump her steadily. Her pussy was extra wet, and I couldn't believe I was finally inside of her. I had dreamt of this since I was fourteen years old, and there I was, feeling the love of the only woman I wanted to be with.

"Awww, awwww, awwwwww, Ricky, give it to me. Deeper, baby, deeper."

Her sweet moan sang in my ears.

I pumped, rolling my pelvis around, thrusting my dick inside of her, and then pulled out quickly when I felt the eruption coming.

I squirted on her pussy hairs. "Ahhhhh, ahhhhhh, ahhhhhhh," I groaned and breathed deeply. It hadn't lasted long, but that was because of the super build-up from wanting her so badly.

I went down on top of her and kissed her again. She welcomed my tongue. I stood and she sat up and smiled at me before she slid off the table.

"I wanted this for a long, long time," I confessed.

"Well, I wanted this since seeing you again yesterday. I don't know, Ricky. Yesterday, it was like my best friend returned. I missed you being around when you left. I had no sexual feelings for you at all back then, so don't get me wrong. But seeing you yesterday, all grown up and handsome and confident, I was turned on. I've been thinking about you all day. And now that I had it, I want more." She smiled again.

"Ms. J, I—"

She cut me off. "Char."

"Char," I smiled. "I didn't plan this. I mean, I wanted it. I wanted it bad, and for a very long time, but I didn't plan for it to happen like this."

"I believe you. I'm just scared that what we've done will make a lot of people angry. We crossed a dangerous line."

"I know, but I want you, baby, and I don't care about anyone else right now."

"I'll tell you what," she said, "let's just have our night, and worry about everything and everybody else tomorrow."

"Okay," I agreed. "I like that idea."

We locked up, turned out the lights, and went up to her bedroom. We showered together and fucked all night. The next morning when I woke up, reality hit me. I had made love to my best friend's mom and I had no regrets.

# CHAPTER THREE

I stood in front of my bathroom mirror smiling. I was in awe and kept telling myself that it wasn't a dream. I had really done it. I'd had a night of passion with Lil' Ricky, well … Ricky. This was my son's best friend and I wondered how in the hell I hadn't recognized him when I first saw him again. He had changed so much. He was short back then, with glasses and braces, and it's amazing how he turned out to be so damn sexy. So damn fine. I mean, he looks like a new person, not that scrawny kid that graduated with Trey. Trey was already damn near six feet at graduation, but Lil' Ricky wasn't.

Now he was a six-foot masterpiece. No more pimples, no more glasses, no more braces, and he now spoke so eloquently. His demeanor was confident and cocky, not like that shy teen he was when Trey would try to recruit him a girlfriend. He walked with a walk that said, "I'm the man," and as much as I hated to admit it, I liked it.

"If they could all see you now," I said and reached for my toothpaste and toothbrush. I freshened my mouth quickly and then grabbed my robe. Singing, I went down to fix us some breakfast. I felt better than I had in years, thanks to him. I hadn't had a date in months and I hadn't had sex in over a year; my body felt good, rejuvenated, not sore like I expected.

He had flipped me, licked me, and had my legs over his shoulders and then over my head. I don't know what school of lovemaking he had attended, but I figured he had to have graduated with honors. In all my days and all the men that I've been with, I'd never been done so well.

I was floating and beaming until my phone rang, scaring the living shit out of me. I felt like a teen being busted by her father on the couch making out with her boyfriend. The phone brought me back to the harsh reality that the night before was a secret I'd have to die with.

I looked at the caller ID and saw it was my sister. My nerves were uneasy and out of control; I felt like she knew something was up. I let it ring, and a moment later, my cell phone rang and I remembered it was still on the dining room table. Determined to make sure she didn't expect a thing, I rushed to answer it.

"Hello," I said.

"Morning, sis," she sang.

"Hey, Cat."

"Hey, are you going to church?"

Damn!

I forgot it was Sunday and I forgot all about church. "Not, this Sunday, girl, I'm too tired. You know the kids were over last night." I couldn't believe I just said the word kids. Ricky wasn't a kid, child, or baby. He was a grown-ass man. "And you stood us up.'"

"Girl, you know me and Judge Garrett have been trying to hook up for weeks. Last night, he called, so, hey … It was a choice between getting my coochie wet or playing cards."

"Well, I hope you got your wish."

"Child, please, not even a nipple twist." We laughed.

"What?"

"Yes, and I hope my nephew is not too mad with me."

"You're good, sis. He was talking a little shit, but I told him to stay out of grown folks' business."

She laughed. "I know that's right. So how was the game without me? Did Bernie or Mo' come by?"

I smiled. "Girl, no. Ricky was my partner, and we held it down."

"Ooooowweee, Lil' Ricky. I still can't believe he turned out to be so damn good-looking, Char. That boy wasn't a good-looking kid."

"Well, he is good looking now, with a body that won't quit. And he asked that we not call him Lil' Ricky anymore. He now goes by Rick. Now I can't do Rick, but I can stop calling him Lil' Ricky. I mean, he is a man now, and ain't nothing little about that man."

"You are so right. If I wasn't old enough to be his momma."

"Girl, you wouldn't do nothing," I joked.

"Maybe not, but it's fun to dream," she said.

I laughed. If she only knew about the sexual convention I'd had with him, she'd scream. I was too anxious to spill, so I decided to change the subject.

"So how was your date with the judge?"

"It was nice, you know, same ole same. We talked about cases and more cases and more cases and I was wondering if I could meet someone not associated with the law. He's nice, but I want spice. I'm only forty-three and I do want to get married again. I felt like I was with my ex-husband last night, because all we talked about was work."

"Ouch, your ex was boooorrring! I used to hate to get cornered by him. He thought he knew every damn thing."

"I know, and I want something exciting, something that's going to get my coochie wet." Catherine laughed.

"You are so nasty, but I know how you feel, girl!" I said looking up in the air, enjoying the vivid memories of my exciting night with Ricky.

"Girl, but where is he?"

"I don't know, sis. Why didn't you change the subject?" I walked back into the kitchen, remembering that I had been about to start breakfast.

"I did change the subject, ten times maybe, but somehow we'd end up back to court cases. Hell, as soon as I finished my food, I waved for the check. Then he says, 'What's the rush?' I said, 'No rush, I just thought we'd go and listen to some music or go dancing,' and his reply was, 'I wish I could, but I got church early in the morning.' Girl, it took all I had not to roll my eyes at him. I was home by ten-thirty."

"Well you should have come by. We were up until after one."

"I started to, but by the time I made it to my side of town, all I wanted was merlot and my tub."

"Well, we had fun last night and your nephew-godson was hot with you when you didn't show."

"Well he'll get over it. I'm dateless, horny, and got a pregnant teen. I can't even scold half the hot-ass girls that come before me in the courtroom because my hot-ass daughter done went and did the exact opposite of what we taught her. I just wish sometimes I had Trey and you had Mesha."

"Well, it's not the end of the world. Just don't treat her like Momma treated me. And Trey turned out to be a great kid, when she said he wouldn't."

"Well, I did it the right way and didn't get pregnant until me and Marshall were married, while I was in law school, and even though I became a judge, my daughter got pregnant at sixteen, so Momma was wrong."

"Well, if you tell her that to her face, I'll give you a million bucks."

"Shit, momma is sixty-two, but she is still quick." She laughed.

I jumped when Ricky embraced me from behind. "Look, Cat, I got to call you a little later. Ricky is here to do some measuring for that deck," I lied. Catherine knew Ricky was a contractor and she knew I had been talking about getting a new deck for a while because my current one was in need of an overhaul.

"Ooooh, eye candy. Can I come and watch?"

"Girl, I'll call your crazy ass later." We got off the phone and I turned my attention to him. "Good afternoon." I smiled.

"Good afternoon," he said and kissed my forehead.

"I was just about to make us some breakfast."

"Okay, I'm going to run over to my house and shower and, you know, brush my teeth."

"Okay, I'll go up and shower, and I can cook when you get back."

"I have a better idea," he said.

I was curious. "I'm listening."

"Let's go out and get a bite and then go by my place. I can grab a few things and come back and we can go for a swim. I want to see you in your bikini." He smiled a devilish smile.

"That sounds great."

He gave me another quick kiss on the forehead and left. I went up, showered, and dressed. I took my time and did my makeup. I knew I looked good. I was still a size seven, curvy, and my stomach was stretch mark-free. I figured that having Trey so young and being athletic was the reason my stomach had gone back to being flat before he was five months old. My hair was now short, in a sassy, natural, curly style, and all I needed was mousse to tame it. I was light-complexioned, and people teased me, calling me redbone, but I didn't think I was that light.

My eyes were not hazel, but they were light brown, and sort of had a honey glow. I always wore natural shadows, nothing bold, because I wanted people to notice my eyes more than my makeup. I lined my full lips with a brown liner, put on a light coat of lipstick, and then I glossed over it. I admired myself in my tight-fitting denim strapless dress, and when I slid my feet into my sandals, my doorbell rang. I did my last quick mirror check and hurried down to answer.

"You look gorgeous," he said when I opened the door.

"Hello," I returned, because he greeted me with a compliment, and not a salutation.

"My bad," he said apologetically. "Hey, baby, you look gorgeous."

"Thank you. Come on in. I have to grab my purse."

He stepped in. "I pulled the car up to the door, I hope that's okay."

"It's fine, babe," I said, coming back with my purse, keys, and shades.

"Are you all set?"

I smiled. "Yes."

WE got on the Dan Ryan and headed downtown. I wanted to take her someplace elegant, so I headed to Alinea's. While Charlotte had been sleeping, I called and got us a reservation, hoping I'd get her out of bed on time to make it, but she managed to get up before me. Since I was trying hard to impress her, I silently cheered when they were able to get us in.

We sipped wine, talked about everything, and ate a fantastic meal. We left and headed to my place, and I reached over and grabbed her hand. I felt like I had accomplished everything I wanted in life and the only thing left was to make Ms. J mine.

I had a horrible childhood because I was always teased by some kid until I met Trey. He and I became best buds quickly and he always took up for me. When we went to high school, he was popular, and because of him, kids didn't bother me much then, and never when he was around. He was smart, good-looking, and played every sport our high school allowed, and I was just his sidekick. Trey and Ms. J treated me better than my own parents, and I loved them like family. But I always had a special love for Ms. J. She was the only woman who never called me ugly and the only woman who understood when I felt out of place.

Prom—ha, I didn't even go. After we saw Trey and La-La off, she and I had dinner together. I remember she took me to Outback Steakhouse and told me to order whatever I wanted. She let me order a virgin Pina Colada, and I fantasized I was her man and we were out on a date. I was seventeen and awkward, but she made me feel like I was a fine prince. When dinner was over, she put her arm in mine and said, 'Are you ready to go, baby?' and we walked out the restaurant.

She told me that looks didn't matter to real women, they were attracted to intelligence. I felt good about being smart then, instead of being handsome like my peers. In the fall after we graduated from high school, Trey went into the military and I went away to school. I wanted to be an architect and design houses and I did just that. When I was in my third year of college, my acne was completely gone and I tried contacts. By graduation, I'd had a growth spurt and the braces were off. I began to hit the gym hard. I went overseas and did contracting work for a while to build up some cash, and then my dad passed. I moved back home and I took the money I received and started my very own construction company. Only a year-and-a-half in business, but it was growing rapidly. Now successful and considered handsome, the women came. Beautiful and smart, but none of them was the woman I desired. All that was missing from my happy ending was Charlotte, and I wasn't going to give up on that goal either.

I opened the door to my loft and let her walk in before me.

She looked around. "Wow, Ricky, this is beautiful. I mean, your place is fantastic. How could you leave something so exquisite to live in your family's old home?"

"Well, I have work to do to get it sold. After the remodel, who knows? The loft may go on the market." I tossed my keys and wallet in the bowl on the table near the door. That was my way of keeping up with them.

"Well this place suits you. And the view …" she said, rushing over to the large window. I lived on the twenty-eighth floor, and I will admit the view was phenomenal. "The view is breathtaking."

"Thank you," I said. I headed for the kitchen, grabbed a bottle of water, and went over to hand it to her. "Take a look around and make yourself at home. I'm going to go and grab a few things."

I went to my room and I grabbed my smallest piece of luggage. I grabbed a few pairs of jeans and button downs. Those were for hanging out with Charlotte, because I worked in my coveralls. I grabbed a few toiletries, and just before I was done, she appeared in my doorway and tapped on the frame.

"Can I come in?" she asked.

"Sure. I'm almost done." I zipped my luggage and put it on the floor.

She sat on the bed. "So, are you single, Ricky?"

"At the moment, yes."

"Why is that? I look at you and see this gorgeous man. You said your business is doing well, you drive a very nice car, and your place is amazing. You're young, yet you're still single. What's up with that?"

I hunched my shoulders and bit the corner of my lip. "I don't know, really." I sat. "I have dated a lot of women. Liked a couple of them a lot, but nothing ever really developed for me. I just could never get close or fall deep enough. It's kind of hard to explain."

"So how do you know you're in love with me?" she asked with one brow raised high.

"I just know. I never forgot you, Charlotte. I mean, the way you walked. The way you'd always make up your own words to songs in the car when we'd go places. Trey and I would crack up, in the backseat. All the encouraging smiles you'd give me when I'd try to be in the background because I didn't want anyone to crack a joke about my glasses or my braces. And when Trey would invite girls over and when their friends met me and wanted to go home, you'd say, 'I didn't like her anyway.' I just know. Back then, it was a terrible boy crush, but as I got older, I missed having a woman who treated me so well.

"I compared a lot of women to you. I mean, your cooking, your sassiness, your walk, how you used to take the time to straighten my tie before we left for church. You showed me how a woman was supposed to treat a man. And when you dated what's his name ... Clearance? Cleveland?"

"Cleofus," she corrected.

"Yes, that guy. Man, I wanted to kick his ass. Every time he'd come around, I'd get so jealous and mad, and when he stopped coming around, boy, was I happy."

"Well, he was the king of the liars. He lied about everything, even where he lived."

"And then I remember senior year, you started dating Matt. By the time we graduated, y'all were still together and I hated it. When it was time for me to go away to school and Matt was still around, I was heartbroken," I confessed. We got quiet.

She slid closer to me. "I had no idea those thoughts were going through your head, Ricky. I don't know why I didn't see it or know that you felt that way, but if I had, I'd have told you to stop it."

I looked at her. "Why?"

"First, you were a pimple-faced kid and I'm not a pervert, and secondly, our age difference. I wouldn't have wanted to put your heart on hold for me."

"Well it's too late. I am a man now, and I'm finally glad I can act on my feelings. And you are all the woman I want and need." I ran a finger across her collarbone.

"I know that this is not the norm and will be frowned upon, but I'm feeling you too. And I can't say that I'm in love, that would be a lie, but I'm attracted to you enough to spend time to get to know the man you've become." I continued to caress her skin. She closed her eyes. "I want us to spend some time getting to know each other for who we are today and see where this goes."

I planted a soft kiss on her shoulder and cupped her left breast. I didn't think my quick stop home, would land us in bed.

I kissed her neck and made my way up to her lips. She pushed me back and climbed on top of me. I wrapped my arms around her and she kissed me deeply as my hands began to touch her all over. I rubbed and squeezed her ass and she grinded against my rod. I pulled her dress up over her ass and she spread her legs and rubbed her body against mine. I wanted our skin to touch.

"Take off your clothes," I panted between kisses.

She got up and pulled her dress over her head. Again, no bra and the sight of her nipples made my mouth water. I quickly undid my jeans and kicked off my shoes. She reached for me, pulling both my boxers and pants away and my dick pointed toward my stomach. I had close to ten inches, no doubt, but she turned me on so much I swore it grew longer.

I sat up and didn't bother to undo the buttons on my shirt. I just pulled it and my tank over my head. She climbed back on top of me and we kissed again. She rubbed her wetness on my pipe and I wanted to go for it and slide right in, but I decided to enjoy her and make our love scene last. She licked down my chest and stroked my man. My eyes opened wide when I felt her lips wrap around my head. She began to jack my shaft and make circles with her tongue around my head. I couldn't hold back groans of pleasure.

She began to bob up and down on it, and I mechanically reached for her head. "Yes, baby, y-y-y-esssss! Your mouth feel s-s-soooo good, baby ... Do that, suck that dick, baby!" I gripped the comforter with my other hand and my pelvis moved up and down on its own accord. I was ready to explode, so I grabbed my pole and pulled away.

"No, babe, I'm there. You are amazing and I can't take anymore," I huffed. I lay still and few seconds later, the urge to splash subsided. "Come here," I instructed and pulled her up. "Sit on my face."

Charlotte stood and pushed her thong away from her waist and down her thighs, then stepped out of them. She got into position and my tongue and lips were surrounded by her wetness. Her sweet sexual scent hit my nose and I went to work, flicking my tongue over her swollen clit and moving it up and down her slit. She rolled her hips and moaned and went to massage her own breast. Her raisin-like nipples got harder when she pinched and tugged on them. I reached up with both hands to help her out. I was so greedy and hungry for her that I wanted to lick her clit and suck on her nipples at the exact same time.

After moments of squirming and moaning, my dick was feeling neglected, so I told her to turn over. She was now ass up, with her pussy back into position over my face for me to lick her. Happy my dick was back in her wet mouth, I pushed up, trying to hit her throat. She sucked and slurped and I sucked and licked. Her hotbox contracted, giving me a gush of her juices, and when I started to lick it some more, she rolled off.

"Oh no," she said breathing heavily, "I got one and you are not about to kill me with that tongue of yours."

"Well open up and let me inside," I ordered.

I got up with my erection in my hand, ready to please. She scooted closer to me and opened wide for me. I rubbed her and pushed my finger in first. She was soaking wet and my dick was anxious to slide in. I positioned myself over her, resting on one arm, and circled the outside of her slit then guided myself inside. After I was in deep, I went into a push-up position and found a steady rhythm.

"Oh yes," she called out. "Oh-oh-oh-oh y-y-y-yesss, baby. Awwww, yes, that feels so fucking good." She opened up some more and held my waist to pull me in deeper. I pumped and pumped, watching her breasts bounce to my beat. Her eyes were closed, but the expression on her face let me know I was getting the job done. I slowed, came down on her, and pushed my tongue in her mouth. Her kiss heightened the sensation as I rolled around deep inside of her.

"Ummm, ummm, ummm," she moaned while I kissed her.

I moved to her neck. "Is it good, baby?" I asked and sucked her skin.

"Yes, Ricky, it's good." She continued to moan. "Your dick feels so g-g-g-good inside of me."

I flipped over onto my back and she squatted and came down on me. With her hands on her knees, she began riding me effortlessly. Her tits were bouncing around in circles and I was going crazy. I reach for them. "Ahhhh, Daddy, ahhhh. Your dick is good. Oooooh, baby. Ummm, it's good."

She stopped bouncing and started rolling on me then put her knees down on the bed and came forward. Her ass went up and down on me, and after a few more pumps, that was it. "Pull out, baby, I'm ready," I groaned. She got up and jerked it. "Awww, awwww, awwwwhhhhh," I grunted as I shot it on her stomach. She rubbed my head in it smearing it on her skin. I had to catch my breath. "Woman, what the hell are you doing to me? You are unbelievable."

She smiled. "I'm just trying to make you feel good and have some fun. Are you having fun?"

"Oh, hell yes." We both laughed. I went to get a wet towel and came back and wiped her stomach. After I did a quick wipe down of myself, I got back in the bed with her and we laid and talked for a while before going for another round. Then we showered, dressed, and went to dinner. When we got back, we were shocked to see Trey and La-La pulling up to her house at the same time.

"Oh shit," I said.

"Damn, why they have to pull up right now?"

"I don't know. What do we say?"

"Umm, we went to dinner?" she suggested.

"Won't that be weird?" I asked nervously. Trey was my best friend and I could see him tackling me if he found out the things I did to his mother.

"No, just say you came over to see if any food was left and I told you I wasn't in the mood for leftovers, so we decided to go out to eat."

"You think that will work?"

She opened the door. "I don't know, but the longer we sit here, it will probably make it worse." She got out.

I was trembling. I didn't know how to conduct myself around Trey now. It was no longer me wanting his mother, I had his mother.

WE got out and walked towards the porch. Trey was unlocking the door. "Hey you two," I yelled behind him.

"Hey, y'all. Where y'all just coming from?"

"Oh, we just went out for a bite to eat," I said. "Tired of leftovers, and since Ricky was at his dad's doing nothing, I walked down and asked him to go with me. Since my other son has been too busy with his girlfriend to hang with me." I laughed.

He opened the door and we all walked in.

"Well it's hard not to, Ma. I mean, I've been deployed for eighteen months." He smiled.

I knew my son had needs I couldn't please. "Boy, that is TMI." l laughed again and thanked God he didn't suspect a thing. "Y'all want something to drink or something?" I grabbed a bottle of white wine.

"A glass for me," La-La said.

I grabbed two wine glasses. "And you two? We still have beer."

"I'll have one," Trey said.

Ricky cleared his throat. "I'll take one."

"So, Ricky … Man, what is up? We haven't had a chance to hang, so this weekend, clear your schedule."

I went to hand them both a beer.

"Cool," Ricky agreed.

"And you have to let me meet your girl. I know you got somebody special, huh?" Trey laughed.

"No, not at the moment. I'm chasing this one particular one, but you know how it goes. It's still early." His eyes were on me.

Staring at me was not the move. "Well, you need to bring her by, so I can see if she is worth it," I chimed in. I knew he was making small talk with Trey, but I'd be hella jealous if he even thought of bringing a woman around.

We had a few more drinks and Ricky left before Trey and Lavitra, but after they had been gone for thirty minutes, he came back. We ended up in my pool with me riding him. I knew I could fall hard for Ricky. He was everything I wanted and needed in a man, and somehow, I didn't feel the age difference between us.

It was like being with someone my age; each moment spent with him was like magic. We came close to getting caught a few times, because it was so hard to keep my hands off of him. But we hid our relationship well, and when Trey left to go to Fort Hood, there was no more bobbing and weaving.

AFTER six months, I still hadn't told Trey. I had finally confessed to Catherine and Mo' because it was just too hard to keep it a secret, and they promised they would let me be the one to tell my son. It was Christmas time and he was coming home, so my nerves were extremely bad. I didn't know how to tell him or how he'd react. All I knew was I had to tell him.

I was madly in love by then and Ricky and I were talking marriage. I prayed to God every day to make my announcement easy, but the closer the day came for Trey to arrive, the more afraid I was.

# CHAPTER FOUR

"Hey, I thought I was supposed to pick you up from the airport?" I said when Trey walked in two hours early.

"I got an earlier flight out, so La-La picked me up."

Rolling my pie dough, I let him kiss my cheek. "Where is La-La? I swear all she talks about is this big wedding you two are having next June."

"She had to do some last-minute shopping, but she'll be back."

"Okay, well, I did make you some dinner before I started my Christmas cooking. Your plate is in the microwave."

"Thanks, Ma, because you know I'm hungry."

"Well, take your bags up and wash your hands."

"Ma, I'm grown. I know to wash my hands and I'm going to La-La's tonight.

"Son, you just got here."

"I know, Ma, but she misses me and I miss her."

"Enough said."

He went into the fridge and got a cold beer after washing his hands in the sink. Then he heated up his food and sat at the island so we could talk while I finished my pies.

"Hey," Ricky yelled from the front door when he came in.

My heart raced. I hadn't told Trey and I didn't know how I was going to explain Rick having a key. "We are in here," I quickly yelled and he walked into the kitchen.

"Hey, I got—" He stopped when he saw Trey. "Trey, man, what's going on?" He placed the bags on the counter.

Trey tilted his head and stood. "You're using a key now? What's going on?"

I jumped in. "Trey, you know Ricky has been working around here on long overdue repairs. Since he is two doors down, he makes sure I'm good, so I told him to keep the key," I lied.

"Oh, okay. Thanks, man, for looking out for my moms."

"No problem, bro," Ricky said and they hugged.

"I hope I got everything you needed, Ms. J. If you need anything else, just text me," he said, turning to leave.

"Ricky, come on now, man. Relax your coat, grab a beer. We've been so consumed lately we barely speak."

"I know, man."

Ricky took off his coat and put it on the back of the vacant chair. I handed him a beer and tried to ignore their conversation. I was nervous as hell. He and I had done it all over my house, been on a couple trips, and been in sexual bliss for the last six months, and here we were, in my son's face like nothing had ever happened. We had even managed to hide it from La-La.

"Well, since you are my best man, you are going to have to make sure shit is going smooth here and help La-La out."

"Trey, La-La is fine," I said, putting my three pies in the oven. "That girl doesn't even want any help. I've tried, but she says, 'I got it, Ms. J,' so I just stopped offering."

"I got you, Trey, no worries," Ricky said. I could tell he was just as uncomfortable as I was. He kept looking at me like he wanted me to say something, but I kept signaling him to stop looking at me.

I had to get out of there. It was too weird. "I'm going to go up to shower, son. If you have anything to do, you know you can use my car," I offered. I wanted him to go somewhere, anywhere.

"I'm good. I'm just gonna chill and wait for La-La."

"Well, why don't you go down and see the renovations in Ricky's house. I mean, it's totally different now and it's beautiful."

"Oh yeah," Trey said.

"Yes, we are just about done," Ricky said. "Come and check it out."

The two of them got their coats and left. I let out a deep breath when they were gone and went up to shower. I was terrified and I knew he'd be furious with me for hiding my relationship. I decided to tell him the day after Christmas. I didn't want to ruin our Christmas.

"HEY, son, what's up?" I said, quivering.

Unfortunately I hadn't told him. It was the thirtieth and I was still creeping.

He was supposed to be at La-La's, and we were shocked to hear him come in. I barely got my nightgown over my head, while Ricky rushed into the bathroom to put on his sweater and fasten his jeans. I started flipping through the channels to take it off the R&B channel.

We had been sipping wine and listening to music until I climbed on top of him. He removed his sweater and undid his jeans and I pulled my gown over my head. He was sucking on my nipples when we heard the door, and we both scrambled like roaches when the light comes on. He grabbed his sweater and ran in the powder room just off the den and I sat like we were just chilling.

"Nothing. What's going on?" Trey asked.

"Nothing, baby. Just sitting here with Ricky watching some TV," I lied, hoping he would let it go.

Ricky emerged from the rest room. "Hey, Trey, man, what's up?"

Trey stared at me. His jaws flared. "Ma, what did I walk in on?"

"Nothing, son. I thought you'd be at La-La's. Did something happen?"

"No, I came by to get some baby pictures of me. La-La said she needed them before I go for some program and slide show."

I hopped up. "Okay, I'll get that for you."

"Hold on, Ma. Why is your gown on backwards?"

Oh shit!

"Huh, what?" I tried to play it off. "Ricky, why you didn't tell me my gown was on backwards." I laughed. "I'm so embarrassed."

Looking suspicious, with his head tilted and brow arched, Trey said, "Okay then, I'll ask you, Ricky. What in the hell did I walk in on?"

"I said nothing, son," I yelled.

"I'm talking to Ricky," he yelled louder.

Ricky didn't sit down. He just went for his coat. "Uhh, Ms. J, it was nice. I will be going now."

"Not so fast," Trey said.

My heart was racing. It was a bad scene and I knew I needed to fess up, but I was a coward.

Ricky stopped and turned to him. "What's up, Trey?" Ricky asked.

"You wouldn't lie to me, would you, man? We have been boys for too long for you to not be straight up with me. I mean, what's going on? Are you smashing my mother?"

Defensively, I said, "Look, son, I told you nothing. You got questions, you ask me."

"No, Ma, I'm talking to Ricky."

"And I'm talking to you. Goodnight, Ricky. Let me talk to my son."

"No. If I need to know something, he should be an honorable man and say it to my face!"

He moved in Ricky's direction and I got in between them. I didn't want them fighting. I knew it was time to talk to my son and tell him the truth.

"Goodnight," I said to Ricky. "Leave so I can talk to my son," I pleaded.

He backed away. "Goodnight. I will be at the house if you need me."

"She's good. I don't need you looking out for my mother!"

I got in Trey's face. I was a small woman, but my son had enough respect for me not to challenge me.

I let out a breath when I heard the front door close. I softened my tone. "Okay, it's me and you, son. What do you want to know?"

He backed down and sat. "The truth. Are you messing around with Ricky, Ma? Do you two have something going on?"

"Yes," I whispered.

He jumped up. "I knew it. I fucking knew it. I'm going to whip his ass!" he roared.

"Calm down, Trey, and lower your damn voice. Who in the hell you think you're talking to, dammit? Sit your ass down now!" I yelled.

"I'm going to kill him!"

"You are going to sit down and hear me out."

It took him a moment, but he finally flopped down. "Ma, how could you? How could you do something so foolish? He is my age, Momma."

"I know, son, and I didn't plan for this to happen. Things just … I don't know, Trey. I wanted to tell you, son, I did, but I didn't know how."

"When did it start, Ma?"

I looked down. There was no reason to lie at that point. "The night we played cards when you came home from Iraq."

"When I was on leave, Ma? Six fucking months ago?"

My eyes bulged. My son had never talked to me in that manner. "Trey! I know you're upset, but you are not going to talk to me like that. I won't stand for it."

He put his head down. "I'm sorry, Ma. I'm just so angry. Ricky and I grew up like brothers. You and him together is sickening, Ma, and you have to stop. Who else knows about this?"

I let out a deep breath. "Auntie Catherine and Mona."

He put his face in his hands and began to sob. I hadn't seen my son cry since he left to go to Iraq.

I sat down beside him and tried to comfort him. "Son, I'm sorry I didn't tell you and I'm sorry I went behind your back, but we are in love—"

He leaped up from the couch. "In love?" he yelled in disbelief. "In love? Ma, do you hear yourself? This is Lil' Ricky. The kid from two houses over with acne, glasses, and braces. You practically raised him!"

"No, he's not that kid anymore, Trey. He is a man. He makes me happy. He puts a smile on my face each and every moment of the day. He is the first and only man that has this effect on me. I love him, Trey. Whether you want to hear it or not, I love him, son, and we are happy."

"No, Ma, no. You have to shut this down. You are not some old, ugly, desperate woman. You're nobody's cougar. You're my mother."

"I'm your mother, Trey, but I am now Ricky's woman and I am happy. You can't come here and asked me to give up what makes me happy because it makes you uncomfortable. That isn't fair."

He shook his head. "I can't believe my ears." He rubbed his head. "Mother, I'm disgusted and disappointed, and right now, I need some space." I sat there wondering what that meant. "I'm going back to La-La's. If you decide to shut down this foolishness, we can talk, but if you choose to continue this sham of a relationship with Ricky, I'm done with you." He turned to walk out.

I ran behind him. "Son, you can't mean that. I'm your mother. You are supposed to have my back, no matter what."

He paused. "Yes, Ma, I do. But this thing with Ricky is disgusting. Ricky and I were friends, and what you and he are doing is disturbing. Tell him that he doesn't have to worry about being my best man. Even if you do shut it down, I'm done with him, Ma." He walked out and slammed the door.

Trey and I had always been close and I knew I was wrong to hide my affair with Ricky. And I knew he wouldn't like it. I broke down in tears. My one and only child was disappointed in me for the first time. All the things I had done in my life to be a good mother, a great provider, and have a successful career didn't mean shit anymore because my relationship with Ricky tainted my image in his eyes.

My son thought the worst of me as if he had found out I was hoeing or out stripping on a pole. What was I supposed to do? I didn't want to go back to being lonely. I didn't want to go back to being by myself. Ricky was perfect for me. He was just born in the wrong year. If I could have tacked fifteen more years on his age, I would have, but the reality was I was in love with a man my son's age. For the first time, I felt ashamed.

I never wanted to hurt anyone. I never wanted to cause any pain. I just wanted to be loved. And now that I'd found it, I lost my son. My one and only son.

#  CHAPTER FIVE

I tried to talk to Trey for two days, but he refused to talk to me. His mother was devastated. I wanted him to be angry with me, not her. If he wanted to punch me in the face, I'd let him. Even though I didn't want to even think of not having Charlotte, I'd leave so she could have her son. It would kill me, but to be with her and know Trey hated her would hurt more. I was going to try to get through to him; I just hoped I could.

"Thank you, La-La," I said when she let me in.

"You're welcome, Ricky. He's downstairs. Just talk to him. I'm sure you'll get through to him."

Not confident at all, I replied, "I hope so La-La." She took my coat and pointed me to the stairwell. I went down and found Trey sitting on the sofa drinking a beer. "Trey, we need to talk."

He looked over his shoulder. "Man, you better get your ass out of here right now." I sat down anyway. "Man, are you hard of hearing? We have nothing to talk about. You are not welcome here."

"We do, Trey, and I'm not leaving until we do."

"That damn La-La. I told her I didn't want to see you, but she is so fucking hard-headed."

"Don't blame La-La, okay. I talked her into it. Char is d—"

He leaped from the sofa. "Char? She is Ms. J to you, nigga!" He hovered over me.

I knew he wanted to whip my ass, so I had to calm him down. "You're right, man, you're right, okay? Chill, sit down!"

La-La came down with two cold beers. She didn't speak, she just set them on the table and then hurried back up the stairs.

Trey breathed heavily and took his seat. He was fuming. "What do you want man? My blessing, huh? You want me to tell you it's okay to fuck my mother?"

"Trey, I know you are not happy with me and Ch—I mean, Ms. J's relationship, but your mother is a great woman. She loves you to death. You are like her lifeline, and she is in so much pain right now because you won't talk to her."

His eyes welled and he put his head down. "Why my mother, man? Huh? How did you fall for my mother? She is my mother. You are fucking my mother." I could see he was hurt.

"Come on, Trey, if you want to hash this out, we can hash it out, but you can't minimize our relationship into something dirty. And we are still talking about your mother, so chill with that. If you want to talk, let's talk, but no crass comments or dis-respect to Charlotte."

"Okay, Ricky. Tell me how you and my mother became involved. I want to know what the hell were you thinking when you crossed that line with her."

I took a drink and cleared my throat. "It was me, man. I had a thing for your mother long before seeing her six months ago. I started liking her when we were teens."

"Ricky, my mother was like a mother to you!" he yelled.

"In your eyes she was, because she is your mother Trey. She is not my mother. The times she cooked and straightened my tie and took me out to dinner when you were on prom and talked to me when girls dogged me, I saw her as a woman treating me like I deserved to be treated. She showed me what love was supposed to be like back then. You'd never look at your mom like a teen would. You can never see how sexy your mom is or seductive she can be, like I do. When I sat across from her and she'd cut my steak, I wasn't looking at her like a mother. She was always this sexy woman who wanted to make me feel good."

Trey's nose flared.

"I know it makes no sense to you," I continued, "but I've never thought of Charlotte as a mother. When I went away, I thought I'd eventually get over her, but that didn't happen. I dated and compared every single woman I was with to her, and not one of them ever compared. When I saw her, the day you came home, I knew it wasn't a crush, Trey. I know you want to punch me in the face, but I knew it was not an old crush and that I loved that woman. I've always loved her and I want to be with her."

I waited for him to attack me, but he didn't move. We sat in silence for a while and he finished his beer.

"I knew, Ricky. I knew you loved my momma, but I honestly thought it was a stupid crush. I'm not a fool, I saw how you'd gaze at her. Or how, if you were mad or upset about something, you'd forget all about whatever it was when my mother stepped into the room. I paid attention to how you'd break your neck to help her with the groceries or clean the pool or shovel the snow before I could get to it, just to impress her.

"You were just a different dude when my mom was around. You'd be shy as hell around everybody else, but you'd talk my mother's ear off. I'd make excuses to get out of cleaning the basement, but you be like 'I'll do it, Ms. J.'" He changed his voice, mocking me.

I chuckled. "Trey, I didn't mean to hurt you, man, or lie to you or keep this from you. Trust, I have all the respect in the world for you, but this was the hardest thing for your mother and I. Not telling you was stressful for the both of us, and as much as I love Charlotte, I don't want you to shut her out because of me. I want her to be happy, and without you, your mother is miserable."

He was quiet. I hoped he understood. I knew he may not have liked it, but I wanted him to understand.

"I need another beer," he said and called for La-La. He told her we needed two more. She brought them and went back up in a flash. "Look, Ricky, this is still a disturbing feeling for me. I know you and my mom claim to be happy, but I can't accept this. I heard everything you've said and I know you love her, but I can't." He let out a deep breath. "I can't see you two kissing or touching. Just the thought of you touching my mother… I-I-I-I just can't."

"You can't stop and consider how we feel, Trey? Better yet, how she feels? Your mother has always been on your side, Trey, through it all."

"It's not the same thing, Ricky!"

"Being there for someone is being there for someone. It doesn't matter the situation."

"This is different."

"At least talk to your mom. If you want to hate me, Trey, hate me, but let Charlotte be happy."

He shook his head. "Nah, no thanks. I can't stomach this fiasco."

"So that's it?" I said.

"Pretty much. You ought to be lucky I didn't beat yo' ass."

"No, I'm not. If punching me or whipping my ass will make you feel better, come on and hit me with your best shot. The only thing that matters to me is your mother's happiness. I thought it mattered to you too."

"It does, but what you two are doing is not natural and I'm not going to budge."

"In your opinion, Trey. We haven't done anything wrong. We are both two consenting adults and we are free to love who we want to love."

"You're right, Lil' Ricky, but that doesn't mean I have to support it. Thanks for the talk." He stood. "I'm done."

I tried one last time. "Can you just please talk to your mother? She is so upset."

"Unless she is telling me you and her are done, we don't have anything to talk about." He put the beer bottle on the table and went upstairs, leaving me alone.

I hated I couldn't get through to him. The only thing left to do was break up with Char. I loved her to death, but coming between her and Trey wasn't the move.

# CHAPTER SIX

I sat in my window seat with a blanket, listening to Aretha Franklin. I had lost my son over a man and I was still scratching my head. I'd always said I'd never let a man come between me and my son, but that was before I fell in love with one. Ricky was my match and I felt he had paid attention to me for so long that he knew what to say and what to do to always make me feel good.

He knew my comfort foods, favorite shows, and my taste in everything. On my birthday, he showed me the night of my life with my favorite fragrance, favorite flowers, and favorite restaurant. He could finish my sentences and he always knew how to make me feel better. He even knew when I just needed a little space. I didn't want to give him up. I didn't want to be alone. He gave me that spice that I craved and I didn't want to go back to how it was before him.

But at what cost? Losing my son, my only son. Why was Trey being so selfish? He had La-La, the only women he'd ever loved, why couldn't Ricky have the only woman he'd ever loved?

I took a drink and went back to singing along with Aretha. I was belting out the lyrics when the volume went down. I jumped.

"Hey, baby," Ricky said, taking me by total surprise.

"Hey," I said and looked down. I dabbed the corners of my eyes. I had been crying off and on all evening.

"I see you're listening to Aretha. I told you not to listen to anything that makes you even sadder."

I looked up. "I know what you said, Ricky, but it doesn't matter what I listen to, I'm still going to feel sad."

"I know, so I came to do the right thing."

"The 'right thing'? Baby, what do you mean? What are you talking about?"

"I'm sorry you're hurting, baby, and it's because of me. I should have never kissed you. I should have never crossed those lines with you."

I paused. I didn't expect to hear him say those words. "Baby, no, don't say that. We did nothing wrong. You don't have to apologize for revealing your love for me."

"I do, Char. I mean, Trey is furious about this entire thing, and I know we should have been up front and honest, but even if we had told him then, he'd still opposed to it."

Scared of where this was going, I said. "Ricky, please, baby, hold me. This thing with Trey will blow over. He'll adjust."

He shook his head. "Baby, it won't. And I don't want to come between you and him."

"Well, I'm not letting you go. I deserve happiness, Ricky, and as much as I love my son, I want to be loved too. In a few months, he is going to marry the love of his life, and I refuse to let him piss on my happiness. I raised him and I did what I was supposed to do. I'm his mother, he is not my father and he can't tell me what to do.

"As a man, he decided to walk out on me and demanded I make a choice. I chose you. I'm not going to be sad and lonely while he's somewhere happy with La-La, living his life like he chooses."

"I can't ask you to do that, Char."

"You're not asking me, Ricky, I'm choosing for myself. I love my son, and he is going to have to accept my choice. But if he doesn't, what can I do? I am not going to be miserable. I just wanna be loved. You are my love."

"So you and I are good?"

I ran over and hugged him tight. "Baby, we are good."

He pulled away. "I'll be right back."

"Where are you going?"

"I have to get something from the house real quick."

"Can it wait?"

"No, so why don't you run up and get out of this granny gown and hair wrap and I'll be back."

He grabbed his coat.

"Ricky—"

"I'll be right back, baby, I promise."

I went up, and after taking a look in the mirror, I snatched my scarf off. I turned on the shower and got in, making sure the water moistened my hair. It was easier to style wet. I got out and did my daily regimen, and quickly applied a little makeup. The last couple days, I'd been down, but I had to get out of that funk. Trey was probably somewhere with La-La having an orgasm, so forget him. "He'll come around," I said out loud.

When I went back down, Ricky had lit a few candles and changed the track from Aretha to the Isley Brothers.

I smiled brightly. "This is nice, baby."

He handed me a glass of red. "Thank you, babe. Come over here and sit." When I did, he knelt down in front of me.

My hands started to shake. "Baby, what are you doing?"

He shook his head and put a finger over my lips. "No, listen to me." He cleared his throat. "A couple of days ago, when we almost got caught fooling around on the sofa, I thought to myself, 'I'm twenty-six years old and I'm running in the bathroom to hide because I can't tell my best friend that I'm in love with his mother.' I stood in the mirror before walking out and said I was going to man up and tell him, but when I came out and saw how terrified you were with telling him the truth, I decided not to say anything. I said I'd let you make the decision on how you wanted to handle me and Trey, and I'm glad I did.

"Charlotte, I love you and I'm so glad you decided to fight for us. You showed me that you love me just as much as I love you, so..." He pulled out a small jewelry box. "You know what this means, right?" He held up the ring.

"I do, but I still want you to ask me." I beamed.

"Charlotte Evelyn Jones, will you marry me?"

"Of course I will, Ricky," I said, surprisingly calm.

He slid the ring on my finger and my eyes watered. I was happy, but sad that the first person I'd normally call with good news, I couldn't. It was a bittersweet moment, but I celebrated it as best as I could.

#  Chapter Seven

"Ten, nine, eight, seven, six, five, four, three, two, one! Happy New Year!" we all shouted. We were at Catherine's house and I wasn't surprised when my son didn't say hello to me and Ricky. I showed off my ring and wanted to tell my son my news, but I didn't. Ricky continued to assure me it would be okay, but every time I looked at my son, he looked away.

"Hey, Ms. J, I heard the news. Can I see your ring?" La-La asked.

I held up my finger. "Yes, you sure can."

"It is lovely. I'm so happy for you."

"Thanks, La-La. I wish your fiancé felt the same."

"He'll come around. He's just hurt."

"I can understand that, La-La, but he's my son. There is absolutely nothing that he can do to make me turn my back on him, and it kills me that he'd turn his back on me."

"Don't worry, I got this. I love you, Ms. J," she said and gave me a tight squeeze.

❤ ❤ ❤

I felt a hard tap on my shoulder. "I need to talk to you," La-La demanded.

"Right now?"

"Yes, right now," she snapped.

I wondered what I had done wrong. I followed her upstairs to where it was quiet. The only persons upstairs was Mesha and her baby.

"In here," she said. I followed her into my Auntie Catherine's office.

"What's the big emergency?"

"You need to apologize to your mother."

"Are you serious? I'm not apologizing to her, and I can't believe she'd come here with him."

"Do you love me, Tracy?"

"Yes, Lavitra, since we are using birth-given names."

"If you love me, you will apologize to your mother."

"What? Come on. That has absolutely nothing to do with how I feel about you. This is between me, my mother, and Ricky's backstabbing ass."

"How did he backstab you, Trey? Did he go behind your back and sleep with me? No. He just fell in love with a woman who happens to be your mother."

"And that is disgusting."

She laughed. "You are unbelievable and selfish and high-minded. Trey, that is your mother, not some whore or some street lady. She is your mother and she wants to be happy. Ricky makes her happy, Trey, and that's all you should want for her."

"I do, La-La, but why him?"

"Why not him?"

"He is my best friend."

"And the best man for her."

La-La made sense, but I wasn't going to change my mind. Their relationship was just wrong and I wasn't going to accept it. "Look. I'm done with this conversation."

"Well, our engagement is off." She took off her ring.

"Are you fucking serious?"

"I'm dead serious. I don't want to marry a man who is so selfish that he'd turn his back on his own mother because he doesn't approve of someone she loves. Tracy, Ms. J is free to love and be with whomever she wants. It's not your decision. What if she didn't like me and asked you to choose, huh? What? Would you leave me? Huh, Tracy? Would you kick me to the curb?" She got in my face.

"No," I whispered.

"Why not?"

"Because I love you."

"Exactly! Your mother has been there for you through it all. How about showing her the same courtesy? If you can't, we are done. If you'd abandon her over this, you'd abandon me for less, because I know how much you love yo' momma." She put the ring in my hand and walked off.

I stopped her. "Here, put this back on and give me a minute. I'll be down and I will do the right thing."

She kissed me. "Thank you, baby, and I love you. Your mother is a great woman, Trey, and she deserves his love as much as you deserve mine."

"I love you too, La-La, and you're right. As much as I don't like it, you're right."

My fiancée left and I sat on my aunt's leather couch for a few moments to get myself together. I looked around and saw a photo of my mom. She was smiling so beautifully in the photo and looked so happy. I wiped my eyes. I was hurt by their relationship and hated that I felt that way.

Ricky and I were tight growing up and my momma and I were closer than any son and mother I knew, and I was treating her like she was a stranger. She was my mother, but she was still a woman, and I had to love what she loved. Unfortunately, that was my best friend, Ricky.

I gathered my thoughts, wiped my tears, and headed back downstairs.

TREY tapped his glass. "Alright, alright, alright, everybody gather around. I have something I want to say."

I started not to move, but Ricky encouraged me to get up and see what my son had to say.

Bernie muted the music and we all waited to see what Trey had to say.

"Okay, everybody, I want to say a few things."

"Go ahead, nephew," Catherine yelled.

I looked at him and I was surprised he looked at me. Even more shocking, he smiled at me.

"First, to my momma, Charlotte Evelyn Jones, you are the baddest woman on the planet." La-La swatted his arm. "She is, baby, and you can and will learn a lot from this woman. My mother is a no-nonsense kinda woman. She had me at fifteen and didn't have much of a life because she had me so young. Over the years, she put my needs first and made many, many sacrifices for me. And all I want to say is thank you for all you've done to mold me into the man I am today."

Everyone clapped.

"Hold on," he said. "Hold on, I'm not done. I did a bad thing, y'all," he confessed.

"Oh, Lord," Mo' shouted.

"Wait, wait, wait. Y'all hear me out. And if your shoes are too tight and your feet hurt, sit down, because this may take me a while," he said. We all laughed. "My mother, Char as you all call her, has stood by me through it all. When I made decisions she wasn't cool with, she'd say, 'I don't like it, but I got your back.' When I decided to go into the Army, she was livid. Oh boy, she was livid. She cried for days and kept telling me, 'You're my one and only son and you just can't go into the army.' But yet again, she said, 'Son, I don't like it, but I got your back.'

"The point is, as soon as my mother made a decision I didn't like, I cursed her out and threatened to be done with her. I walked out on her without considering how she felt or what she wanted. Momma, I'm so sorry." My eyes welled as he spoke. "It's my turn to say to you, Ma, I don't like it, but I got your back." He came over and hugged me tight. "You are an awesome mother, and I will never turn my back on you, no matter what. I will never speak to you that way again and I'm sorry. I want you to be happy, and just like you always wish me well, I wish you well."

"Thank you, son," I cried.

Everyone clapped and Bernie turned the music back on. We danced and we didn't get home until five in the morning. Ricky and I climbed into my bed exhausted as hell. The next day, I didn't want to move, so my fiancé made me breakfast in bed. We stay in bed all day and that evening, the party was on at my place.

The next couple days we spent with La-La and Trey, playing

cards, drinking, and eating. We all rode to the airport to send Trey back to Fort Hood. I was sad to see him go again.

We spent the next few months planning Trey and La-La's wedding and even took a road trip down to visit Trey in Fort Hood. He and Ricky weren't as close as they were before Trey found out the truth, but they were getting there.

The wedding was beautiful and afterwards, we saw both of them off. They went to Jamaica first for their honeymoon and then to Fort Hood.

Ricky and I married and things were perfect for us. I conceived again at forty-four and gave my husband a healthy baby boy. It was odd that Trey and La-La's son was almost a year older than his uncle, but over time, things were all good.

We all deserve to be loved, and sometimes love comes in an unexpected package. Mine came in a package fifteen years younger, but there is not a day that goes by where he or I have any regrets. I wanted to be loved by someone who loved me and Richard Eugene Collins Jr. loved me just that much.

Thinking back on it, I'd have never imagined it would be him, but I'm so glad it was. The heart wants what the heart wants and I'm so happy that Ricky's heart wanted me.

If you enjoyed these short stories as much as I enjoyed writing them, please take a few moments to post a review.

Thanks and Happy Reading.

Hooks in Me is coming soon. Go to the next page for a sneak peak!

# Hooks in Me

*EXCERPT*

# Prologue

"DANA, PLEASE DON'T do this." She had me at gunpoint and I didn't want to move, because I was afraid to death that she'd shoot.

"Don't beg now, you bitch!" she barked. "It's because of you my marriage is ruined. The only way for me and Matthew to ever be happy is for you to be out of the picture!"

I was shaking so bad, I couldn't concentrate. All I could think of was my parents, my lil' brother, and Matthew … Oh my God, Matthew—the reason I had a loaded barrel pointed in my face.

I tried to reason with her. "Dana, you and Matthew won't be together if you do this. They will put you away forever and you will never see Matthew or your son again if you go through with this."

"Shut up! Just shut up, you bitch!" she screamed and began to pace. "I swear I will shoot you in your fucking mouth if you don't shut the fuck up!" Her hand holding the gun trembled, and I obediently complied. I could tell she was nervous, because she kept twirling her hair. She continued to pace. "All I wanted was a family with Matthew. All I wanted was for him to get over you, but he's never going to get over you, you selfish bitch. Why didn't you just back off after he married me," she yelled.

At that moment, I wished I had. At that moment, I wished I had done the right thing because I was about to lose my life over Matthew. The only man I had ever loved. I promised myself each time that it would be the last time, but it never was.

"Dana, please … I'm sorry," I cried. Tears streamed down my face.

"Save it. Viv! You and Matt can rot in hell!" She pointed the gun at me again.

I held up my hands in surrender and then I heard a loud bang. I hit the floor, yelling in pain.

Boom.

She got off another shot, and I thanked God that one missed me. My left shoulder burned with pain and my blouse was soaked with my blood.

I didn't want to die. I was too young to die. There were so many things that I didn't get a chance to do.

"Dana, please," I begged, "call 911. Please don't do this to me." My shoulder was hurting like hell and I didn't want to feel another bullet enter into my flesh.

"Shut up," she yelled. "You deserve to suffer for what you did to me."

I sobbed and prayed that she'd spare my life. I was too afraid to even get up from the floor. I didn't want her to pull that trigger again.

"Do you know how much pain and misery you have caused me? Do you have any idea how it feels to know the man that you are madly in love with loves someone else?"

"I didn't break you two up," I cried.

"You did!" she screamed.

I sobbed and held my shoulder. "Please, Dana, just go. I won't tell anyone it was you, I swear."

She narrowed her eyes and pointed the gun at me again. She squeezed the trigger, but Matthew tackled her at the same time and she missed me again. They struggled on the floor and I crawled over to the phone. I scream in agony when I raised myself up from the floor, because my wound hurt so bad. I'd had fights before, but never had I felt such physical pain.

I grabbed the phone and dialed 911, and there was another bang.

"Matthew!" I screamed as the operator asked what my emergency was.

He stood to his feet, while Dana lay on the floor wailing in pain. The 911 operator asked what my emergency was again and I whispered, "There was an intruder in my house and I've been shot."

Matthew took the phone from my shaking hand.

# Chapter One

IT STARTED WAY back when I met him freshman year at DeKalb. I was lost and didn't know what direction to go to find my literature class. I bumped into him because I was looking around trying to figure out where to go and not looking where I was going.

Embarrassed as hell, I said, "I'm so, so sorry." After seeing how fine he was, I was even more embarrassed. He was sexy as hell and his eyes had a gleam in them that I would never forget, even years after I first laid eyes on him.

"Oh, it's okay, sweetheart." He gave me a handsome smile.

"No, no, I'm so sorry. I mean, I-I got turned around and I have no clue where I'm going and, man, I'm really sorry."

"Look, relax, okay? It's no big deal. Where are you trying to go?"

"To my Lit class. I'm already late. I found it with no problem yesterday, but I guess I got turned around."

He took my schedule from the top of my books. "Let's see here," he said. "Oh, Professor Ingram, he is just four doors down that way." He gave a point in the right direction. "I had him my freshman year."

I was so grateful. "Thank you so much," I said and hurried to class. I made my way to an empty chair and Professor Ingram shot me a look over his glasses. I put my head down and opened my book quickly. I had already missed ten minutes, so I had no idea where the hell he was, and I didn't know anyone in my class I could ask what I missed. I half listened to him because my mind was on the fine-ass guy I had damn near knocked over trying to find my class. I fantasized about his light bronze complexion and the dimple he carried in his left cheek. His tall frame and broad shoulders were not his best features, but they were great assets to have. I figured he was an upper classman, because he said he had Professor Ingram his freshman year, but I wondered how far up he was. When the class came to an end, Professor Ingram got my attention as I stood.

He said, "Young lady?" I knew he was talking to me.

"Yes, sir," I said nervously.

"What is your name?"

"Vivion … Vivion Ford," I said, trembling. It was only my third day there and everything and everyone was foreign.

"Well, Ms. Ford, I don't like it when the door opens and I've already begun my class. I understand that you are a freshman, but if you know you need a little more time to be punctual, I suggest you head over to class a little early."

I wanted to run. "Yes, sir."

"Good day, Ms. Ford."

"Good day, sir." I hurried out of his class. I moved so fast I bumped into him again and thought, this is madness. "Oh my gosh, I am sorry. How do I keep bumping into you?" I asked, thinking that was highly impossible.

"Well, I was waiting around for you," he said taking me completely off guard. "You ran off so fast, and I wanted to know your name."

I knew I looked a mess. I didn't have time to glam up before I left my dorms, trying to make it on time.

"Huh, my name?" I said, sounding like I was slow.

"Yes, your name. You do have one of those?"

I laughed. "Yes, yes I do. It's Vivion."

"Vivian," he said.

"No Vivion, like on, not an," I corrected him, like I'd had to do all of my life. I wondered why my mother didn't just use the damn 'a.'

"Okay, Vivion," he said, stressing the last syllable. "I'm Matthew Abrams, but everyone calls me Matt." He flashed his gorgeous smile again.

"Matt, okay. It's nice to meet you, and if I don't get a move on, I know I'm going to be late for my next class."

"So what's next?" he asked.

"World History," I said.

"With who? I can get you there on time if you'd like. No sense getting lost again when I'm free."

I looked at my schedule. "Walker."

"Come on, I'll walk you." I quickly accepted because I didn't want to be late. I made it on time with a few minutes to spare. "This is it," he said, stopping in front of the door.

"Thanks, Matt, that was very kind of you."

"Hey, not a problem. Will you need help with your next class?"

"No, I will be done for the day after this one."

"Okay, well, can I have your number?"

I was amazed that he dove right in. "Wow … my number," I said. He wasn't wasting anytime and I hated to admit it, but it was a turn on.

"I'm sorry, do you have a man or something?"

"No, and since you're asking for my number, I can assume you don't have a woman," I said, hoping that was the case.

"Yeah well, I don't. Just had a bit of a breakup, but I saw it coming a long time ago."

"Okay." I had to get inside. "Listen, my class is over in an hour, can you meet me after?" I didn't really want to give him my number just yet. He was super fine, but it was only my third day on campus and I didn't want to go running with the first guy I met.

"Actually, I can't, because I have a class in about thirty minutes and I won't be out before you. But I'll tell you what, if you can find your way there," he said, flipping over my schedule and writing his classroom number down, "you can meet me after my class."

"Okay, Matt, I will definitely try," I said and went into my class.

I set the thoughts of Matt to the side while I listened carefully to my Professor. When I got up to leave, I remembered telling Matt I'd find my way to his class. Since he wasn't due out for another two hours, I decided I'd go and spruce up a bit before meeting him. When I got to the corridor of his class, I sat at a nearby table and waited.

He walked out with a group of guys and I stood. I guess he didn't recognize me, because he was about to walk right past me. I had thrown a few curls in my short bob and put on a halter top and jeans. I didn't wear much makeup, but I was dedicated to mascara and lip gloss back then.

"Matt," I called.

He stopped and turned to me. "Wow, you clean up nicely." I took the smile on his face as an indication that he was happy with my minor makeover.

"Yeah well, I had some time to kill, so, you know…" I gave him the same smile in return.

"So can you go with me?"

"Go with you where?"

"To my place."

"Where is your place?"

"Not too far from here," he said, moving toward the parking lot. I automatically walked along.

"Sure, I guess," I said. I wasn't too sure, but thought, why not. We walked to the lot and he stopped at a parked SUV.

"What year are you in?" I asked.

"Third. I've been here a while," he said.

He helped me in and closed my door. We rode to an apartment complex just minutes from the campus.

"So do you have any roommates?" I asked as we approached his door.

"Nope. I live alone." He opened the door.

I stepped in and wondered what he did for money because his place was nice and I knew his Tahoe was a recent model. "So what are you, a rich kid or something?" I asked looking around.

He laughed. "Not exactly, but my parents don't do too badly. I do work, but my parents do a lot for me."

I smiled. "I can tell. I mean, your truck is what? It looks brand new."

"Well, it's fairly new, and my parents are loaded, to be honest. I have luxuries, but they still make me work."

"So how did you end up here at Dekalb and not some fancy overpriced university?"

"Well, my parents both attended this school and this is where they met, so they decided a long time ago that this is where I would go."

I nodded and just stood near the door, trying to take it all in. I didn't expect his place to be so nice, and on top of that, clean. He was a college dude.

"You can have a seat. Would you like a drink?" he offered.

I went towards the sofa to sit, but misunderstanding his drink offer, I replied. "No, I'm not twenty-one yet."

He burst into laughter. "I mean a pop, or juice," he said. "I've never had a woman to tell me that before, even if they were under twenty-one."

"Okay, well I'm a dork," I joked. "I'll have some juice." I felt goofy. "I've never taken a drink in my life," I confessed.

"Really, not even a cooler?"

"Nope, not even a cooler," I said, being honest.

"Wow, you are a dork," he joked and headed for the kitchen. He came back and handed me a bottle of Minute Maid grape juice.

"Shut up," I joked.

"I'm just joking," he said and sat on the couch with me.

"You're not going to have anything?" I asked and took a sip.

"I was, but you just made me feel like an alcoholic, so…"

I almost spit out my juice. "I'm sorry," I said wiping my chin and laughing.

"It's cool. I won't drink unless you drink. And since you're not twenty-one, there will be no drinking tonight."

I felt comfortable with him. "Well what do you have? Maybe you can introduce me to something?"

"Naw, no way. You're not going to blame me in five years when you have a drinking problem." We both laughed again.

"You are hilarious." I set my juice on the end table next to where I sat.

"I'm serious," he said.

"Listen, why don't you have your drink and I'll have my juice. Just make sure you are able to take me back to my dorms."

"Deal," he said. He went into the kitchen and came back with a red mixture of something.

"Wow, what is that?" I asked.

"It is vodka and cranberry," he said and hit the power on his stereo system.

"Can I taste it?"

He paused. "I don't know. I don't want to get in any trouble giving liquor to minors." His lips twitched and I could tell he was holding back a laugh.

"Come on, I'm nineteen, okay, and I'll be twenty soon."

"Yeah, twenty, not twenty-one."

"Come on, Matt," I begged. "I won't tell anyone. I just want to taste it." After a moment or two he finally handed the glass to me and I took a big gulp, and frowned.

"Hey, take it easy. You were supposed to sip not gulp."

"I'm sorry," I said, frowning. It tasted awful. "How can you drink that stuff?"

"Well, it takes some getting used to," he said. He got up and I watched him refill his glass. The glass was small and I damn near killed it.

"Can I try another?"

"I thought you just said it was awful?" he asked me with a brow raised.

"It was, but how can I get used to it, if I don't drink it?"

He got up to make me a drink. He poured a very small amount for me, and after three glasses, I was all over him.

He pulled away. "Vivion, baby, you need to chill. I know you're only reacting to the vodka."

I giggled. "I know, but I just feel so good and your kisses are so good and I promise you I know what I'm doing." I went back to kissing him. He tried to stop me a couple more times, but then he just gave in. After fooling around on the sofa, he asked me what I wanted to do.

"Matt, I know I'm buzzing, but I am very at-attracted to you.

I think we should stop, but I really don't want to."

"I know we should, so here, sit down and I'll get you some water." He got up and went toward the kitchen.

I followed him. "I want to," I said and started kissing him again. He squeezed my ass and his erection pressed against me.

He stopped and looked at me. "Vivion, we don't have to do anything. That is not why I brought you over here." I believed him.

"I know, and this is not why I came, but it is what it is, right?" I wanted him.

"Yeah," he said softly and took me by the hand.

We went into his bedroom and we fucked. It was explosive and passionate and we had the sheets wet from the good sex we had. My hair was soaking wet. When we finally collapsed, I realized what I had done and knew that what I used to do with my old high school boyfriend, Charles, wasn't shit. I had just been fucked by a grown-ass man, and I knew I'd want him again.

I closed my eyes when the room started to spin. I felt sick. I prayed and asked God to help me to not vomit, but I felt it coming on.

"Matt, the bathroom, where is it? I don't feel so, good." I lay there with my eyes closed, intoxicated from the sex and the vodka. I didn't want to move, but I knew if I stayed there, I'd throw up in his bed.

"It's down the hall to the left. Are you okay," he asked as I struggled to get up.

"No I don't feel so good."

"Viv, it's the vodka, I know it." He got up and he helped me up. He showed me to the bathroom and stood outside of the door while I blew chunks in the toilet. He tapped softly, and when I opened the door, he handed me a towel.

"Viv, hey, are you okay? I shouldn't have let you drink," he asked sounding concerned.

"Yeah, I'm … fine. I'm …" I paused. I thought I had more to come out, but I was finished. I felt a little better, but my head was banging. I turned on the faucet and rinsed my mouth.

"Viv, I'm sorry. I never should have given you anything to drink. This is my fault." He opened the cabinet and gave me a new toothbrush.

I ripped it open and picked up the toothpaste that was on the sink. "Hey, Matt, I'm good. I've just got a headache, but it's not your fault. I asked for it. I just had no idea it would make me feel like shit." I began to brush my teeth. He gave me two aspirins and went into the kitchen to get me a glass of juice. "Thanks," I said and took the pills.

"Come on and lay down. The aspirin should kick in soon," he said.

I don't know if I was the first woman to get sick in his place and I was embarrassed. He didn't act as if he was grossed out at all, but I still felt horrible. He helped me into bed, lay close to me, and held me. He kissed me softly on my cheek and gently rubbed my head and I was sleep within minutes.

# About the Author

**Anna Black** is a native of Chicago and the bestselling author of the Now You Wanna Come Back series. Her desire to become a published author didn't develop until her late twenties, and she didn't take her writing seriously until several close friends and family members encouraged her to go for it. After signing with Delphine Publications in November 2009, Anna became a bestselling author for her debut release, Now You Wanna Come Back, within a matter of weeks.

She has since released eight novels and two short stories. I Just Wanna Be Loved is her third short story under her own publishing house, Black House Publishing, which was launched in May of 2013. As she forges her path to success, her goal is to offer aspiring authors an opportunity to publish their page-turning tales under a new, up and coming label.

This award-winning author currently lives in Texas with her husband Chris, daughter Tyra, and her adorable Yorkie, Jasmine.

www.ingramcontent.com/pod-product-compliance
Lightning Source LLC
Chambersburg PA
CBHW071123170626
46809CB00002B/478